PROJECT ARMA

KYE

NYSSA KATHRYN

KYE
Copyright © 2022 Nyssa Kathryn Sitarenos

All rights reserved.

An NW Partners Book
Cover by Dar Albert at Wicked Smart Designs
Edited by Kelli Collins
Proofread by Marla Esposito

❀ Created with Vellum

Sometimes it's in the depths of hell, that one finds their angel.

Samantha Jacobs thought she was aiding her government. She believed the chip she created, the one that could change the world, would be used for the good of mankind. But it was all a lie…and she discovered the truth too late. Now, Samantha will suffer dearly for her mistake.

Former SEAL Kye Hade has been hunting the people behind Project Arma for years. He never expected to fall back into their hands, waking in a cage alongside a beautiful, brainy woman.

The enemy wants the unthinkable—and the clock is ticking. Freedom won't come without a fight, but when your rivals have proven they don't die easily, Kye and Samantha might just pay the ultimate price.

ACKNOWLEDGMENTS

Thank you to my incredibly talented editor, Kelli. I always feel confident releasing my books to my readers once you've edited them.

Thank you to my proofreader, Marla. Yet again, you caught dozens of those pesky errors that slipped through the million and one rewrites and edits.

Thank you to my beautiful husband, Will. Thank you for supporting me in all the ways I need you to. And thank you for loving me.

Thank you to my daughter. This is all for you and our family. You teach me about the purest love.

Thank you to my wonderful ARC team. Your kind words inspire me to write the next book.

Thank you to my readers. You have made completing this series possible. Without you, Kye would not have gotten his story.

PROLOGUE

 wo Months Ago

SAMANTHA'S HEART jackhammered against her ribs hard and loud. She pushed the door open silently, even though there was no one around to hear, and stepped into the building.

It was a Sunday. No one should be here. *She* shouldn't be here. If someone saw her…

She couldn't think about that right now.

She'd hacked the building security system from the car. Both the foyer and tenth floor should be safe. *She* should be safe.

But…there were no guarantees when it came to safety.

Samantha made her way up the stairs quickly.

She had a PhD in Physics, obtained from the Massachusetts Institute of Technology. But it was her masters in biomedical engineering that made her qualified to shut down the building security and surveillance effectively. Still, fear crept into her limbs. Causing her knees to tremble and her teeth to chatter.

Fear of being caught somewhere she shouldn't be. Of not being able to destroy what she needed to destroy.

No. She couldn't let the fear take over. She had to be brave. It was her fault such powerful microchips were in existence.

God, she was stupid. Stupid for believing the lies. For not questioning the man who'd hired her. She'd been told she was working for a government department. But she should have done her own research.

She'd only learned the truth yesterday when she'd left her office to grab something. It was while walking past Hylar's office that she'd overheard the words he'd said to someone on the phone.

Samantha swallowed at the memory.

"If she doesn't complete the job, you know what to do."

There had been something in his voice, something dark and menacing, that made Samantha's skin turn icy.

That's why she'd returned to her office, taken encrypted files she wasn't supposed to take, and placed them on a drive to hack at home.

She'd also switched on her GPS tracker so that she knew exactly where this top-secret facility was located. Just in case her fears were confirmed, that something else was going on here, something sinister, and she needed to return at a time when she wasn't supposed to...

Samantha was only a couple floors from the top when she stopped to take a breath. Air was moving in and out of her body quickly and her vision was bleary from staying up all night hacking the files.

She scrunched her eyes at the memory of what she'd found. Information about a project that Hylar had hijacked.

She'd known about the DNA-altering drugs. But they hadn't been created by an enemy of the country, as she'd been told.

Everything she'd read had been proof that Hylar wasn't working for the government.

His goal?

Decimate the US Army.

It was terrifying.

It had taken too damn long to hack the file. It wasn't until the early hours of this morning that she'd finished reading everything. Driven straight to Tori's house and warned her.

Christ, she'd all but pushed her out of the house.

Had her friend gotten away?

Samantha shook her head and began moving again. She did. She had to have.

Sweat beaded her forehead when she reached the door to the tenth floor. Her workplace. It should open easily, just like the door downstairs. Saying a silent prayer, Samantha placed her fingers around the handle and pushed.

Access.

The dark, familiar hallway greeted her. The same hallway she'd walked down five, sometimes six days a week for almost five years, each day thinking she was creating something great. Something for her country that would revolutionize warfare. Tip the odds in their favor.

Stupid.

She moved straight to her office, which doubled as her lab. It was positioned at the end of the hall and contained all her work, including the microchips she'd already created.

Tugging the door open, she sat in front of her computer and powered it up.

Destroy the chips, destroy the chip blueprints, and run. Get out of town and never return. That was the start and end of her plan.

Samantha opened her work. Years' worth of designs sat in front of her. Work she'd poured her blood, sweat, and tears into. Destroying it should be easy after finding out what it would be used for.

It wasn't. Everything in her rebelled against the idea. Burning the place to the ground would have been easier. But there was no guarantee the fire would destroy everything. That Hylar's men wouldn't get wind of what was happening and save her work.

She needed to make sure it was gone. All of it.

Her fingers hovered over the keys. Hesitated...

Just do it, Samantha. It's all saved in your brain anyway.

Giving herself a little shake, Samantha started deleting.

It took a while. The chip blueprints were extensive and in-depth. The minutes felt endless. And every second that passed felt like a lifetime.

When she was sure it was all gone, she planted a virus on the computer just to be sure. Nothing could be salvageable. No one could recreate this for Hylar.

While the virus was activating, Samantha turned her attention to the stored chips. She'd only recently perfected the microchip. All the old, imperfect versions had already been destroyed.

Samantha shook her head, still stunned that she was only just realizing it wasn't her place to play God. She should have come to that conclusion earlier. So much earlier.

Sliding the backpack off her shoulders, she took out the large bottle of hydrochloric acid. Then, one by one, she took out the trays of microchips and poured the liquid over them.

It didn't take long. A couple of minutes, tops. Something that had taken her years to perfect, ruined so quickly.

There was one last thing she needed to destroy. The wireless remote that activated the chip. It was the powerhouse. The connector between the input and the device receiving the instructions.

Opening the top drawer of her desk, she stilled. It wasn't there.

What the hell? This was where she kept it. *Always.* There was nowhere else she would have put it.

Had someone taken it?

Breathing out a shaky breath, she quickly rummaged through

her other drawers before glancing at the door. She left the room quickly, heading over to Hylar's office. She tried the knob. It didn't work.

Dammit.

He'd taken it; he had to have. It was the only thing that made sense.

It's fine, Samantha. You've destroyed the blueprints for the chips. If the chips can't be recreated, the remote is useless.

Moving back to her office, she noticed the virus was still installing. It would probably take a while longer but would be done by the time everyone returned to the building tomorrow.

Giving the office one final glance, again feeling the weight of her mistake on her shoulders, crushing her, she grabbed her bag and left the room.

The irony was, her entire life, people had been telling her how smart she was. How damn brilliant her mind was.

Well, for once, she didn't feel brilliant. She felt like she'd been blind her entire life, and it was only now that someone had ripped the blindfold off and exposed her to the real world. The one where people were seen as mere tools of warfare. The world where all it took was one mistake and everything changed.

She didn't want to contribute to the evil. She couldn't.

Samantha was halfway to the door leading to the stairs when she stopped. She'd never explored other parts of the tenth floor. What did Hylar have hidden behind closed doors?

One look. It would take barely a second. One peek into what she had walked past every single day.

Reaching for the handle closest to her, she pushed it open. A small gasp escaped her lips. A cage sat in the center of the room. It was huge. Floor-to-ceiling bars that were so thick, they looked unbreakable.

Jesus. Had they put anyone in that cell? Or was this just waiting for the first victim? Maybe this was where Hylar planned to keep Oliver, the man her best friend had been tasked with bringing in.

Had he then planned to have the microchip—her microchip—inserted into him?

Nausea washed through her stomach, making her want to bend over and be sick. She just stopped herself. She closed the door firmly behind her, not wanting to see any more. Knowing none of it would be good.

Focus on running, Samantha. Disappearing and never resurfacing.

Samantha reached for the door to the stairwell when suddenly it opened on its own.

No. Not on its own.

Her breath caught in her throat, and she took three hurried steps back as Carter, Hylar's right-hand man, came to stand in front of her.

She'd always had a bad feeling about the guy. And now she knew why.

"Samantha. So nice of you to come in on your day off."

Samantha swallowed in an attempt to wet her dry throat. "How did you find out I was here?"

Carter smiled. It made her skin crawl. "You disappoint me. Here I was, thinking you were some kind of genius, yet you didn't even think to check whether Tori's house was under surveillance before you so bravely tried to save her."

Her skin turned to ice. Not because of the comment about surveillance, but because of how he'd worded his statement. "*Tried* to save her?"

Kip entered the hall, moving to stand behind Carter. "Adrien's taking care of your friend right now."

Samantha's heart stuttered. Maybe he'd be too late? *Please, God, let Tori get away...*

Carter took a step forward. "Anything that you've damaged or destroyed will need to be recreated."

"No." The word left her mouth in a whisper. She wouldn't

recreate anything for these people. She'd risked everything to come back here. Destroyed her work. That couldn't be in vain. She'd rather die than be responsible for millions of good men being micro-chipped and controlled.

"I'm afraid you don't have a choice."

She took hurried steps away, but Carter was too quick, grabbing her arm and tugging her back to him.

He tilted his head to the side. "Where are you going?"

"Either get your hand off me or kill me. I won't be doing anything else for you people."

Carter's fingers tightened. Digging into her skin. Bruising her. "Yes, you will. Even if we have to break you in the process, you will."

CHAPTER 1

 *resent Day*

KYE WATCHED the steady rise and fall of Samantha's chest as she slept, her large blond curls splayed across the flat pillow.

She slept on a tiny mattress with a thin sheet to cover her. It was nowhere near thick enough for what she needed in this cold cell.

What was more, it was clear she'd been wearing the same clothes for weeks.

His jaw tensed at the frustration of it all.

He'd slept for a couple hours. That was all he needed. All he was willing to spare each night in this four-foot-wide cage. He didn't want to close his eyes any longer than necessary.

He scanned the bars that separated them for the thousandth time. His cell sat beside hers, both small and empty, other than a toilet and small basin, and her mattress, pillow, and sheet.

A week had passed since he'd woken up here. A week of cold concrete floors, of having no way to escape. And a week of her.

Not that she was in her cell much. Whenever she woke, Carter wasn't far off. Taking her away to work on the damn microchips.

He needed to ask her more questions about that. Find out exactly how they worked and how powerful they were.

The problem was, when Samantha was here, the woman was exhausted. She spent most of her time sleeping.

It was a hell of a lot better than when she wasn't here, though. Watching her sleep sure beat counting the metal bars. Staring into the camera on the other side of the prison bars, knowing he was being watched.

It also didn't hurt that the woman was gorgeous. Even in her unkempt state, her intelligent blue eyes lit up the whole damn place. In combination with her cute button nose and full lips... the woman was stunning.

He looked across to the door that led to the hall. Carter would arrive with food soon. It was always the same routine. He brought breakfast, then Samantha had ten minutes to eat before she was whisked away to some damn lab.

Hours. Maybe twelve. That's how long he estimated she was gone before she was finally brought back with barely enough energy to eat dinner.

He tapped his foot lightly on the concrete floor.

Christ, if he had to remain here much longer, he might lose his goddamn mind. Either that or die from boredom.

He had seven teammates. Men who were more brothers than friends. They would be searching for him. In the meantime, he needed a backup plan.

No, he needed to pull off a damn miracle and get their asses out of here.

Then he would destroy anyone who'd played a part in his and Samantha's capture.

At the shift in Samantha's breathing, Kye's gaze went back to her. She was stirring. Slowly, her eyes fluttered open. Her bright blue gaze went straight to him.

A slow smile curved his lips. The woman hadn't said the words out loud, but he knew she'd been through hell. He had a feeling she needed his smile like she needed air.

"Morning, beautiful."

She carefully pushed up into a sitting position before pulling the hair band from her wrist. He loved the moment she first woke. When her wild hair framed her face and tumbled down her back. It was the sunshine the concrete walls stopped him from seeing.

"Good morning."

"Sleep well?"

A ghost of a smile tugged at her lips. "You ask me that every morning."

He lifted a shoulder. "Maybe I hope your answer will change."

"The one about sleeping as well as I can in a cold cell? Afraid not."

Even though Kye smiled on the outside, he raged on the inside. Carter could have at least ensured the woman had adequate clothing and bedding. As it was, she wore jeans and a thin tank top, both with tears in them.

"Maybe tomorrow." He winked before pushing to his feet and walking to the bars. "I wonder how long until Bane delivers our food today?"

"Bane?"

"Bane. The man who wants to overthrow Gotham's elite. The completely flawed villain in *The Dark Knight Rises* who had an incoherent plan from the start."

She frowned. "You think Carter's plan is incoherent?"

"Any plan that involves capturing me and thinking he can change me is flawed."

Her gaze quickly shot away. Clearly, the woman didn't agree. But then, she'd created the chip, so if anyone knew, it was her.

"Tell me about what you've created, Samantha."

He'd avoided asking too much about it up to this point. The woman worked on it all day. While she was here, caged with him, he tried to take her mind off everything.

But he needed to know.

Sighing, she cast her gaze down as she spoke. "Hylar approached me a little over five years ago. I was doing my thesis on human microchips at MIT. He asked me to work for his government department and create a chip like the world had never seen. He spoke about 'making a difference' and 'tipping the odds in our country's favor.'" She shook her head. "It was a huge acceleration for my career. So I didn't think twice."

And clearly, she beat herself up about that. "If he had all the right credentials, there's no reason you would have questioned him."

She didn't look like she agreed but continued anyway. "It took me a long time to get the chip to where it is now. Then we needed a simple connector between the chip and the controller. Something that was mobile and allowed Hylar, or whoever was in control, to access it while in the field. I created a wireless remote. A code is entered into the remote, then it's voice-activated to gain control of the host."

Kye tried not to cringe at her wording. "Control the host" just didn't sound right. But she felt bad enough; she didn't need his judgment added on.

"Only one voice can gain control at a time, and the remote needs to be in reasonably close proximity to the person in control. The only one who can then deactivate the voice is the user. And me, because I know the codes."

Kye nodded, as if what the woman described was completely normal, when it was anything but.

"The main issue with the original chips was that female voices worked better for some reason. Hylar didn't like that, obviously.

It was only about four months ago that I finally perfected it so that male voices could activate the chips."

He tilted his head to the side. "How were you able to create the chip in just hours in Killeen, when they were holding Oliver and Tori, when it's taking you weeks now?"

"When I went back to destroy my work, I couldn't find the remote. I later found out that Hylar had taken it." She shook her head in disgust. "The blueprints didn't take long to re-write. It's all in my head. The remote takes a lot longer."

And of course, Carter wouldn't have the remote. That had been seized by police when the building had been raided, and it was now in a secure location, only known to a few...including Kye and his team.

"How's the chip inserted into its...host?"

God, that was hard to say.

"The microchip is so small that the insertion point is barely noticeable. A surgeon is still required though, because of how exact the placement needs to be. The surgeon inserts it just below the shoulder blade. The chip then attaches to nerves that connect to the brain."

Yep. Sounded just as evil as he'd suspected. "Can it be destroyed once inserted?"

The sound of the door opening cut off any response Samantha may have given. Carter stepped inside the room carrying two trays of food.

"Morning, sleeping beauties." He placed their food on the ground in front of each cell, his gaze sliding to Samantha. "You have ten minutes to eat, then I'll be back."

He turned, his hand on the door when Samantha spoke. "Could I have some salt?"

Kye almost laughed. She'd asked for salt every day, and each time she'd gotten the same answer. Carter seemed to be getting progressively more annoyed by it.

"No." The door slammed shut behind him.

"Still holding out hope for salt?"

Samantha lifted a shoulder. "A girl needs one luxury in this hellhole."

"Is it really that much of a hellhole if I'm here, though?"

Another small smile touched her lips. He swore one of these days he was going to get a big one.

They both went to the bars. There was a small hatch that allowed food to slide through. Unfortunately, it wasn't big enough to use in any form of escape attempt.

Grabbing his food, he sat in his normal spot. Every morning was the same. They placed their trays of food directly opposite each other and ate together. It was almost comical, how normal they looked...if one ignored the bars.

Kye shoved some of the stew into his mouth. They'd been living off stews and soups since arriving. "Damn, it's another good one."

How the hell was all the food in this place so goddamn tasty?

"It's weird, isn't it. That everything else is subpar, yet we're fed well."

"Can't let the brainiac or super-soldier starve."

Another small smile touched her lips. He was living for those at the moment. He shot a look at the door, then back to Samantha. "What do you see out there?"

She followed his gaze. "Outside of this cell? Not much. We walk down a long, dark corridor. There are a couple of doors on either side. The few times I've glanced inside, I've barely been able to see anything. One time, though, I'm pretty sure I made out a seat with restraints."

He didn't miss the way her body gave a small shudder.

"Since then, I avoid looking. At the end of the hall, we turn right. That hall is really short, and at the end is the small lab I work in."

"Any windows?"

She shook her head. "None."

Everything she said confirmed his suspicions about the type of location where they were being held.

Her spoon paused midway to her mouth. "Do you know where we are?"

Either the woman was a mind reader, or he was terrible at concealing his thoughts. "Geographically, no. But based on what I've seen in this room, these cells, in combination with the fact that I can't hear anything, it could be a deserted black site."

She tilted her head, a blond curl falling onto her cheek. "What's a black site?"

A place no one wants to go. Yet here they were.

"A facility controlled by the CIA and used by the US government for covert operations. The locations are only known by a handful of people. There was a CIA agent who was involved in Project Arma. He might have known about this place and shared its location with Hylar and Carter. Your description of what you've seen fits."

Kye doubted Carter had taken them out of the country. That would have taken too much manpower.

"Have you ever seen anyone else out there?"

She shook her head. "Never. I haven't heard anyone either. There's only ever been silence."

It was looking more and more like Carter was alone in all this. The question was, why?

"Have you seen the microchip in action?"

Pain flashed across her face. It was fleeting. "Yes. Hylar used criminals as test subjects. At least, men he *told* me were criminals. Hylar said the men had agreed to trial the chip in exchange for shorter sentences. I guess that was a lie." She shook her head again, almost looking repulsed by the likely truth behind it all.

"He brought in this one particular guy..." She pushed her food around her plate, suddenly not looking so hungry. "One second he was himself. Swearing at Hylar to let him go. Tugging at the restraints around his wrists. Then Hylar ordered him to stop, and he just went completely still. *Statue* kind of still."

"And he could do that with his voice, because he'd activated the remote?"

"Yes."

He saw a myriad of emotions on her face. Anger. Frustration. Regret.

Without thinking, Kye reached through the bars and placed his hand on top of hers. He felt her immediate flinch. It was the first time he'd touched her. He'd been talking with the woman for a week, sleeping right beside her, but had yet to touch her soft skin.

Until now.

He waited patiently for her to look up. When her eyes finally landed on his, he ran his thumb over her hand. "This isn't your fault. Any of it. From the start, you thought you were working for a government department doing military research. I knew Hylar. I can just imagine how genuine his job offer would have seemed."

Samantha didn't pull her hand away. "I should have seen past the facade. I'm smarter than that."

"Samantha, Hylar was my commander for years. I saw the man every day. Trained under him. Followed every directive he gave me. Do you know how many times I questioned him before I started feeling the effects of the drugs? How many times I questioned the true nature of Project Arma? Not once. I'm *trained* to be better than that. Yet I couldn't see what was right in front of my goddamn eyes."

He hadn't questioned the drugs that had been pumped into his body. The program he'd been signed up for. Not until he was stronger than he should have been. Faster than humanly possible. What kind of a SEAL did that make him?

"You didn't question him because you cared about him."

Kye smiled, but this time, it was pained. "Kind of makes it

worse, doesn't it? Caring about a man who saw you as a tool rather than a human. Being fooled not by a stranger, but by a guy you had misplaced your trust in."

And ultimately, killing that man. Because it had been Kye who'd pulled the trigger, shooting his former commander dead. And he hadn't batted an eye.

"I don't think caring for another person is something you should ever regret." Samantha turned her hand over and threaded her fingers through his. "The mistake is his for not appreciating you."

Kye held her gaze, letting the weight of her words sink in. It was the first time in years that anyone had told him what he'd felt for Hylar wasn't a mistake.

He opened his mouth to respond, but yet again, the door to the room opened and Carter interrupted them.

Time was up.

"Well, isn't this sweet."

Samantha un-threaded her fingers from his and stood as Carter made his way to her cell. Kye stood as well, anger welling in his gut at the way the guy grabbed her arm too roughly and tugged her from the cell.

Kye growled. "You don't need to fucking manhandle her. She's never resisted."

Carter grinned. "Where's the fun in being gentle?"

The door slammed behind them after they exited, and the room was once again plunged into the silence he'd become so familiar with.

CHAPTER 2

*C*arter's fingers remained firmly around Samantha's wrist as he tugged her into the corridor. They dug into her skin, causing pain to radiate up her arm.

She didn't say anything. It wouldn't save her. She knew from experience that the second she made a sound, even the quietest of objections, his grip would tighten.

The man was evil to the core. He enjoyed inflicting pain. Enjoyed the reactions he got.

So instead of tugging at her arm or cursing at the asshole, Samantha grit her teeth and internalized the pain. Something she'd become quite good at lately.

"That was a nice intimate moment you were sharing with soldier boy." Carter's words were laced with sarcasm.

What would he say if she responded with, "Yes, it *had* been nice"?

Ha. He'd probably laugh in her face. It was the truth, though. Kye's hand on hers was the first gentle touch she'd felt in months. The first touch where the intent wasn't to hurt or manipulate.

Maybe that's why her entire arm had tingled with awareness.

Yeah, if she mentioned any of that to Carter, she was sure he'd find some way to turn it into something ugly. Either that or separate them. Maybe even force her to sleep in the lab.

She couldn't let that happen. Her few minutes with Kye each day were the only things keeping her sane.

She felt Carter's eyes on her at her continued silence. "I wouldn't get too attached. That man won't exist much longer. And you may be dead soon."

He'd told her about her impending death many times. Even before they'd arrived at this mystery location, *other* people had been telling her, warning her, that she didn't have long. Adrien, Hylar...

But *they* were dead now, not her.

"This environment doesn't exactly encourage love connections. I think we're safe."

Carter chuckled. "Neither of you are safe. You'd have to be stupid to think you were."

Samantha had definitely thought of herself as stupid more than once in recent months.

His chuckle was worse than his words. A reminder that he enjoyed her fear.

"Were you always like this?" she asked as they turned the corner.

The words were out of her mouth before she could stop them. Not that he seemed bothered. They came to a stop in front of the lab door. "You mean have I always been relentless in the pursuit of my goals? Yes."

Okay, but there was a difference between being goal-orientated and having a complete disregard for others. "Do you have family?"

When the door was opened, he shoved her in. "I was raised by my father. He was a drunken, abusive asshole."

Ah. So he'd learned the art of inflicting pain early. "And you didn't feel the need to be better than him?"

Samantha realized her mistake the second the words were out

of her mouth. But it was too late. The backhand was sudden and sent her flying backward into the wall. Her cheek immediately throbbed, her back crying out at the impact with solid brick.

Carter crouched in front of her, glaring. "I am *nothing* like that asshole. He was weak and never had a goal in his life. That's why I killed him."

Samantha blanched at his statement. "You killed your own father?"

"Of course I did." No hesitation. No empathy. "He used me as his personal punching bag for eighteen years. The second I was capable, he was dead."

She opened and closed her mouth, but no words came out.

Then he continued. His words chilling. "I dragged it out, too. Made the man beg for death before I finally let him take his last breath. One of the sweetest moments of my life."

She swallowed. The man was a psychopath.

Carter straightened, heading back to the door. Samantha was slower to rise. Ignoring the soreness in her body, she headed to the standing desk, powering up the computer and getting to work.

Carter remained behind her, fiddling with his phone. She knew what he was doing—checking that surveillance was working. He did it every day before he left. Always watching her.

Samantha lifted a hand to her swelling cheek, immediately flinching away from her touch. Anger pulsed through her bloodstream and she had to grit her teeth to stop from cursing at the man by the door.

"You've got three more days to complete the remote."

Samantha spun toward him. "Three? I'm supposed to have six, according to the timeline you gave me at the start. That's what I've been working toward."

He lifted a shoulder. "Things have changed."

Was the guy joking? She couldn't fit the amount of work she still had to do into half the time...

Carter opened the door. Samantha took a quick step toward him. "No, Carter, you don't understand. There's literally no way I can have it done by then. It's impossible."

His body went still. *Remained* still for a good few seconds before turning. When he faced her, she almost stepped back. He looked every bit the deadly predator she knew he was.

It took a great deal of effort for Samantha to remain still. To not run and find something to hide behind.

"I've been pretty easy on you since you've been here, haven't I? You haven't had any of that earlier torture."

Her breath caught in her throat at the use of the word "torture." She'd endured a lot in Killeen. Hylar had used methods that would haunt her nightmares for years to come. All to try and force her to recover the work she'd destroyed.

"You haven't had to." Her words were quiet. Barely a whisper. "I've done everything you've asked."

He took a slow step forward. "That's right. You've been very obedient. Do you know what happens if that obedience stops?"

More mental and emotion scars to add to the collection? "Nothing good."

Carter stepped closer again before reaching up and trailing his finger down the cheek he'd just bruised. His touch was light, but still pain throbbed from the area.

A shudder she couldn't suppress ran up her spine.

"Kye was correct. This is a deserted black site. You know what its primary function was? Psychological and physical torture against enemies." Carter's lips slowly pulled up into a sinister smile. "If you're not working with me, you're working against me. That makes you an enemy, Samantha. Those rooms we walk past every day...they have everything I could ever need to destroy you," he leaned his head down, hovering his lips near her ear, "without killing you."

Ice burst through her chest. She'd survived everything they'd done to her in Killeen. The waterboarding, the electrocution, the sleep deprivation...she wasn't sure she could do that a second time.

His hand trailed down to her neck, fingers wrapping around lightly. "Do you understand?"

Repulsion and fear swirled through her gut. "Yes."

"Good." Carter straightened, his hand dropping from her skin. Turning, he left, and the air whooshed out of her chest.

Samantha understood what he wanted. The problem was, it wasn't possible.

∿

KYE COMPLETED another set of pushups. He'd lost count of how many he'd done. Regardless of the exact number, it was a lot. Yet he hadn't broken a sweat and wasn't tired. In fact, he felt like he could go for hours more.

He'd been working out most of the day. Doing what he could in his four-by-seven-foot cell. There was little else to spend time on.

Kye tried to push his body to the limit, to the point of pain, but it was impossible. Hell, even with a fully stocked gym and the help of his team, it was impossible.

He'd had years to get used to his altered DNA. And not just to the strength. To his speed, his ability to heal quickly, and hear things he shouldn't.

He *wasn't* used to it. And he doubted he ever would be. Most days, his body didn't feel like his own.

Kye tuned into his heart rate. It wasn't elevated. His breathing was completely normal.

He performed the next set one-handed. He increased his speed. He needed an outlet. Something to take his mind off being trapped.

He'd just finished another twenty when the creaking of the

door sounded. He was on his feet in seconds, watching. Waiting to see her.

Carter walked in first. That stupid smirk he often wore stretched across his face. Behind him, Samantha trailed in.

Kye's body immediately tensed at the sight of the red bruise that marred her left cheek. Anger thrummed through his veins. "You fucking hit her."

It wasn't so much a question as a statement. Kye could see the asshole had, and it made *him* see red.

Carter opened Samantha's cage and shoved her in. "Surprised? You shouldn't be. You know I'm a sick bastard."

Yeah. Kye knew. That's why, eventually, he'd tear the guy to shreds. Rip his heart right from his chest.

Kye ran his gaze up Samantha's body, checking that the rest of her remained unharmed. Bruises in the form of fingerprints colored her wrist. When his gaze returned to hers, he saw more anger than fear.

That's it, honey. Don't let him break you.

"Maybe you should let me out so you can hit someone as big and mean as you. See what happens."

Carter scoffed as he headed back to the door. "Don't flatter yourself. You don't come close to being as mean as me."

"Put me in a room with the right person and I'm the meanest son of a bitch you'll ever come across." The guy would be dead within minutes. Kye didn't even need a weapon.

Carter stepped through the door but didn't immediately shut it. "As tempting as it is to show you the complete inaccuracy of that statement, that's not what we're doing here."

The door closed with a resounding bang.

Slowly, Kye turned to see Samantha lowering to the mattress. Rather than lay straight down, she remained sitting as she untied her hair.

"Are you okay?"

"I'm okay."

Her response came too fast. Lie. The widening of her pupils and hitch in her voice gave her away. "Does it hurt?"

"The bruise? Not really."

Truth. Interesting. So something else was bothering her. Had Carter done more than hit her?

His jaw ticked at the thought. "What else did he do to you, honey?" He barely controlled his voice.

Her brows lifted. "Do? Nothing."

Another truth. Relief rushed through his system. He hated the idea of any man hurting a woman. Touching her in a way she didn't want. He especially hated the idea of it happening to Samantha. They'd only known each other a week, but in this kind of environment, it felt longer.

"What are you not telling me?"

She sighed. A heavy sound that made his gut clench. "He's giving me three more days to finish building the wireless remote."

He studied her face. "And that's not enough?"

It was a question. But it wasn't.

Samantha scrubbed a hand over her face. "It will be hard for me to meet that deadline."

She gave a nervous glance to the camera before turning to Kye. He understood. It wasn't hard. It was impossible. "And if you can't meet that deadline—"

The door opened, and Carter walked back in carrying two plates. He placed the trays at the normal spots before meeting Kye's gaze. "Pain. That's what happens."

Kye heard the slight acceleration of Samantha's heartbeat at Carter's words.

Carter was almost at the door when Samantha asked the same question she always asked at mealtime. "Could I have some salt?"

"I've said no the last ten times, what makes you think I'll say yes now?"

She lifted a shoulder. "Empathy?"

He chuckled. "That's not an emotion I'm familiar with."

Carter left the room. Samantha lay down and started pulling her sheet up.

"Eat with me." After taking his tray, Kye took the same spot he always took.

Samantha was already closing her eyes. "I'm sorry. I'm tired."

"You need to eat. And I need someone to remind me what a conversation is."

There was a small smile on her face. Her eyes were shut, but he was still claiming it as one. "You seemed to do just fine with Carter."

Kye growled. "Anything said to that bastard doesn't count."

"True." She remained under the covers for another beat before pushing up and moving toward him. Victory. "What's for dinner?"

Kye swirled the contents of the bowl. "Soup." He lifted a spoonful to his lips. "It's good."

"Now I have high expectations." She sat opposite him, less than a foot away. When she tasted her own, her eyes momentarily shut. "God, it *is* good. Cauliflower soup. And maybe zucchini."

"Still need salt?"

She chuckled. It was the first chuckle he'd heard from her, and it made his heart do a funny kick. "Yeah. I still need some salt."

Kye didn't. The stuff was perfect.

He studied the bruise on her cheek again. Now he was going to hate when she left him even more. He would be wondering the entire time if she was okay. "I'm sorry he hit you."

She frowned. "Why are *you* sorry?"

"I wish I could have been there to protect you." It wasn't a lie. "Why did he do it?"

She stirred the soup around in her bowl. "He told me his father was abusive. I made a stupid comment about it."

"Whatever you said, it didn't warrant being hit." When she remained silent, he tried changing the subject. "Do you know the irony of me being here? My team actually calls me Cage."

Her eyes shot up, questioning. "Like a nickname?"

He nodded. "Yup. Me and a couple other guys got captured in Somalia while doing a mission. Got thrown into a cage. I just so happened to have a small hair clip in my pocket. I was able to use it to pick the lock and get us out. Although, to be fair, it wasn't a high-tech cage."

Not like this one.

"I'd ask where you got the hair clip, but I feel like I know."

Whatever Samantha was thinking, she was likely right. He'd pulled it out of a woman's hair the night before at the hotel bar.

"Got any hair clips now?" Samantha jokingly asked.

He shook his head. "Fresh out." He leaned forward. "But I *will* get us out." He didn't care if Carter heard. In fact, he welcomed it. Let the asshole know his days were numbered.

Samantha studied his face. Probably wanting to trust him but scared to hope.

She lifted a shoulder. "Either way, I'm glad I met you."

She didn't believe him. That was okay. He'd just have to prove it to her.

CHAPTER 3

*I*n a matter of seconds, the room shifted from quiet to chaos. Violence filled the space.

Samantha watched in stunned silence as Oliver threw another punch. Just like the last, it was blocked by Adrien.

She shot a quick glance at the door, praying that his friends chose that moment to walk in. Save her and Tori, and destroy the men who had held her captive for so long.

When another second passed and they didn't arrive, she switched her attention to her friend. Her best friend. Tori stood inside the cell, fear on her face as she watched the man she loved fight for his life. A man who could throw a blow yielding the strength of ten.

When Tori looked her way, Samantha took a step forward to go to her, but strong hands suddenly wrapped around her waist, halting her. Tugging her in the opposite direction.

She struggled against the hold, at the same time watching in horror as Hylar moved toward Tori.

No...The man was pure evil.

Samantha shoved an elbow into the body behind her. She threw her head back.

Carter barely reacted. Not only was he a head taller, he was miles stronger.

In one swift move, he yanked her from the floor, tossing her over his shoulder. Then he was moving.

Oh, God. No! She couldn't be taken again. She wouldn't survive it. Not when she'd had a glimpse of freedom.

Samantha kicked and screamed. She ignored the whisper in her head that said there was no point. That this was a fight she wasn't going to win. Desperation gnawed at her insides, consuming her.

Doors opened and closed. Then he stopped in front of...a window?

Her heart stuttered in her chest. He couldn't be...could he? He was strong, but strong enough to scale a ten-story building? It would be a risk to both their lives.

"Carter, what are you doing?"

The sound of the window lock disengaging echoed through the room. He didn't speak.

"No! Carter, don't do this. You'll kill us both!"

Her heart was now soaring in her chest. She was so breathless and lightheaded, it was entirely possible she'd pass out right there on his shoulder.

He sat on the edge of the open window. "Hold on tight."

Then, displaying his immense strength, Carter closed the window with one arm, before lowering them with the other.

Terror coursed through Samantha's veins as rain pummeled her back. Had her stomach had any food in it, she was sure she would have thrown it up.

He placed his second hand on the ledge and continued to hang. She waited in terror for him to move. Drop. Something.

He didn't. They remained where they were—suspended from a window ledge.

Seconds passed before his left hand dropped from the ledge and he yanked something out of his pocket. A small whimper escaped her throat. She scrunched her eyes shut, not wanting to see how far from the ground they were. She had no idea what he'd taken out of his pocket, and she didn't care. Whatever it was, it reduced them to one hand on the ledge. One hand as their lifeline.

As seconds turned to minutes, she finally realized what he was doing.

Waiting. Waiting for the floor to be empty, assuming that the storm around them would block out their heartbeats. Their breaths.

She didn't know how long they hung there. It probably wasn't long, but every second felt like an hour. Her life literally hanging in the balance.

Don't look down. Don't look down. Don't look down.

Three words that she repeated in her head like a mantra. Every bone in her body was tingling with terror.

Finally, after what felt like a lifetime, he lifted them up, pushed the window open, and threw Samantha inside. Every inch of her body trembled. Her stomach tried to rebel, but it was too empty.

Carter tried to grab her, but she lunged backward, needing to get away. Her escape from the man only lasted a second before his fist was colliding with her face, sending her to the floor.

She was in a daze, barely conscious, when she was again thrown over a shoulder.

Samantha wanted to cry. To scream. But she had no energy left for anything. She was being taken again. Her life was a nightmare she couldn't wake up from.

KYE WOKE to Samantha's soft cry from the other side of the bars.

She was having a nightmare. It wasn't the first. In fact, she usually had multiple a night. The first night, he'd woken her each time. But he'd soon realized that if he kept that up, the woman wouldn't sleep.

What had they done to her to make her so scared? To fill her subconscious mind with such terror?

Kye gritted his teeth as he pushed into a sitting position. He wasn't going back to sleep. He estimated he'd had about three hours. He was done. But Christ, did he hate that he'd have to sit here and listen to her pain.

Another cry sounded. Her face contorted in fear. Her breaths rushing in and out of her chest in quick succession.

He tried to focus on something else. Tried to grind his teeth to block out the sound of her fear.

God, he hated them. Every one of them. He wished he could go back and kill Hylar a second time. A bullet to the head had been too kind. The man deserved to experience the pain he'd inflicted. They all did, Carter included.

Her body jerked beneath the thin sheet. Her heart pounded loud and hard in her chest. Even if he had the senses of a normal man, he was sure he would be able to hear her heart working overtime.

When another minute passed and she still hadn't calmed, Kye growled. *No.* He couldn't do it anymore. He couldn't sit here and listen to her pain.

Moving close to the bars, Kye reached his arm through and gripped her arm. His touch was light, wanting to wake her gently. "Samantha."

Nothing. Nothing but terror-filled breaths.

He applied more pressure, gave her a light shake, and raised his voice. "Sam! Wake up."

Still nothing.

Trailing a hand up her arm, he stopped at her face, holding her cheek in the palm of his hand. His fingers overlapped onto her neck, and with his thumb, he stroked her skin. "Sammy. Wake up."

He used the name that he knew Tori used. A name she would associate with safety.

Her body stilled. Her breathing, although still too quick, lost some of its jagged edges.

Slowly, she woke, bright blue eyes looking up at him.

Confusion. Fear. Pain. He saw all of it in her gaze.

His thumb continued to stroke her cheek. "You okay, darlin'?"

He wished he could tell her she was safe. That he would look after her. But with the bars between them, that was a promise he couldn't guarantee.

She remained still for another few seconds. He began to wonder if she planned to answer. Then, slowly, she pushed into a sitting position. She looked at him for only a few seconds before dropping her face into her hands.

"I'm sorry." Her voice was muffled, but he could still hear her sorrow.

"Talk to me, sunshine. What was your dream about?"

Not dream. Nightmare. But he wanted to soften his words.

She looked at him, tears glistening in her eyes. She shook her head.

His hand twitched to touch her again. Offer some kind of comfort. What he wouldn't give to break down these bars, take the woman in his arms and hold her.

"Talking about it might help." He kept his voice gentle and reassuring.

She swallowed. "They won't leave me alone. The nightmares. It's like my subconscious is continuing to punish me for what I created. Making me live the worst moments of my life over and over again."

He could see her madly swallowing, forcing the emotions down.

If she told him what she'd been through, he knew it would make him angry. Murder-level angry. And here, where there was no way to release his rage, that was a dangerous thing.

Regardless, he needed to know what this woman's demons were. "What did they do to you, Samantha?"

"Nothing good." Her eyes were downcast, and she wrung her hands in her lap. "They tried a few different methods to make me do what they wanted. Believe it or not, one of the hardest was being locked in a cold dark cage for days. It was tiny and damp and sleep was impossible. There was this dripping sound that made me crazy. I honestly thought I would lose my mind. It makes this cell feel like luxury. They hoped I would break. Lose my mind and ask them to take me out."

"One of the hardest?"

She lifted her gaze. "You probably know their methods. You had the same training as them."

He *did* know. That's why such a crazed storm brewed in his chest. This woman shouldn't have been exposed to any of that. "So, your nightmares are about the torture you had to endure at their hands?"

"Most of the time." She paused. "Tonight, it was about Carter, hanging off the side of the building in Killeen, with me on his shoulder."

Reaching his arm through the bars, Kye squeezed her knee. "It must have been terrifying."

"The worst part was, a couple days earlier, I had convinced myself that I didn't care if I lived or died."

Kye tensed at that. Hating that she'd all but given up.

"Then, in the space of a few minutes, everything changed. The power went off. You guys arrived. For the first time in, I don't even know how long, I had hope."

She paused, but Kye understood what she was saying. Hope can be dangerous. Because once that thing you hoped for was gone, it could be soul destroying.

"And you had to once again accept the reality that you weren't going to be saved. Not yet, anyway," Kye finished for her.

She nodded. "Exactly."

"But, things have changed again, Samantha. Hope isn't so dangerous anymore."

One side of her mouth lifted. "Because you're here."

"Damn, you catch on quick."

She didn't believe it. Sighing, she glanced around. "I don't know if I'll be able to fall back to sleep."

That wasn't good. Not when the woman needed all the rest she could get. "Lie with me."

Kye lay down first. Samantha watched him for a second before resting beside him.

Reaching through the bars, he took her hand. Christ, it felt small in his. Small and delicate. "Maddie and Giorgia are going to love that I missed our weekly game night."

From his peripheral vision, Kye saw Samantha's head turn toward him. "Maddie and Giorgia?"

"My younger sisters. We have a game night every Sunday evening via Skype. It was my turn to choose the game this week."

"Will they be worried about your absence?"

"No, my team will make something up and ensure they're not." He turned his head toward her. "I'm usually the winner, so they'll be pretty happy I'm missing."

She smiled. "Humble, too."

He chuckled. "Humble has never been in my vocabulary." He heard Samantha's soft return chuckle. Best fucking thing he'd heard in here. "They'll probably give me shit about running scared. There's a lot of banter in my family."

Kye moved his thumb gently over her hand once again. It was fast becoming one of his favorite things to do in here.

"Tell me about them."

That was easy. Kye could talk about his family all night. "Maddie's the bossy one. She likes to think she runs the family. We let her believe it to keep her happy. She's also the organizer. She was the one who created the game nights. It's no wonder that she became a lawyer. Giorgia, on the other hand, is easygoing. She runs a doggy daycare and is obsessed with animals. I kid you not, her house is like a farm."

Kye felt Samantha's hand begin to go lax in his. He continued talking about his family, about their holiday traditions and crazy antics. It wasn't until her breaths had completely evened out that he went silent.

He didn't remove his hand though. That small touch made him feel just a bit better. Like he was helping her in some small way.

CHAPTER 4

*S*amantha rubbed her tired eyes. The exhaustion of the day was weighing on her. She'd tried to work faster. Tried to achieve double the work in half the time.

It was impossible. She was nowhere near where she needed to be to get the remote completed by the end of tomorrow.

Tears of exhaustion and fear stung the back of her eyes. Unless she or Kye could pull off a miracle, bad things would be in store for her.

Pain. Torture. Both physical and emotional.

God, she was going to be sick.

Samantha was gulping unsteady breaths, trying to keep the panic at bay, when the door to the room opened and Carter stepped in.

Usually, the man was composed. An arrogant smirk almost always etched on his face. Right now, that wasn't the case. In fact, he looked angry, frustrated...and maybe a little stressed.

He was just closing the door—when another voice stopped him.

"Carter, you get back here right now."

Samantha started at the new voice. It was female and completely unfamiliar to her.

Carter blew out a frustrated breath before walking back outside the room. He pulled the door closed after him, but the latch didn't catch, allowing Samantha to hear the conversation.

"I don't want to wait any longer. Those boys are smart. They'll find us. When is it going to be done?" The woman just about growled the words.

"I've given her until tomorrow."

"And if she doesn't meet your deadline?"

Carter's voice lowered. "She will."

Samantha's stomach convulsed. She didn't have to be a genius to understand the underlying threat in his words. It almost made her think he'd left the door open intentionally...

"Fine. I want new chips made in the next week. Then we'll collect the others."

Oh, God...

Footsteps echoed down the hall as Carter stepped back into the room, looking just as frustrated as before.

"Shut down the computer. Let's go."

Samantha swallowed, doing as he asked. "Who is she?"

She almost wanted to bite her words back. But curiosity was killing her.

"She's none of your goddamn business." He fiddled with his phone.

Okay. Message received loud and clear.

She stepped to the door, and Carter immediately wrapped his fingers around her arm. His grip was punishing, immediately causing her to wince and instinctively attempt to rip her arm free. Her efforts only made him tighten his hold.

"Why are you doing this? Hylar and your team are gone. You're a free man."

He scoffed. "I don't want freedom. I want power."

He tugged her down the hall. Her arm started to numb.

"You *have* power. With your altered DNA, you could do a lot of damage in the world."

"I could do a lot more damage with men below me, following my command. And I had that. Loyal soldiers. Kye and his friends took them from me." A sadistic smile stretched his lips. "It's only fair he's the first man forced to follow my orders."

The guy was deranged. "Why is power so important to you?"

He glanced down, towering over her. There was a small beat of silence. "I was born a peasant, Samantha. I want to die a king."

The explanation had a chill sweeping across her skin. "Something tells me that's not the first time you've said those words."

He tugged her around the corner. "I live by them. Growing up trailer-park scum, I had to believe in something."

"You could believe in doing good."

His hold tightened even further. Samantha cried out. "There's nothing *good* inside me. There hasn't been since the day I was born."

She tried to tug away again. "You don't need to hold my arm, Carter. I can walk on my own."

He spun toward her, slamming her against the wall. His face was so close she could feel his hot, angry breath across her skin. "You don't tell me what to do. The next time you try, it'll hurt. Got it?"

Hurt *worse*, he meant. She kept those words to herself.

It took two attempts before she was able to make her voice work. "Got it."

"Good." He grabbed her arm again in the exact same spot.

Samantha ground her teeth and breathed through the pain. The walk to the end of the hall felt long. The moment they stepped into the room, Kye's gaze fell on her, then to the hand on her arm.

His eyes narrowed, fire lighting across his cheekbones. She could see he was about to say something. Immediately, Samantha gave a little shake of her head. Any words from him and she was sure Carter would take his frustration out on *her*.

Kye's mouth snapped shut, his jaw clenching with anger as Carter threw her into the cage.

She fell heavily onto her knees. An immediate growl sounded from Kye's cell. Still, he remained silent.

Samantha pushed to her feet as Carter disappeared back into the hallway, the door slamming closed after him. She moved her hand to the place his own had just been, immediately flinching at the touch.

Christ, it throbbed. Almost like he'd bruised the bone.

"Are you okay?"

Her head snapped up at Kye's words. He held the metal bars that separated them, looking large and angry. The guy was all power. And she was sure he was a man of action. It must be killing him to be caged, unable to do anything.

"I'm okay."

"Come here, sunshine."

Even though she was exhausted and in pain, she couldn't stop the small kick in her chest at the endearment. He'd used it a couple of times already, and each time it soothed her just a little bit.

Like her feet had a mind of their own, they moved toward the bars, stopping once she stood in front of him.

Tipping her head back, she was reminded of just how tall he was. He had to be about six and a half feet. Miles taller than her five-foot-six.

Reaching through the bars, he stroked her upper arm. She expected pain. Heck, she'd only just touched the area and it made her flinch.

His touch was so soft and gentle that she barely felt it. Yet, at the same time, she felt it right down to her toes.

Was that possible?

"Does it hurt?"

Yes. "No."

He detected the lie. But she knew he would.

His hand lifted to her face, thumb stroking below her eyes. "Always tired."

No. Always *exhausted.* Working twelve-hour days, sleeping on a cold, flat mattress and living in a perpetual state of fear would do that to you. Not to mention the nightmares that plagued her sleep.

She opened her mouth, but before she could speak, the door flew open once again. Kye's hand dropped, and she swallowed the disappointment over losing his comforting contact.

Carter stepped into the room and placed a tray outside each cell.

When Samantha looked down at the food, she couldn't help the soft gasp of surprise.

Salt.

The small shaker sat beside her bowl.

Carter scowled at her from the open doorway. "It's your final fucking dinner."

The door slammed shut and there was silence.

When she looked back to Kye, it was to see absolute fury all over his face. But the moment he glanced at her, it cleared.

Something told her he did that a lot. Concealed his true feelings in an attempt to lighten everything.

A small smile tugged up one side of his lips. "Let's eat before you crash."

It was like there were two of him. The deadly soldier, ready to kill his captor at the first opportunity. And the sexy man with the gentle touch, who was able to soothe her in the depths of hell.

She was grateful for both.

Heading over to the food, she sat down. She'd just lifted her fork when Kye's voice sounded.

"It's not, you know."

Looking up, Samantha frowned. "Not what?"

"Your last meal."

Yeah, she knew it wasn't. Because she knew that she wouldn't be able to code the remote fast enough. She needed a minimum of three more days. She'd told Carter as much.

"I know."

Samantha lifted the saltshaker. Rather than shake it straight onto her food, she twisted the lid off and tipped half the salt into her hand. She could feel Kye's gaze, yet she was almost certain he wasn't looking directly at her. "Tell me about your team."

With the hand that was angled away from the camera, Samantha pretended to rub her leg, sliding the handful of salt into her jeans pocket.

Luckily, she'd lost a lot of weight since being held captive so it wasn't a difficult task.

When the lid to the salt was back in place and on the tray, she finally looked up at Kye. She wasn't sure what she was expecting to find. Confusion? Suspicion? Maybe even a little wonder...

He looked exactly the same as he always looked.

He shoved some food into his mouth. "I have seven team-mates, and they're the best men I know. We were SEALs together, we went through Project Arma together, and hunted and destroyed Hylar together."

"And you're sure he's dead?" Because the man had been larger than life. It was hard to believe the world could exist without him in it.

"I shot him in the head. Saw his lifeless eyes looking up at me. The man's definitely gone."

Good. One less evil.

"Carter said something tonight. He said, 'I was born a peasant, I want to die a king.'"

The fork paused halfway to Kye's mouth. "His mother left his abusive father after he was born. He lived in a trailer park. You think he's doing this for power or money?"

Samantha tasted her soup. Another tasty meal that didn't

actually need the salt she'd added. "He said he wants men to follow his orders. You took that from him, now you'll replace them."

"So after being powerless at the hands of his father, he wants other people to feel his fear."

Samantha took another sip of her soup. "There's something else. There was a woman here."

Kye's body stilled. "A woman?"

"Yeah. I only heard her voice, didn't see what she looked like. I have no idea who she is, but she wanted to know when it was going to be finished."

"Did Carter say anything about her?"

"I asked him but he wouldn't tell me." She stirred the soup in the bowl. "It was strange. She was annoyed…bossy even, and Carter seemed to want to reassure her."

There was a tinge of frustration on Kye's face. She could tell he tried to mask it, but it slipped through.

She was almost certain she knew why.

He'd thought, *hoped*, Carter was the last man standing. The final piece of the puzzle. If there was a woman, that meant another person to take down.

It also begged the question, were there others?

Argh, it was all too much for Samantha's tired brain to compute right now.

"I'm pretty wiped. I might go to sleep."

Kye's eyes softened. "You sleep, sunshine."

That endearment…it was everything in this place. *He* was everything.

She gave him a small smile before heading to her bed. Dropping onto the mattress, she tugged the sheet over her body. Just before she shut her eyes, she looked across at Kye. "If you see me having another nightmare, can you wake me?"

If? Yeah, she may as well just say "when." They plagued her subconscious mind like they owned her.

Kye didn't smile, but his eyes remained gentle. "Sure."

Closing her eyes, Samantha ignored the desperate wish for the sheet to be warmer. For the mattress below her to be thicker. Because there were bigger things to worry about.

Tomorrow, Carter would come and get her. She'd need to act. To save both herself and Kye.

~

KYE LISTENED as Samantha's breaths evened out. Tomorrow, she was going to do something. What, exactly, he wasn't sure.

His heart crashed against his ribs at the idea that she could get herself into trouble and there was nothing he'd be able to do to save her. Not from inside this damn cage.

He watched as the worry lines smoothed out on her face. She always looked so calm before the nightmares hit. Ten years younger. Like she didn't carry the weight of the world on her shoulders.

One day, honey. You'll feel that again.

Kye was a born protector. And seeing the woman he'd gotten to know over the last week suffering, seeing her hurt by this godforsaken project, made him angry. Angry enough to kill.

Once his bowl was empty, Kye lay down beside her. She was within reaching distance, just the way he liked it.

CHAPTER 5

*N*erves threatened to consume Samantha, nearly to the point where the screen blurred before her eyes.

It was almost time. Any second, Carter would walk through the door, stand beside her, and ask if she was done. If the remote was complete.

Her breath stuttered in her chest. Should she tell him the truth? That she was still at least a couple days off completion? Or should she remain silent? Not even attempt a response.

It didn't really matter what she said. It mattered what she *did*.

The salt felt heavy in her pocket. She could still recall the way Kye had watched her this morning. He hadn't said a word, but his intense black eyes hadn't left her. Like he was waiting for her to say something. Reveal her plan.

The truth was, she barely had one. All she had was a desperate idea in her head. She'd wanted to enact that idea this morning, the moment her cage was opened, but Carter had shoved his keys back into his pocket too quickly. She'd had no choice but to wait.

Oh, God. She needed to calm down. To *not* pass out.

Her fingers trembled against the keyboard. Not just out of fear of what she was about to attempt, but out of fear that it wouldn't secure her freedom. That she'd end up in one of those torture rooms. Experience more pain that was sure to unleash new demons into her soul.

Samantha scrunched her eyes shut as memories of water being thrown over her cloth-covered face came back to her. Choking her. *Drowning* her. She was sure she would never again be comfortable with the feeling of water raining over her face. Nausea welled in her stomach just at the thought.

She pushed it down and gave herself a mental shake. She couldn't think about that right now. She had to focus. Focus on getting the upper hand with Carter. Slowing him down. At least until she could free Kye.

The clink of a key being inserted into the door had the fine hairs on Samantha's arms standing on end. Carefully, she slid the hand that faced away from the door into her pocket and pulled out a handful of salt.

She didn't take her eyes from the screen. Focused on regulating her breaths.

In and out.

Samantha didn't look at Carter as he came to stand beside her, but she felt him. Felt his stare bore into the side of her head. His body heat penetrate her side.

"Is it done?"

No. And it would stay that way.

At her continued silence, a strong hand clenched her shoulder. "I said, is it done?"

He spun her to face him. Mid-turn, Samantha lifted her hand and threw the salt into his eyes.

It hit him full force.

His hand dropped from her shoulder, and he growled in pain, scrubbing his closed eyes.

In the next second, Samantha yanked the knife from his harness and plunged it into his neck.

Carter spluttered and choked, the keys dropping from his fingers.

Yanking the knife out, she grabbed the keys from the floor and ran.

She didn't stop to look at the blood. The wound. The man barely breathing. She didn't stop to think about the fact that *she'd* done that.

The only thought in her mind was *run*. Free Kye, before Carter stopped her.

With trembling legs, she sprinted down the hall, her feet pounding the hard floor. Her breaths moving in and out of her chest in short, quick succession. Reaching the intersecting hall, she immediately turned the corner.

There it was. The door to the cells. Only a few feet away. So close she could almost cry.

Her legs moved faster.

She'd almost made it when a strong arm encircled her waist, yanking her backward.

Air whipped across her face, the keys and knife slipping from her fingers. For a second, she was airborne. Then her hip hit the concrete floor hard.

Groaning, she immediately rolled to the side.

A shadow cast over her. She looked up to see Carter looming. Blood still oozed from his neck. His breaths were coming out in short gurgles—and fury clouded his eyes.

He opened and closed his mouth like he wanted to speak, but couldn't. The knife wound had somehow stolen his voice. Silencing him.

He looked ready to kill.

Shuffling back, she tried to put space between them. But with every inch of space she created, he doubled it, closing the distance easily.

Terror swelled in her chest as he bent and wrapped his fingers around her throat. Yanking her to her feet, he shoved her against the wall. His hands clutching so tightly that her air was cut off.

His grip was too firm to breathe. His strength impossible to fight.

Both her hands went to Carter's wrists. Pulling and tugging.

It did nothing.

Fight, Samantha!

Her arm felt heavy as she released his wrist, moving her hand to the wound on his neck.

In almost slow motion, Samantha dug her fingers into the open cut.

A wave of nausea rolled through her stomach. Carter's face contorted in pain and his hands released her.

A dark haze still blurred her vision as she dropped to her knees. She didn't have time to recover. She had to move.

Grasping the keys from the floor, she stumbled her way to the end of the corridor. Three times she tried to get the key into the slot. Three times her trembling fingers missed.

Slow, heavy footsteps sounded behind her. Gagging breaths.

Come on, come on, come on!

Her heart was in her throat, her limbs boneless with terror.

Just when she was sure he was going to grab her, sure he was close enough to yank her back again, wrap his unrelenting fingers around her throat, the key slotted into the hole and she all but fell into the room.

Her gaze caught Kye's. Immediately, he was on his feet. Hands on the metal bars and eyes alert.

She took three steps toward him before she was lifted off her feet and thrown sideways into the concrete wall.

The air was knocked out of her chest, pain cascading through her skull where it collided with the wall. She tried to push up, but her arms gave way.

Come on, move, Samantha! You have to move!

Yet again, she heard Carter nearing her. This time it was

accompanied by Kye's angry shouts in the background. His threatening words, all directed at Carter.

She tried to block out all the sounds. She needed to focus on making her limbs work. If Carter reached her, he wouldn't spare her any pain. It would be game over.

She couldn't let that happen.

Carter was a foot away when he stumbled. His powerful body tumbling to its knees. He was losing blood fast. It coated his shirt. His pants. The stuff was everywhere.

Samantha tried to push to her feet, but her knees gave way. A small whimper escaped.

"Crawl to me, sunshine!"

Kye's gentle words cut through her foggy brain. Remaining on her knees, she moved around Carter, giving him a wide berth. Blood gurgled from his throat as he crouched on his hands and knees.

The man was dying.

She didn't spare a thought to the fact that his blood still coated her fingers. She'd never taken a man's life before, and the idea of his death being on her hands was too much.

Her eyes scanned the floor.

Where were the keys? They'd slipped from her fingers when she'd been thrown.

Crap, she needed to find them. Carter might gain another wind and come for her. With frantic eyes, she scanned the area.

"There."

She looked up to see Kye pointing to the corner. Of course. They'd skidded to the farthest spot.

Every muscle in Samantha's body hurt. Her energy was nonexistent. There was also the agonizing pain that radiated from her head, back, and hip. Yet she pushed herself to continue crawling.

Not much farther. Get Kye out, then you can rest.

She'd felt worse pain. Could experience worse pain again, on the slim chance Carter survived this and got to her.

Finally, her fingers closed around the silver metal.

When she turned around, it was to see Carter standing. He took slow, uneven steps toward her, looking like he could fall to his knees again at any second. But she was sure her strength was still no match for his.

She needed to get to her feet.

Samantha pulled herself up, her knees threatening to buckle yet again, but this time she didn't let them. She staggered toward Kye's cell as quickly as possible.

She'd almost made it when Carter was suddenly in front of her.

His fist flew, but he wasn't as quick as usual. Samantha dropped to her stomach and threw the keys along the floor to the cage, missing Carter's punch.

She didn't get a chance to see if the keys had made it before strong hands latched onto her shoulders, shoving her onto her back. Then Carter was on top of her, his now cold hands once again wrapped around her throat.

Droplets of blood dripped from his neck, splattering onto her chest. Her face.

Her air was cut off. Consciousness began to slip as darkness edged her vision. Her bloody hands were on his wrists, but they were slipping.

Samantha was seconds from drifting into oblivion when the heavy weight of Carter's body lifted.

Air rushed through her starved lungs. She gasped it in greedily, scrunching her eyes closed as she did, grabbing her neck and coughing.

When she finally looked up, it was to see Kye throwing Carter against a wall. The guy barely put up a fight, hitting it hard before dropping to the ground.

Kye stalked toward him, lifting him again.

Suddenly, a loud siren filled the room. It made the pain that already pounded through her head that much more intense.

Christ, what the hell was that?

Kye was scanning the room when Carter reached for something on his hip.

"Kye!"

Samantha's scream had Kye turning in time to see the gun being drawn.

That's when he snapped Carter's neck.

Before Samantha could process what she'd just witnessed, Kye hurried over to her.

A hissing noise sounded.

It took her a second to recognize that gas was being shot into the room from somewhere near the roof.

Kye cursed loudly before sweeping her into his arms. "Dig your head into my chest, close your eyes and hold your breath."

Samantha did as he ordered. The air shifted around her. She didn't look up but knew they were moving fast. The sound of gas hissing continued throughout the building.

Doors opened. Thirty seconds, maybe more, passed before fresh air brushed against her face.

When she looked up, it was to see that they'd entered the dark night. Unpaved ground surrounded the building, leading to thick forest beyond. In the distance, she could just make out some mountains.

Kye didn't speak as he began moving toward a break in the trees.

She opened her mouth to ask what the plan was but quickly snapped it shut. Exhaustion and pain weighed on her. She trusted Kye and whatever plan he had.

As he ran through the darkness, her eyes fluttered shut. She let the steady beat of his heart lull her to sleep.

Finally, there were no bars separating them. For the first time in months, she felt safe.

CHAPTER 6

*K*ye's feet pounded the uneven forest floor as he made his way through the trees. He didn't pause. *Hadn't* paused in hours. He had one goal.

Get as far from the building as he could, as quickly as possible.

It would have been faster to take the road. Flag someone down and get in a vehicle. But where he'd have gained ease, he'd have lost a level of obscurity.

There was no guarantee Carter had been alone at the location they'd just left. *Someone* had been watching. Someone realized they were about to escape and set off the gas.

They would likely assume Kye had taken the road. Exactly why he hadn't.

He hated the idea of people coming after the woman sleeping in his arms. She was damn strong. The way she'd taken on Carter...almost single-handedly killing him...

But if he could save her from another battle, he sure as hell would.

Whoever *they* were could be close. And they could be many. Hell, for all he knew, there could be an entire army of enemies he didn't know about. Kye couldn't risk that. If he and Samantha were found, there was no guarantee he would be able to keep them both safe.

The smell of pine trees penetrated his nose as he sped past more than he could count. The trees provided a layer of protection from possible eyes above.

Kye tuned into Samantha's heart rate and breathing. Normal. Fortunately, she didn't seem too badly hurt. Angry red bruising covered her neck, and he'd felt a bump on her head, but no other visible wounds, thank God.

She needed rest though.

Kye ground his teeth, trying not to think about what that asshole had done to her. When he'd thrown her against the wall, Kye had damn near lost his mind. Then his fingers had wrapped around her neck, trying to choke the life out of her...

It made Kye see red.

No—it made him want to turn around, go back, and tear the guy's heart out. Burn his body to ash. If that goddamn gas hadn't been released, Kye would have made the man's death slow and painful.

There had been a couple of times where it almost seemed like Carter was trying to speak. What had he been trying to say? Whatever it was, it died with him.

He shot a quick glance at Samantha's sleeping face.

So damn strong.

He wasn't sure exactly what had taken place outside their cells tonight, but somehow Samantha had managed to pull off the impossible. Injuring a man who should have been almost unbreakable. Slowing him down. Getting the keys to Kye while remaining alive.

Man, she was something.

Admiration hit him in the gut like a bag of bricks. The woman was brave. Smart. Determined. He'd never met anyone like her.

Now it was his turn to save them.

At the feel of raindrops on his shoulders, Kye's arms tightened around Samantha's body. He cursed under his breath as the thin material of his undershirt quickly stuck to his chest.

He moved his body faster, trying to outrun it, but when the rain became heavier and thunder rolled through the sky, Kye began to search for shelter. Somewhere they could wait out the storm.

He shot a quick look over his shoulder. Other than the occasional sound of wildlife moving through the forest, he hadn't heard a single noise. He'd taken plenty of twists and turns to throw off anyone who might try to track them.

It should be enough for a short break.

Four minutes passed, maybe five, before Kye spotted what looked to be a shallow cave. Plants had begun to grow on the outer surface of the rock, covering half the entrance. When he came to a stop, he had to duck his head to step inside the small space.

Dry. Exactly what he needed.

Crouching, Kye placed Samantha on the ground. There was a small sigh from her lips, but other than that, she barely stirred.

Gently, he grazed her cheek, pushing a tendril of hair from the side of her face. *So delicate.*

He glanced down at his clothes. Soaked. Samantha wasn't as wet, but she definitely wasn't dry. Luckily, he didn't feel the cold much. But he'd have to share his body heat with her.

Making a split-second decision, Kye removed his wet clothing, everything bar his briefs. Then he carefully removed Samantha's shirt, jeans, and shoes.

He made a conscious effort not to look at her nakedness any more than he had to, but it was impossible to miss the array of bruises scattered over her body.

His jaw ticked.

Lying beside her, he curled his body around hers, cocooning

her. He made sure to put his back to the entrance of the cave, protecting her from the wind.

The soft purr that released from her throat had his blood turning molten.

The tiny woman felt good in his arms. Too good.

Stop, Kye. Shut it down. This isn't the time to be feeling that stuff.

When a small shiver racked her small body, Kye pulled her closer. There were no bars separating them now. And finally touching her the way he wanted was doing strange things to his insides.

A LOUD CRACK penetrated Samantha's ears, pulling her from sleep.

Was that lightning?

It couldn't be. The sounds of nature didn't penetrate the concrete walls of her cell.

She wriggled her body, a small frown marring her brows. She wasn't cold. She'd been cold for weeks. Months even. Yet, right now, she was almost too warm.

Had Carter finally given her a thicker sheet?

Lifting one of her hands, she tried to feel around her.

Wait. Was that...a forearm?

"Samantha?"

Her breath caught in her throat at the sound of the deep voice. Not just any deep voice. Kye's. Did that mean...?

"We got out." She whispered the words as memories suddenly funneled their way back to her. Of throwing salt in Carter's eyes and stabbing him...his fingers around her throat...throwing the keys to Kye. "You got us out."

"No." His response was immediate. "*You* got us out."

At the feel of his breath on the back of her neck, the hairs on her arms stood on end. She swallowed. Then, slowly, she shifted onto her back. Everything was pitch black. She couldn't see a thing. But she could *feel* him. His body pressed against her side.

The heat of his skin was intense as he hovered over her slightly.

Instinctively, she raised her hand, touching his face. She moved her fingers over his forehead. His cheeks.

Kye didn't say anything, and he didn't pull away. He remained completely still. Allowing her to explore.

"I threw the salt in his eyes. Salt creates a hypertonic solution in the tear film, which draws moisture from the corneal surface." She didn't know why she was going into such detail. Maybe because she was in shock that she was finally free. "Then I grabbed his knife and stabbed him in the neck."

"You did good, sunshine."

Was that admiration in his voice? She'd acted out of desperation. Anyone who'd been through what she had would have done the same to avoid history repeating itself.

She should ask where they were. How much time had passed. But none of that seemed to matter right now. She was out. Away from the evil.

They'd been holding her for so long, she'd believed her days were numbered. Some days, she'd even *hoped* they were. She'd thought she'd never feel the warmth of another person again.

"How are you feeling?" His voice was soft.

Her fingers trailed to his neck. "I've felt worse." A lot worse. Her mild headache and dry throat were nothing compared to other injuries she'd incurred. "Are we really free? I mean, I know we're free right now...but do you think they'll find us?"

She almost didn't want to know the answer. Because if she was dragged back there, she would lose the tiny tendrils of sanity she had left.

"Hylar's dead. Carter's team is dead. And so is Carter. When the rain subsides, we'll keep moving and find a town to contact my brothers."

Dead. All of them. Every man who had held her in that hell. Every man who had laughed at her pain. Her fear. Gone.

When her fingers grazed his chest, she could have sworn his breath shifted.

She couldn't stop touching him. She needed the physical reminder that metal bars no longer separated her from safety.

"Your clothes were wet, so I removed them," he continued, his voice deeper. "I hope that's okay."

"It's okay. Did I have any nightmares?" Usually, she woke with the taste of terror in her mouth. Not necessarily remembering what she'd dreamed about but remembering the fear the nightmare had incited.

"We've only been in this cave about an hour but you didn't stir once."

Her fingers rose to his shoulder. So large and powerful. Just like the rest of him. When her fingers grazed down his chest once more, he whispered her name.

"Sam…"

Rain thrummed against the outside of the cave. She heard the groan of the trees swaying in the wind. She didn't pay any of it one bit of attention. She couldn't. Not with Kye so close.

She craved closeness with another person. Connection. Intimacy. She craved *goodness*.

Slowly, she lifted her head and pressed her lips to his shoulder. His quick intake of breath penetrated her ears. She pressed another kiss beside it. Then another.

"Samantha…what are you doing?"

"I—I want to feel something good." Something gentle. Tender. *Him*.

Silence followed.

He didn't want this.

Of course not. They'd just killed a man. Were running for their lives.

Giving herself a mental shake, Samantha dropped her head back to the ground. "I'm so sorry. I shouldn't have—"

Before she could finish, Kye's lips found hers. His touch was light. Like he knew she needed softness.

She moved her lips against his. Closing her eyes against the darkness and breathing him in. He deepened the kiss. Pressing his tongue between her lips and tasting her.

The band that had been around her chest, suffocating her for so long, loosened. In this moment, she could almost forget everything before now.

When her hand slid to his chest, just above his heart, she felt the rapid beat against her palm. It was steady and powerful, just like everything else about the man above her.

His masculine scent surrounded her, mixing with the smell of forest and rain.

His hand lightly grazed her side. Then slowly, almost tentatively, he shifted his hand and enclosed her breast.

Samantha immediately arched into his touch. Moaning softly as he massaged the soft mound through her bra.

One of her legs curved around his hip, his hardness pressing into the junction between her thighs. For the first time in months, her heart beat wildly from something other than fear. Her body craved something other than freedom.

His mouth shifted to her neck. Her shoulder. Every touch remained soft and gentle and healing. The kisses were featherlight yet burned across her deprived skin.

Reaching behind her, Kye unclipped her bra and slid it off. His head quickly replaced the material, his lips closing over her peak. This time, Samantha didn't moan. She cried out into the darkness, desperately wanting more of this man.

He switched to her other breast and another round of pleasure took over. His hand moved to her core, his fingers slipping inside the thin material covering her.

At the first touch, sparks flashed behind Samantha's eyelids.

She scrunched her eyes tighter, blinded by the pleasure the man enticed from her body.

He continued to thrum his fingers. Playing with her. Pushing her higher and higher.

"Kye…" His name was a strangled cry on her lips.

"What do you need, sunshine?"

Need. That word was so fitting. She'd moved past "want" long ago. "You. Inside me."

She wanted to feel the man. All of him.

Within seconds, the last scraps of material that separated them were gone. He lay above her. His weight anchoring her to the ground.

Anticipation hammered in her heart as he paused at her entrance. "Are you sure?"

"Yes." So sure, she thought her heart might explode.

Slowly, he sank into her.

It was earth-shattering. The only sound from either of them was the soft hiss of breath escaping her chest.

He paused inside her. She didn't move a muscle. Never wanting this moment of peace and pleasure to end. Seconds passed, then he lifted his hips before pushing back into her. He did it again.

Ecstasy. Utter and complete ecstasy. It coursed through her body, rivaling the thunderstorm that raged outside the cave.

A few days ago, Samantha never thought she'd feel anything but pain again. She'd thought lightness would never touch her soul.

This was lightness. This was everything.

Kye continued to move inside her in long, slow strokes.

He kissed her again. This time, harder. Her center now aching. Her heart jackhammering in her chest.

She knew she wouldn't last long. Knew she was teetering dangerously close to the edge of the cliff, waiting to fall off. But she didn't want it to end. She needed this goodness to last as long as possible.

Kye's hand returned to her core. He'd barely touched her when her spine arched. A soft cry flew from her lips, and she shattered beneath him.

Kye thrust two more times before his own body tensed. He shuddered above her before going still.

She held him tighter. A light inside her, which she'd assumed had well and truly died, flickering to life.

CHAPTER 7

Samantha's feet sank into the damp earth, mud coating her shoes. She could hear Kye's footsteps behind her. She didn't need to turn her head to know that he was close.

The sun was almost setting. Kye had jogged the entire day with her in his arms, only lowering her to her feet a couple of minutes ago at the sound of traffic. She could just make out the road through the break in the trees ahead.

Kye had said he was going to contact his brothers. *How* he planned to do that, exactly, she wasn't sure. She probably should have asked. But her mind had been filled with something else.

Last night.

She shot a quick peek over her shoulder. Kye's gaze moved from the break in the trees to Samantha. He smiled. Then he winked. Samantha quickly swung her head back around in an attempt to hide the rosy pink that tinged her cheeks.

He'd been acting completely normal all day. Like they hadn't woken from a night of earth-shattering lovemaking. Well, earth-shattering for Samantha at least.

She could have brought it up. But what would she say? Thank you for having sex with me? For reminding me that human touch can feel nice? Healing even?

Because it *had* been healing. She still had a long way to go, and she was almost certain she would never be the same person she once was…but still, her heart felt a little less heavy today.

"You doing okay?" Kye's voice penetrated the silence.

"I'm okay." Tired, hungry, in desperate need of a shower…but so much better than she was yesterday.

Suddenly Kye was beside her, taking her hand in his as they reached the road.

Although it looked like a highway with multiple lanes, there were barely any cars. Across the highway, she could see an access road with a gas station and some small shops.

Kye tightened his hand around hers as they crossed.

He remained silent as he led them down the two-lane road and past the stores. A couple of streets beyond the highway were some spaced-out homes on big lots.

She shot a quick glance up at him. "What should we do?"

They were both dirty, especially her. She didn't even want to know what she looked like, but it couldn't be good. Anyone who saw them would probably assume they were homeless.

"We need to find a phone so I can contact my brothers."

She loved that he referred to his teammates as brothers. "I think of Tori as a sister, too."

She was unbelievably grateful that her best friend was alive and safe. If Hylar had killed her, it would have been entirely Samantha's fault. She had only become embroiled in all of this because of Samantha's involvement.

She never would have been able to forgive herself if anything happened to Tori.

"How long have you known each other?"

She couldn't even remember. "Six, maybe seven years. We ran into each other a lot in the oncology ward where our moms were receiving treatment. It didn't take us long to get to talking. We figured out we had a lot in common—our moms were both sick, neither of us had siblings or a father around, and we were both trying to remain positive even though we were terrified of losing our only family. Even when she was away in the Army for a while, we still kept in regular contact. Leaning on each other. I don't know what I would have done without her."

And what had Samantha done to thank her? She'd gotten her friend kidnapped, electrocuted, and almost killed.

She sucked in a deep breath, not wanting to think about that right now. At least Tori had met Oliver. The man who had saved her life and fallen in love with her.

"It's not your fault."

Samantha frowned at Kye's words. Had she spoken her thoughts out loud without realizing it?

"I can tell you're blaming yourself right now for her kidnapping."

Was the man a mind reader? Or was she just wearing her remorse for the world to see? "How can you tell?"

"Your quick intake of breath. Your sudden silence."

Ah. So just very observant. "Oliver loves her, right? He's going to take care of her?"

"The man's besotted with the woman. She's in very good hands. The best, in fact."

Good. That's what mattered. That's what she deserved. "I can't wait to see her."

She'd probably cry her eyes out. Then grab the woman and never let go.

Kye's voice softened. "I think she's going to be excited to see you too."

At his gentle words, she couldn't help but tighten her hold on his hand.

When Kye suddenly turned off the road and started heading up the driveway of a house, she shot a quick look at him. "Are we going to ask to use their phone?"

Instead of moving toward the front door, he headed around the side toward the back.

Wait—were they about to break in?

Nervousness unfurled in her stomach. What if someone was inside?

He stopped at a back window. It took her a moment to realize what he was doing.

Listening.

"No one's home," he said after a couple of seconds.

His hands went to the base of the window and he pulled. It opened easily. So easily, Samantha was sure he hadn't even broken a lock.

Kye climbed in first before helping her. He went straight for the kitchen counter, where there were both unopened letters and a landline phone.

"Don't see many of them anymore," she said with a small chuckle. In fact, since moving away from home, Samantha had never even had a landline, always content to just use her cell.

Kye ignored the phone for a moment, instead lifting a piece of mail. "Forest Hill, Louisiana."

WYATT CLOSED the door to his apartment. The rich smell of Bolognese bombarded his senses.

The sight of Quinn turning her head to smile at him from the stove made some of the weight on Wyatt's shoulders a bit more bearable. It had been a long day of searching for Kye, with nothing to show for his efforts.

"Hey there, handsome. Dinner's almost ready."

God, he was so grateful for her. While Kye's absence had been tearing him apart, tearing the entire *team* apart, Quinn had been holding him together. The woman was everything. He honestly didn't know what he'd do without her.

Stepping behind her, Wyatt pressed a kiss to her neck. "Smells amazing." Not just the food. The woman in his arms smelled better than a meal ever could.

She chuckled. A soft, lyrical sound. "It's spaghetti Bolognese. Not sure amazing is the right word for it. Quick, maybe? Easy?"

"God, I love you." He told her at least a dozen times a day. He couldn't stop.

Her voice softened. "I love you, too."

He nuzzled her hair with his face. "How was work?"

Her job at Mrs. Potter's Bakehouse was her newfound passion. She'd come to love baking and making coffee. Not to mention the social interaction with customers. There was usually at least one of the guys watching her, to keep her safe, which wasn't hard to organize when the bakery was on the same street as their self-defense business, Marble Protection.

"Busy. Filling the people of Marble Falls with caffeine and sugar is a big job." She turned, remaining in his arms. When her hands wrapped around his neck, the humor slipped from her face. "Any new information?"

His jaw ticked. If only. "Not yet."

Her expression didn't change. She felt his pain like it was her own but rarely did she show it. So damn strong for him.

Quinn pressed her palm against his cheek. "Soon."

It had to be. Wyatt refused to believe that this was it. That Kye was now with Carter for the foreseeable future, God knows what happening to him.

The buzz of his phone ringing sounded from his pocket.

Reluctantly, Wyatt released Quinn. He glanced down at the screen, noticing it was an unknown number. Taking a step into the living room, he answered the call. "Hello?"

"Jobs. It's me. Cage."

Wyatt's body went completely still. Blood began to pump through his veins twice as fast as seconds earlier. "Is this a secure line?"

"Yes. I found an unoccupied house. Their mail was piling up in the mailbox, so I think they've gone away."

"Where are you?"

"Forest Hill, Louisiana."

Grabbing Quinn's phone from the counter, he did a quick search.

It was a six- to seven-hour drive. Not close, but hell, he'd take that over the other side of the country. "Are you safe?"

"Carter's dead."

Wyatt's eyes immediately shuttered, relief flooding his system. Finally. Their last enemy gone.

He felt Quinn's hand on his back, calming as always.

"We have nothing but the clothes on our backs, though," Kye continued. "We look like hell. I think the safest thing for us to do is wait here for you."

We. So Samantha was with him. Good. Tori and Oliver would be relieved. "We'll fly over—"

"No." Kye's response was instant. "I think you should drive here to pick us up."

Wyatt paused. The only reason to avoid airlines was to keep their movements under wraps. Kye was telling him there was still an enemy out there.

Dammit.

He pushed aside the disappointment, focusing on his friend. "Give me your address, we'll leave now." Wyatt's heart continued to beat wildly in his chest. Disbelief that he was actually talking to his friend coursed through his limbs.

The last week had been the longest of his life. So many times, he'd wondered if this was the time he was actually going to lose one of his brothers.

Wyatt was about to hang up when he stopped himself. "Thank you, Cage. For getting yourself out."

"I didn't. Samantha did."

CHAPTER 8

*K*ye shut his eyes as the soft latex mattress sank beneath his body.

Goddamn heaven. That's what the bed felt like. After weeks of sleeping on a hard concrete floor, no blankets, no pillow, sitting on something so soft was the best damn thing.

Not that concrete was the worst thing he'd ever slept on. Hell, when he was on active duty, he'd had to sleep out in the elements more times than he cared to remember. Returning to a real bed never got old.

He swung his gaze to the bathroom again. Samantha was on the other side, taking a bath.

No one had returned to the house, so as he suspected, it seemed to be theirs for the night.

He didn't feel bad about sleeping in someone else's house. Eating food from their freezer. It was survival. Other than some chicken and corn, and a couple of clothing items, the home-owners hadn't lost much. Whereas they'd gained plenty.

The sound of the plug being pulled from the tub filled Kye's ears. The room was small, with a king-size bed and connected bathroom. Samantha had offered him the first shower, claiming she wanted a long bath.

There was something about the way she'd said it, though…He almost thought he'd heard a tremble in her voice.

Why? He wasn't sure. But unless she volunteered the information, he didn't want to push. The woman had been through enough, she'd open up if, and when, she was ready.

He scrubbed a hand over his face, leaning back against the headboard with a sigh.

Why had he had sex with her?

Actually, he knew the answer to that. There'd been something about the way she'd been looking at him. Touching him.

Desperation mixed with vulnerability.

She'd needed him. And Christ, he was a weak man and hadn't been able to say no. Not just for her sake, but because she'd been all but naked. And when she touched him, it damn well set his blood to blazing.

But he should have said no. The woman was recovering from trauma. She'd been locked up for weeks. *Months*. She needed time to heal. He couldn't help but feel like he'd taken advantage of that.

Idiot. He could kick his own ass.

There were other bedrooms in the house, but for safety reasons, they needed to share. If he had to get them out quickly, he needed her right beside him.

Shuffling noises sounded from the bathroom. She hadn't eaten much of the food they'd heated up, but at least she got a chance to wash.

Kye's eyes shot up when the bathroom door clicked open and Samantha walked out. His mouth went dry.

Samantha's golden curls cascaded over her bare shoulders. Her face was clear of dirt, and she looked five years younger than she had.

She wore bed clothes she'd found in a drawer. The shorts

showed way too much of her long, soft legs, and the tight under-shirt...Kye struggled to keep his eyes off her chest.

A fire began to burn in his gut. The woman was sexy. There was no two ways about it. But then, he wasn't surprised. He'd found her sexy after months of imprisonment. Freshly bathed and smelling like citrus, she was a damn aphrodisiac.

Shut it down, Kye. Leave her alone and give her time.

He clenched his jaw. "Was the bath okay?"

She smiled. It made his chest tighten. "I feel clean for the first time in...a long time. It was nice."

She moved to the other side of the bed and slipped under the covers, her bright blond locks splayed over the pillow, her face turned away from him.

He twitched to put his arm over her. Tug her body into his.

Giving himself a mental shake, he rose and went to the bathroom.

When he re-entered the bedroom, he noticed the soft rise and fall of her back. Already asleep.

Switching off the light, Kye was just about to crawl under the covers when he saw the first flicker of movement. He didn't need to wait to know what was coming next. A flinch, quickly followed by a soft cry.

Another nightmare. They haunted her.

For a moment, he was torn. Torn between simply waking her or taking her in his arms.

When her body twitched again, he made his mind up. Slipping under the sheets, he wrapped an arm around her waist, tugging her body against his.

Almost immediately, a soft sigh escaped her lips. The tightness in her muscles released as she softened against him.

"That's it, sunshine. Sleep. You're safe."

Like her subconscious had heard him, she nuzzled her back closer. Then her hand moved to rest on top of his.

Laying there, holding her, his mind quietened. A calmness he hadn't felt in far too long settled in his chest. When he'd been caged, he'd felt helpless for the first time in years. Unable to protect the woman imprisoned with him.

His hand on her waist tightened.

Never again did he want to be in that position.

This woman was strong. And smart. A damn survivor. And he wouldn't—couldn't—let anything else happen to her. Not when she'd risked her life to save them. He knew she'd been tortured while refusing to make the microchips. While protecting Kye and his brothers.

He ground his teeth, hating that she'd been hurt, but at the same time, in complete awe of her strength.

Kye lay there for a long time, eyes open and appreciating the beautiful, courageous woman in his arms.

Movement in the house had Kye's eyes shooting open. Samantha's cheek lay on his chest, and he could feel her gentle breaths on his skin.

Carefully, he eased out from under her. She hadn't woken from any more nightmares. It was the second night in a row, which surprised the hell out of him. No night had passed while they'd been imprisoned without her waking in terror, her subconscious mind reminding her of what she'd been through.

Kye listened, hearing three heartbeats moving toward the bedroom door. He shot a quick look at the clock. Almost three a.m. He crept toward the door, careful to remain silent. His body was tense and ready for action.

Then he heard it. Quiet words spoken by Wyatt.

Kye relaxed, sighing loudly. His team was here. His brothers. God, he'd missed them. They'd been separated less than two weeks, but it felt like a lifetime when he was used to seeing them every day.

Tugging the door open, he was greeted with the sight of Wyatt, Oliver, and Tori. Wyatt was the first to step forward and tug Kye into his arms.

"Missed you, buddy."

Kye returned the hug, holding his friend tightly. "I missed you too, brother."

When they separated, Oliver wrapped his arms around Kye, hugging him for a solid twenty seconds before parting but keeping his hands on Kye's shoulders. "You okay?"

"Yeah. I'm okay." Now that he was free and with his team again.

Tori stepped forward next, hugging him around the waist. "I'm glad you're safe."

Kye's chest warmed at the hug.

When she stepped back, she nibbled her bottom lip nervously. "Is she here?"

"Yeah, she is."

A watery smile stretched across Tori's lips. She tried to blink the tears away. "Thank you."

"What for?"

"Getting her out."

He could have laughed. "The woman is tough. She would have gotten away if I'd been there or not."

One way or another, he truly believed that.

He heard the soft rustling of sheets moving before light feet hit the carpet. Turning his head, he saw Samantha standing by the bed, hands wringing in front of her. She looked just as nervous as Tori.

Stepping back, Kye was about to usher his friends inside, but Tori was already running. Arms wrapping around Samantha in a hug like no other.

Damn, it was good to see.

"I missed you," Tori whispered to her friend. When she pulled away, she shook her head. "I'm so sorry."

Samantha frowned, tears rolling down her cheeks. "Sorry for what? *I* should be apologizing."

"No. You were tricked. Just like me. I'm sorry for letting you go back the day you told me to run. Then for allowing Carter to take you."

"There was no way you were stopping me from trying to fix my mistake. And Carter and Hylar didn't exactly give us a choice in the whole abduction thing."

"I'm still sorry," Tori said softly.

Samantha pulled her against her chest again. They remained like that for a few silent minutes.

Kye closed the door behind his friends after they stepped inside.

Wyatt dropped a bag on the bed. "We brought you both some clothes if you want to change before we start driving home."

Home. Christ, that sounded good. To sleep in his own bed. Be back with his friends, his community.

Kye looked over to Samantha. "You want to take a quick shower and change?" Not that he would be complaining if she decided to stay in the shorts and tank top. Cute didn't even begin to describe how she looked in them.

Samantha eyed the bathroom, then the bag of clothes. "I don't need a shower. I'll change though."

Tori walked over to the bag and grabbed a handful of clothes, pressing them into Samantha's hands. Once her friend disappeared into the bathroom, Tori moved back to Oliver's waiting arms and leaned into his body.

Wyatt wrapped an arm around Kye's shoulder. "It's so good to have you back. You had us scared for a while there."

Kye scoffed, trying to take his mind off Samantha's vulnerable eyes and bring back some of his usual humor. "You can't get rid of me that easily."

CHAPTER 9

*S*amantha rubbed a hand over her eyes as she sat up in bed. The sun poked through a crack in the curtains. This was her third morning waking in Oliver's spare room. Each morning she'd felt exactly the same...tired as all hell.

The nightmares had returned. They were so bad that she'd woken both Oliver and Tori multiple time.

But...she was free. Nightmares inside Oliver and Tori's home sure beat nightmares from the inside of iron bars.

Samantha ran her hand across the side Tori had slept on last night. What time had her best friend snuck out of the room? Early morning? The sheets were cold, so it must have been at least a couple hours ago.

Sighing, Samantha pushed out of bed.

She hated that she'd been waking them with her cries. That her friend had to slip into her bed at night and try to talk her through the fear.

Walking to the bathroom, she stood in the doorway and studied the shower. Maybe she should give it a try today. Just a second of standing under the stream. She had to eventually, didn't she?

Samantha walked further into the room, pulling open the glass shower door. The second she looked up at the showerhead, sweat beaded her brow. Dizziness clouded her head and nausea rolled in her stomach.

With a quick shake of the head, Samantha closed the glass door and stepped back. No. She wasn't ready. Not yet. She'd have her normal evening bath tonight.

Give yourself time, Samantha.

Turning toward the sink, Samantha pulled her hair up in a band and brushed her teeth. Then she quickly dressed in jeans and a T-shirt. *Her* jeans and T-shirt, thanks to some of the guys driving her and Tori to Samantha's apartment yesterday.

It had been strange walking in there. Like she was stepping back into her old life. A life she didn't quite fit into anymore. The Samantha who had moved in there several years ago had been working for Hylar, had a mother who was still alive, and knew very little about the evil that existed in the world.

So, someone else entirely.

Leaving the bedroom, Samantha made her way downstairs. She was immediately greeted by Charlie. Bending down, she gave Tori's dog a pat and a cuddle.

Rising, she heard Tori before she saw her. Her friend's giggle was quickly followed by Oliver's hushed voice as he whispered words she didn't catch.

Cute. In fact, she'd seen a bucketload of their cuteness since moving in, even when they tried to hide it.

Stepping into the kitchen, Samantha noticed Tori quickly pull away from Oliver's embrace. "Sammy! You're awake."

She slid into a seat at the island. "I am. And you don't need to stop whatever you were doing on my account. Cuddle. Kiss. Do whatever you want. It's your home."

Well, Oliver's. But now that Tori had moved in, it was basically hers too.

Oliver smiled, immediately tugging Tori back into his arms.

"Don't need to tell me twice." He nuzzled her neck while Tori swatted him on the shoulder.

Samantha laughed. It felt good to do that. She hadn't laughed much since coming to Marble Falls, but when she did, it almost made her feel human again.

It took Tori a minute to extract herself from Oliver—or more accurately, for Oliver to release Tori. Then she came to sit beside Samantha. "I was thinking we could go to Joan's Diner for breakfast. We haven't left the house much since you've gotten here. I need to show you the best parts of the town."

"Sounds great. I've been having a huge bacon craving, so if they have it, I'll be one happy girl."

Oliver chuckled. "Oh, they definitely have bacon. My usual comes with a double serving."

A double serving of bacon didn't sound terrible. "I might jump on that bandwagon, Oliver. Good coffee, too?"

He leaned his hip against the counter. "Between you and me, best coffee in Marble Falls."

Between her and him? "Who are we keeping this information from?"

Tori sighed. "Quinn. Wyatt's partner and Mason's sister. She works at Mrs. Potter's Bakehouse, working toward becoming part owner. She makes good coffee."

"But not the best?"

Oliver lifted a shoulder. "It was terrible when she first started." He grinned. "She's gotten better. I just wouldn't go so far as to say it's the best in Marble Falls."

Tori stood. "We can go to the bakery tomorrow and you can compare. Now let's go, this girl's hungry." Tori took Samantha's hand and tugged her toward the door.

The drive to the diner was quick and Tori spent the entire time talking about the people in Marble Falls. Oliver's team. Their partners. Kye had already told her about everyone, and

Samantha had thought the same thing then as now—that there was no way she'd remember all those names.

"Maya's actually gotten me into running," Tori said from the passenger seat as Oliver pulled the car to a stop. "We run together a couple of times a week. Want to join?"

Samantha couldn't help but laugh as she climbed out of the car. "Tori, when have I ever wanted to work out with you? Or do any form of physical exercise? You would run circles around me." It wasn't that Samantha hated exercise. More that she knew how fit Tori was. The couple of times in her life she'd gone to the gym with her friend, Samantha had sworn she was going to die.

No, thank you.

Oliver reached the door to the diner first, holding it open for them.

Tori pouted. "I'll go slow for you."

Yeah, Tori had said those words before. Then proceeded to kick her butt in whatever physical endeavor they'd done. "I'll think about it."

And after she thought about it, her answer would still be no.

By the look on Tori's face, she knew it.

They chose a booth by the window, Oliver sliding in beside Tori, right as her friend rolled her eyes. "That's what you say when you mean no."

Tori knew her too well.

Luckily, the waitress chose that moment to arrive at their table, saving Samantha from having to respond. She gave them each a menu before leaving with their drink order.

Samantha scanned the items, noticing that Oliver was right, just about every item had bacon.

Tori barely looked at her menu before placing it on the table.

Samantha lifted a brow. "Already know what you're getting?"

"I'm feeling hot cakes today."

That didn't help Samantha. She definitely wanted savory. "Oliver?"

"Bacon omelet with a side of bacon."

Samantha and Tori giggled. She should have known.

"Okay, I might just get toast and bacon." That wasn't one of the menu items but surely they'd make it for her.

Tori frowned. "Just toast and bacon? No egg? Or vegetables? No side of avocado?"

Okay, it sounded a bit boring, but it's what she felt like. "Maybe I'll add butter." She grinned.

Tori shook her head as she glanced at Oliver. "She always does this. Orders something boring, then eats mine."

A laugh burst from Samantha's lips. It was true. She'd done that more times than she could count. "Yours always looks better than mine."

Tori leaned forward. "As it will today, if you order buttered toast with bacon."

The waitress popped back to the table with their drinks. "Ready to order?"

Samantha gave Tori a mischievous smile as the words came out of her mouth. "Buttered toast with a side of bacon, please."

Tori rolled her eyes, but her lips tilted up.

Once their orders were placed, Samantha took a sip of her coffee. Mm. It *was* good. In addition to bacon, coffee was another thing she hadn't had any of in the last few months. She'd never been someone who relied on the stuff, but her time away from it had definitely given her a new appreciation.

"It's good," she said to Oliver, placing it on the table.

"Told you." He took a sip of his own before his gaze caught on something by the door. She followed his line of sight, and her belly did a little flip.

There, standing at the door, was the man she'd been thinking about way too much. The man she tried to distract her mind with when the terror of her memories seeped in.

Kye.

He was just as tall, dark, and handsome as she remembered.

His large biceps strained the fabric of his shirt, and his powerful legs were evident even in jeans.

When she looked up at his face, it was to find him looking back at her, a small smile on his face. She flushed before quickly looking away.

Oliver pushed out of the booth. "I'll be right back."

He moved across the room. When he reached Kye, Samantha saw what she'd missed the first time—a beautiful woman standing close beside him. She had long red hair and a flawless hourglass body.

Jealousy hit Samantha hard.

It shouldn't. She had no claim over the man. They'd been placed in a terrible situation together, relied on each other to survive, and now it was over.

What was more, she hadn't seen him since arriving in Marble Falls.

"Who's the woman with Kye?" Samantha asked, not able to hide her curiosity.

Tori looked across the room. "Lexie, Asher's girlfriend."

Relief pierced her chest like an arrow.

God, what the heck was wrong with her? Okay, the man had taken pity on her and they'd had sex. Didn't mean he was going to pursue her.

At the beat of silence that passed, Samantha dragged her gaze away from Kye and looked at Tori. Her friend was watching her closely.

Uh-oh. "What?"

"Did something happen between you and Kye at that house we picked you up from?"

"No," Samantha answered quickly. Way too quickly. Dammit. "Nothing happened between us at that house."

Which was a hundred percent the truth. As long as you classified sleeping in the man's arms all night "nothing."

She hadn't told her friend about their night of lovemaking in the forest. She didn't know why; she usually told Tori everything. Maybe because a part of her wanted to keep that private and between her and Kye. Their secret.

"You spent a good chunk of time together. You also relied on each other quite heavily for companionship…" Tori's voice trailed off. "I wouldn't blame you if you wanted to spend more time with him now. Grab a meal together, maybe."

Kye hadn't contacted her at all over the last few days. If he wanted to spend more time with her, he would have.

And she should *not* be disappointed by that.

"No. He's probably trying to get back to his normal life in Marble Falls." Who knew, maybe she was an unhappy reminder of his time in captivity. "I'm just happy to be free and spending time with you. For as long as you and Oliver will have me, that is."

Tori reached across the table and took Samantha's hand in her own. "You're welcome to stay as long as you want. Oliver said the same. And to be honest, until they know who set the gas off in the building where you were held, I'm not sure the guys would want you on your own just yet."

Yeah, Samantha didn't want to be on her own either. She didn't know Oliver very well, but she did know that he would do everything in his power to keep her safe. Not just for her sake, but for the sake of his team. Because if she was caught and forced to make more microchips, forced to make another wireless remote, no one was safe.

"Thank you. I don't think I've said this yet, but I *love* you and Oliver together. And I love how happy he makes you."

Her face lit up. "Thank you. I feel so lucky. The man is…argh, I can't even explain it. He's everything."

Samantha could see that. "You deserve to be happy."

Less than a year ago, her friend had been anything but. Losing her mom had been just as hard for Tori as it had been for Samantha.

Tori shot a look over her shoulder before leaning across the table again. "If you and Kye got together—"

"Nope." Samantha cut her friend off before she could finish. "I'm not going to participate in 'imagine if our boyfriends were best friends too'."

Tori pouted. "Why not? It sounds fun, doesn't it?"

It did. Especially the part about her dating the oh-so-sexy Kye and double dating with her best friend. Unfortunately, it wasn't reality.

"I'm going to the bathroom." Before Tori started dreaming up double weddings and living in houses next door to each other.

Samantha was out of the booth and across the room before her friend could stop her. She used the facilities quickly, all the while thinking about what she'd just told Tori to stop thinking about.

She shook her head. Kye was a bachelor. He'd told her as much during more than one of their conversations. He didn't "do" relationships—his words, not hers.

Drying her hands, Samantha had just stepped into the hallway when a guy stopped in front of her.

He immediately held out his hand. "Phillip Barret, reporter for *The Hidden Outpost*, nice to meet you."

Samantha was so surprised by the guy's sudden appearance that she automatically slipped her hand into his before quickly pulling it back. "Uh, *The Hidden Outpost*?"

"We're a magazine that exposes the deep, dark secrets in the world that nobody knows about. Nice to meet you."

The guy was tall at maybe six-one. She was sure he would be considered good-looking to most, with his dark brown hair and bright blue eyes. Samantha was totally put off by his smile though. Because it was about as fake as one could get.

"I was wondering if you had a couple minutes to answer some questions for me. It would really help with a story I'm working on."

"Story?"

"Yes, it's about a military experiment involving the guy you're staying with." He chuckled. It was as fake as his smile. "I've called some of the men, but just get hung up on, and it's incredibly hard to catch any women they hang out with alone."

A woman pushed past them to make her way into the bathroom. Yeah, this really wasn't the best place to stand. "I think if you have questions, it's best you ask them—or just drop it."

Samantha tried to step around him, but he immediately mirrored her move, blocking her path.

"Would you know anything about the men possessing above-average strength or speed?"

"No." Her answer was immediate and firm.

She took a step the other way, but again, he blocked her. "Really? Because I have numerous eyewitness accounts stating these men are far from normal."

Okay, the guy was starting to annoy her now. "I find that ridiculous, Mr. Barret—"

"Phillip."

"—and I think you're chasing a fictitious story."

"It does sound fictitious, doesn't it?" His brow rose. "Are you living with Oliver Bolton right now?"

"That's none of your business. Now, I'd like to go back to my table."

She stepped to the side for a third time. Phillip tried to step in front of her again—but a hand on his elbow swung him around, stopping him mid-step.

Kye towered over the man, his eyes dark and stormy. "You weren't about to block her exit *again*, were you?"

The reporter looked up, strangely, appearing anything but scared. "If I say yes, what will you do? Throw me across the room?"

Kye's jaw visibly ticked. "I think it's time you got going."

Phillip turned back to Samantha, but Kye immediately stepped between them. "Now."

Phillip stepped sideways, coming back into view. He yanked a card from his pocket and attempted to hand it to Samantha. When she didn't take it, he shrugged. "Fine. I'll be back."

Turning, he walked away, clearly not intimidated by Kye's size.

Kye turned around and studied Samantha's face. "You okay?"

"I'm fine. But he knew about—"

"I heard." Kye scrubbed a hand over his face. "The problems are never ending."

Placing a hand on the small of her back, he led her back to the table. She felt his hand as if he was touching bare skin. It made her back heat and tingle, and she forgot all about the nosy reporter and his claim of coming back.

CHAPTER 10

"*I* don't understand how they could've let it be taken."

Kye was only just holding on to his calm. The wireless remote, which had been seized by authorities in Killeen, was missing.

Something as important as that should have been protected, dammit!

Wyatt, Luca, Bodie, and Oliver sat with him around the table in Marble Protection's office, all looking equally angry and frustrated.

"Security footage was switched off. Two police officers were shot and killed," Wyatt said, repeating what their CIA connection had told him.

"And there's no evidence of who took it?" Luca asked.

Wyatt shook his head. "The attacks on the officers came from behind. And whoever did it knew how to hack into the security footage."

Goddammit!

Just then, Samantha's sweet voice penetrated his ears from the other room. It was the only thing keeping him calm.

He hadn't been able to get the woman out of his mind since

returning to Marble Falls. She was all he could think about. Her bravery and intelligence, her gentle nature...it was all wreaking havoc on his system.

And if the remote had been taken, how long would it be until they came for *her* next? After all, whoever took the remote would need more chips coded.

"You okay, Cage?"

Oliver's question pulled Kye out of his thoughts.

Was he okay? Nope. He was losing his goddamn mind. "Just thinking about everything." Samantha being everything. "There's no lead on who took the remote. So what about the building in Louisiana? Has Logan made contact?"

Logan and his team were also once Hylar's prisoners. Taken from their homes, given DNA-altering drugs and held against their will for years. Now, they were free and living a couple hours away in Lockhart.

With Kye's help, they'd been able to locate the black site where he and Samantha had been held in Louisiana. Logan's team was investigating the location while Kye and the guys protected their women.

"Yeah, he left me a message. Figured I'd call him back when we were together." Wyatt checked the time on his watch. "I'll give him a call now." Taking his phone from his pocket, he dialed Logan's number. He then placed the phone in the center of the table and put it on speaker.

Logan picked up on the third ring. "Wyatt."

Kye leaned forward in his seat. "Hey, a few of us are here. Find the site okay?"

"Hey. Yeah, we went to the black site yesterday. We're leaving Louisiana today." There was a brief pause, and Kye suddenly got a sinking feeling in his gut. "The place is ashes. There was an explosion."

Curses sounded from around the table. Not that it was

surprising. Destroy any and all evidence was what any smart person would do.

"There's nothing that survived?" Oliver asked.

Kye said a silent prayer that there was. Any small reprieve.

"Nothing. By the car tracks in the dirt, I estimate they blew the place shortly after you left."

Disappointment hit Kye hard.

Bodie sighed. "Even if there wasn't an explosion, the person or people probably took any evidence before they blew up the place."

"There shouldn't have been much," Kye said. "Samantha hadn't started work on any more microchips. Instead, she spent all her time working on the remote."

"Well, that's a positive." Wind rustled over the line. "We're going to pop into Marble Falls before we head back to Lockhart. Jason's keen to see his sister and it would be good to talk about everything in person. I took photos of the aftermath."

Kye nodded, even though Logan couldn't see him. "Thanks, Logan."

"You got it. See you soon."

When the line went dead, there was a heavy silence in the room.

So someone stole the wireless remote from police custody. And the black site was blown up. Kye was reasonably certain the same person had to be responsible for both.

Bodie was the first to speak. "We need to find this mystery woman."

Who the hell knew if she was working alone though? And the woman was both faceless and nameless. "We knew who our enemy was before," Kye said quietly. "Right now, we're blind."

Luca leaned forward. "Chances are good that she is alone, though. Other than the woman who visited, Samantha didn't see anyone else there. And you didn't see anyone in the building when you left. Plus, it was just Hylar and Carter's team who held Oliver, Tori, and Samantha in Killeen."

True. No backup was called—and if there *had been* any backup, they definitely would have been called.

Kye looked across to Wyatt. "You said you and Evie couldn't find any women connected to Hylar or Carter's team?"

Wyatt shook his head. "Hylar wiped all information on his family. Even his sister Tanya had a fake record. Carter only had a father, who died when Carter was eighteen. All the other guys' family members look clean." He took his phone back from the center of the table. "We'll wait for Logan and the guys to arrive, have a look at the photos. There's not much we can do until then, other than watch our backs."

"Done." Luca's gaze shot across to Kye. "Oliver mentioned a reporter."

Kye scowled at the memory of the jerk. "He approached Samantha when she was leaving the bathroom yesterday. Kept blocking her way. He knew about the project. Not exact details, but that we have abnormal speed and strength. Asked about a military project."

Wyatt shook his head. "The asshole has called Marble a couple of times looking for information. I was hoping he'd disappear."

Oliver sighed, having heard the entire conversation as well. "He said there were eyewitness accounts." He shook his head. "Not that I'm surprised. There have been times when we've each exposed ourselves out of desperation. Hell, I did that less than a month ago outside the bar to save Tori from being hit by a car."

"I definitely moved too fast at the fair when I lost sight of Maya in Keystone," Bodie added.

Wyatt nodded. "You're right. I think we've all exposed ourselves at some point or another to save one of our own."

"He has nothing," Kye sneered, hating the guy without even knowing him. "That's why he had to resort to trapping Samantha outside a public restroom. If he comes back, we just deny."

The guy had to be desperate for information. Why else would he have had to resort to what he'd done yesterday?

Luca chuckled, but there wasn't much humor behind it. "Let's hope that if he ever prints anything, the story is so out of left field that people don't believe it."

Wyatt nodded. "I'll do a quick look into him today. I'll also let our contact at the CIA know. Hopefully, they'll shut him down." He was about to stand when he stopped and looked across to Kye. "Are you still doing okay since getting back, Cage?"

Shit. Could his friend see how distracted he was? If he could, he probably assumed it was from Carter's treatment.

It wasn't. Not even a little bit.

"I'm okay."

Oliver frowned. "I'm worried about Samantha."

Kye stiffened in his seat. "Why?"

"She hasn't been sleeping well. Wakes from nightmares constantly. Tori's been spending the second half of most nights with her. It hasn't seemed to help."

Kye's muscles tensed further. He'd been hoping that once out of the cell, her nightmares would dwindle. The ones he'd seen had tormented her every time she'd closed her eyes.

Oliver lifted a shoulder. "I think she needs to speak to a therapist. But..."

Kye knew what his friend was thinking. "But then she'll need to expose us to someone." She would hardly be able to heal without talking about everything.

"I know someone," Luca said. "Evie was seeing a therapist quite frequently after Troy died. She had a great reputation with no red flags. She only works with women, and she specializes in trauma recovery. She's helped Evie a lot. Both Evie and I would trust her with the secrets we keep."

Kye shot a look across to Oliver. "You think she'll be willing to talk to someone?"

"I can ask Tori to suggest it. She certainly hasn't spoken to Tori about any of it."

Probably trying to be strong. Shield her friend from the pain.

"Did you talk to her a lot while you were in your cells?" Bodie asked.

"Not nearly enough. She was gone most of the day in the lab. We only talked for short periods of time, morning and night."

They'd also talked a bit while working their way through the forest.

Not just talked...

Kye quickly shut the thought down. He couldn't think about that right now.

"I'll get Tori onto it. I'll also keep an eye on her," Oliver said quietly.

Kye wanted to be the one keeping an eye on her. But she needed comfort. Tori was her best friend. Basically, a sister. She was the one Samantha needed right now.

If he was being honest with himself, he actually wanted to date her. He'd never wanted a relationship with a woman before...but dammit, he wanted it now. She needed time to heal first. And Kye needed to grit his teeth and give her that time.

The guys pushed to their feet as Bodie spoke. "Once Logan and the guys arrive, we should do a family BBQ. A night of just spending time together, appreciating each other's company and the fact that there are seven less threats in the world."

Luca smiled. "Beer will be necessary."

Kye laughed. "Lots of it."

"How's the wedding planning going?" Oliver asked Luca as they headed out of the room.

Luca had been the first to meet his woman. They were a damn cute couple.

"We're all good to go. We've changed the location to Eden's property, so we'll have all the security we need. Just us, some family. And Logan's team will be there for added security."

That was as safe as it could get. Blake wouldn't be present, because he was remaining with his daughter and her mother, but the guests would still have fifteen DNA-altered protectors.

"Let me know if there's anything I can do to help." Kye wasn't exactly sure what he *could* do. But heck, if his friend asked, he'd do his best.

"Thanks, buddy."

When they stepped into the main area, Kye spotted the women talking by the desk. His gaze immediately zoomed in on Samantha. She was smiling at something Maya was saying. And she was damn beautiful. Her hair, her eyes, the way her face softened when she smiled.

Was it crazy that he actually missed their conversations from those cells? There was absolutely nothing else he missed about that place...only her.

Kye stepped up to the group. "Hey, ladies, are those smiles a result of thinking about my handsome face?"

He got a couple of chuckles and a few eye rolls in response.

Tori shook her head. "Evie was telling us about her flower arrangements for the wedding."

Ah, another topic Kye knew nothing about. "I've never understood the need for flowers at a wedding. Don't they charge you ten times the normal price once you say the word 'wedding'?"

Luca stepped behind Evie, wrapping his arms around her waist. "If flowers make my girl happy, I'll buy a whole damn garden of them."

Evie's cheeks colored pink.

Waste. Of. Money.

Tori turned to look at Kye. "Flowers are beautiful and they smell nice. Nothing wrong with investing some money in them."

He nodded. "That's funny, I'm beautiful and smell nice, too."

When Samantha laughed, Kye's gaze flew to her face. He wanted to hear that sound again and again and again.

Bodie threw an arm around Kye's shoulders. "Think you have a bit too much self-love going on, Cage."

Nothing wrong with that. Especially if it elicited a laugh from Samantha.

Oliver took Tori's hand. "Ready to go?"

Tori nodded, trailing behind Oliver. Samantha followed them out.

It wasn't until they were halfway to the door that Kye caught up and touched her elbow. "Hey." He didn't miss the way her heart rate increased at his touch.

Was that good or bad?

She gave him a smile. "Hey."

"I just wanted to check in and see how you're doing?"

An expression crossed her face. It was so fleeting, he almost missed it. Anxiety maybe?

"I'm okay. Glad to be with Tori."

Kye lowered his voice. He wanted to help but wasn't entirely sure how to do so. "Oliver mentioned the nightmares have come back."

Her cheeks shaded red. She was embarrassed. She shouldn't be. He'd seen her in the thick of her night terrors.

"I'm okay, Kye. But thank you for checking in."

"But if you need to talk to someone…"

"Someone?" She tilted her head.

He was going to let Tori mention this, but he may as well just do it. "There's a therapist here in Marble Falls."

Her eyes shuttered. Did that disappoint her?

"I'll think about it." She shot a quick look over her shoulder. "I should really get going. Thanks again."

Kye watched her leave, wanting to kick his own ass. He should have suggested himself. Should have suggested that *he* listen to her.

Goddammit.

He hadn't, because he wasn't sure if that was the best idea. His feelings for her didn't seem to be decreasing with time apart. But, damn, he didn't want to see that look on her face. Like for a second she'd had hope, only to have him tear it away.

The next time he saw her, he was going to suggest she confide in him. Because he wanted to see that light come back in her eyes. That smile on her face.

CHAPTER 11

*S*amantha sipped the beer in her hand, trying very hard not to stare at Kye. He stood on the other side of Luca's backyard, talking to some of the guys. Logan's team was here too. It made for a lot of large alpha men all in one space.

Tuning back into the conversation around her, Samantha looked across at Shylah. The woman was telling the group about her one-on-one self-defense sessions with Eden.

"He couldn't understand why I kept getting distracted, and I was like, hello, you're all over me. Have you seen yourself?"

Samantha chuckled, knowing she'd be the same way with Kye. Heck, she'd probably go into a state of shock. She snuck another peek at him from below her lashes.

As if Kye felt her looking at him, his gaze immediately clashed with hers. When he winked, her heart gave a little stutter.

Samantha's cheeks heated.

Kye's attention went back to the guys. Before she could glance away, a man beside him looked at her. Samantha had been introduced to all of them but couldn't remember any of their names, including his.

She gave a small smile before turning back to the women.

Kye had explained a very short and condensed version of the other team's story. Men who had been taken by Hylar. Men who had the same abilities as Kye and his team.

Samantha turned to Evie beside her. "So, Hylar held those guys hostage for two years?"

Oliver had seemed reluctant to go into detail. Maybe because it made Samantha's couple months in Hylar and Carter's hands absolutely pale in comparison.

Evie nodded, turning to face Samantha. "Yeah. They weren't kept in cages. Well...at least not until the last couple months, after Logan escaped. Before that, most of their time was spent living on a large estate. They all have military backgrounds and training, but while they were held, they were also trained by Carter's team."

The fact that they had military training was obvious. Not just because of their size, which was impressive, or because she knew Hylar tested strictly on soldiers, but also because of the way they scanned their surroundings. Always looking ready for action.

"They must be happy Hylar and Carter's team are dead."

Lexie, who sat on the other side of Evie, scoffed. "They're probably angry they didn't get to do any of the killing."

"Why didn't they stay in Marble Falls until Hylar was taken down?"

Evie's gaze rose to the men. "Blake, the only one from their team who isn't here, has a daughter. The girl's mom lives in Lockhart, so he wanted to be near them. The team wanted to stick together. Not just for safety, but also to help each other recover from their experience."

"Speaking of children," Lexie scanned the yard. "Where's Fletcher gone?"

Sage chose that moment to walk up to the group, depositing Fletcher in his mother's arms. "This guy keeps trying to make a getaway."

Lexie stood. "He's already walking, can you believe it? It's a wobbly walk, and he falls on his butt every couple steps, but gosh does it make my life harder. Every chance he gets, he's on the move." Lexie shook her head. "I have a feeling this guy's going to test my speed very soon."

Samantha noticed Asher heading their way. He stopped beside Lexie and threw an arm over her shoulders. "That's why you have me. The speedy father."

"And the reason for our physically gifted child."

Almost on cue, Fletcher began to wriggle from Lexie's arms. His feet had barely touched the grass before he was off. Asher chuckled, trailing after his son.

Cute.

One day, Samantha hoped she'd be lucky enough to have kids of her own. Not just one. Two or three at least.

Sure, she'd been happy being an only child, and her mother had given her more than enough love, but she'd craved that sibling love and connection. Especially while her mother had been sick.

When her eyes sought out Kye again, she almost scolded herself.

Stop, Samantha. What the heck is wrong with you?

"He would make beautiful babies."

Tori's quiet words as she shifted her chair closer to Samantha had her smiling. "As would Oliver."

Tori chuckled. "Oh, he would make *gorgeous* babies." She shook her head. "Definitely not now, though. He hasn't said it, but I can tell he's stressed. We can't be adding pregnancy to his load."

"Stressed about the woman who was at the black site?"

She lifted a shoulder. "I think so. Maybe also because Kye was taken. It scared him into acknowledging that he could lose someone he loves." She shook her head. "So, yeah, I absolutely cannot get pregnant and give the man something else to worry about."

"Well, that just gives you something to look forward to in the future."

Excitement lit her friend's eyes. "Hell yes, it does."

From over Tori's head, Samantha saw Oliver heading their way, presumably to give Tori more of those ridiculously sweet kisses he gave her all day, every day.

Argh, Samantha couldn't watch that right now. Not while she was obsessively thinking about a man she couldn't have.

She stood before he got to them. "I might get a drink."

When Tori stood too, Oliver slid his arms around her waist from behind. "Mm, you torture me when you're too far away."

Tori chuckled. "Too far away? You were only a few feet across the lawn."

He lowered his head to her neck. "Yeah, too far."

And that's my cue. "I'll be back."

Samantha wasn't surprised when neither of them seemed to hear her. She wasn't complaining about their constant displays of affection. Tori deserved to be deliriously happy, and if Oliver was the one to make her happy, then she didn't want him going anywhere. She just didn't want to be witness to it all the time.

There was a drinks table outside, but Samantha walked past it and continued toward the house. She needed a couple minutes of silence.

She never used to need quiet. But after months of fear, months of no freedom, suddenly some time to collect herself each day had become necessary.

Pushing inside, she grabbed a glass from the kitchen cabinet and filled it up at the tap. She stood there, sipping her water, watching through a window that looked onto the backyard.

Everyone seemed happy. A handful of people were laughing. Most of those who weren't laughing were at least smiling. No one would look at them and know what they'd gone through. No one would look at Kye and realize that only a week ago, he was being held in a concrete cell.

If he was suffering, it was invisible.

Was hers?

She'd been held for months. Electrocuted, waterboarded, sleep-deprived to the point on insanity by keeping her body at ridiculously cold temperatures…

She closed her eyes, attempting to push the memories down.

She'd survived all of it. Standing firm and refusing to rebuild her work because she'd known how dangerous the microchips were.

It had only been Tori's promise that Oliver's team would save them that had finally made her give in. She trusted her friend with her life. And, evidently, the lives of many others.

"Are you okay?"

The stranger's voice jolted Samantha out of her thoughts, the glass slipping from her fingers. The sound of shattering glass echoed through the kitchen.

Crap.

Cursing under her breath, Samantha quickly attempted to clean the glass out of the sink. Clearly her mind was still elsewhere, because when she grabbed a large piece, the sharp edge cut the palm of her hand, slicing the skin open.

"Dang it!"

The man moved beside her. It was the same guy who had smiled at her from his position beside Kye. He had short, shaggy brown hair. His eyes were a light brown and his skin an olive shade. He stood well over six feet, but then, they all did.

"Sorry, this is my fault." He almost looked angry with himself as he took gentle hold of her wrist. "Hang on, most people keep…" He let her go to open the door below the sink. "Bingo."

The guy straightened, first-aid kit in his hand.

"Good find. If there's a Band-Aid in there, that should fix it."

He smiled, the lines around his eyes telling her he did that often. "I'm sure there is. Come over to the couch, and I'll give the cut a quick clean before we cover it." When she hesitated, his smile grew. "Sorry, I should have introduced myself. I'm Jason. Sage's brother."

Samantha couldn't help but return the smile. "I'm Samantha."

She trailed behind him into the living area, taking a seat on the couch. Jason dropped down beside her and studied her hand.

Even though the guy was good-looking—actually, more like deliriously gorgeous—she didn't get the buzz that zipped through her body when he touched her compared to Kye.

"Don't think it needs stitches, but I could get my sister to have a quick look?"

"Oh, no. That's okay. I think the Band-Aid will do fine."

One side of his mouth lifted. "You're in great hands. I happen to be a master at Band-Aid application." He grabbed a wipe out of the first-aid kit. "You looked like you were deep in thought over there."

His comment threw her for a moment. How long had he been in the room before he'd spoken?

"I was." There was no point in lying. The guy could probably spot a lie like the rest of them.

He shot a quick look up at her before moving his attention back to her hand and continuing to gently dab the alcohol wipe along the wound. His voice lowered. "I do that too. Get caught up in my own mind. In memories."

Memories from when he was kept prisoner? "How do you cope?"

He lifted a shoulder. "Some days are better than others. In a lot of ways, I was lucky. I had my team around me. For the most part, we weren't kept in cells."

"But you were still prisoners."

He dipped his head. "That we were. And we were forced to train. To allow life-altering drugs to be injected into our systems."

"Did they ever..." Samantha swallowed, unsure how to word it. "Did they ever hurt you?"

He put the swab aside and lifted the Band-Aid. "We weren't tortured or beaten physically."

Immediately, she hated herself for almost feeling disappointed. God, could she get any more selfish? To almost hope that someone else had gone through the same hell as her, just so someone else knew how she felt?

"We experienced more psychological torture," he continued. "Our families were threatened. We had to live with the fear of never being free men again. The fear of what would become of us."

Samantha should be grateful that all she'd had was Tori. They hadn't used her against Samantha until the end.

When the cut was all covered, he sat back. "Trauma is trauma, though. And everyone who's experienced it needs to fumble their way back to their own semblance of peace."

Fumbling was definitely an appropriate way to describe how she was dealing with her trauma. "How long did it take you to get to where you are now?"

She prayed that it was a small amount of time. A couple months, maybe? That would give her hope.

Jason ran a hand through his hair. "I'm a constant work in progress." Her heart dipped. "But then, who isn't?" He placed a light hand on her knee. "Talking to people helps. If you ever need someone to talk to, I'm happy to listen."

Samantha smiled. The guy was sweet. And she could tell he wasn't trying to come on to her, he was just being kind. Identifying her pain and offering his help.

She opened her mouth to respond, but before she could, the back door opened and Kye stepped into the room. He took a moment to study her and Jason. Then he looked almost...angry.

"What the hell is going on?"

CHAPTER 12

*F*rom his peripheral vision, Kye watched as Samantha stepped inside the house. Her long tanned legs were fully on display in her denim shorts, and Christ, were they making his blood rush south.

He was about to follow her when Logan clamped a hand on his shoulder. "How are you doing after your time with Carter?"

Reluctantly, Kye dragged his gaze away from the house. "Just glad we could finally end him."

Logan nodded. "I'm almost sad I wasn't there to see him die. And I wish we'd gotten to the black site before it was burned to the ground."

Yeah, Kye wished that were the case too. "We appreciate you making the trip. It's a bit harder for us to leave while protecting the women."

"Happy to be useful. We're just as keen to see the end of all this as you. So you think there's just one woman left?"

Kye took a quick swig of his beer. "That we know of. Samantha heard her voice but didn't see her face."

Mason stood on Kye's other side, joining the conversation. "I don't understand where this woman has come from. There were barely any women working at the Project Arma facility all those years ago. No women have popped up since then, except for Hylar's sister, Tanya."

"We never saw a woman in the estate we were held in," Logan added. "Maybe she entered the game late."

Maybe. But what were her plans now that all the soldiers were dead?

Kye scrubbed a hand over his face, wishing like hell Samantha had seen the woman's face. A voice didn't give them anything to go on.

Logan dropped his hand from Kye's shoulder. "Whoever's left, they had the resources to blow the place up without leaving a scrap of evidence. Everything was destroyed." The group was silent for a moment before Logan spoke again. "Carter was definitely dead when you left though?"

"Samantha stabbed the guy in the neck, and I followed it up by snapping his neck. He was dead." Kye had seen the man's empty eyes looking up at him before getting himself and Samantha out of there.

Kye shot a look back to the house before scanning the yard. Samantha still hadn't returned.

"You sure you're doing okay after everything?" Logan asked again, studying Kye with an intense look.

"All the asshole did was hold me in a cage for a while. I'm fine."

He hadn't been held for years like Logan's team. Hadn't been tortured like Samantha.

Logan shook his head. "I can't believe they're all dead. It's...surreal."

"No shit," Mason said, sipping his beer.

"What are your plans now?" Kye asked Logan.

Logan cast a look around at his team. "Jason's going to remain in town for a bit with his sister. A couple of us might hang around; the others will go back to Lockhart so that Blake's not alone out there. And we'll all be back for the wedding, of course."

"And what about when this is all over?" Mason asked.

Logan sighed, running a hand through his hair. "Flynn's mom is sick. He would move her to us, but the woman has lived in Cradle Mountain, Idaho, her whole life, it wouldn't be fair to uproot her now. Flynn wants to be with her to help with care. If Blake can get his daughter and her mom to move, we might all relocate and open a security business over there."

Kye nodded. "That's awesome. Let us know if you need any help."

He dipped his head. "Will do."

When Mason began talking about the business side of Marble Protection, Kye hung around for another couple of minutes before heading toward the house.

When he stepped inside, he was surprised to find Samantha wasn't in the kitchen. Looking through to the living area, he tensed at the sight of her sitting close to Jason. The guy had his hand on Samantha's knee. And she was looking at him like he was the center of the goddamn universe.

"Talking to people helps. If you ever need someone to talk to, I'm happy to listen."

Kye's fists clenched. "What the hell is going on?"

He didn't try to shield his irritation. He probably should have. After all, the woman wasn't his. He had no right to be angry. But it was all he could do to not leap across the room and rip the guy's arm from his shoulder.

Samantha stood quickly, followed by Jason, but much slower. He moved to stand in front of her, almost like he was shielding her from Kye.

What the hell?

Jason's brow creased. "We're just having a conversation, Kye."

Conversations didn't usually entail touching. Kye took a step forward. Jason mirrored the move. "Why's there a first-aid kit on the floor?"

Samantha's quiet steps sounded as she joined them. "I broke a glass and Jason helped me bandage my hand."

There was a beat of silence. Neither man took his gaze off the other or stepped back.

"I'm going to head back outside," Jason finally said before glancing down at Samantha. "You okay?"

Christ, even the guy's question made Kye see red. Was he insinuating that Kye could pose a threat to her?

She nodded.

When Jason looked back to Kye, he waited for him to step aside. It was the soft touch of Samantha's hand on Kye's arm, her soft voice as she said his name, that finally got him moving.

Stepping to the side, Kye watched as Jason headed outside. Once they were alone, he turned back to Samantha.

She was studying him, her head tilted inquisitively. "What was that?"

That was him losing his goddamn mind at the sight of another man touching her. "I didn't like him touching you."

It sounded even crazier when he said it out loud. He shouldn't care. Had never cared about a man touching a woman before, regardless of what their history had been. But it felt different with Samantha. Everything felt different.

Her brows shot up. "Why not?"

Because you're mine.

The words flashed through his mind before he could stop them. They shook him to his core. But hell…that's how he felt.

"Have you eaten?" He needed to change the subject. He couldn't explain how he was feeling because he could barely understand it himself.

The smallest of frowns crossed her face. She knew he hadn't answered her question on purpose. Would she call him out on it? And if she did, would she tell her the truth? That he'd never wanted to date another woman in his life, but he wanted to date her...

"I haven't."

Kye took her hand, immediately reminded of the cut on her palm. He began leading the way outside. "Is the injury okay?"

"It's totally fine. It was a tiny cut. Jason was just being helpful." She paused at the kitchen. "There's still broken glass in the sink. Should I—"

"I'll come back and clean it up later." For now, he just wanted to eat and drink with the woman and get his crazy overreaction of moments ago out of his head.

SAMANTHA INSPECTED her mountain of meat, salad, and potatoes as they walked away from the table. Man, Kye had really loaded it up. There was probably enough food on her plate to last *three* meals.

She expected them to eat with one of the clusters of people. So when he continued to tug her along, walking right past them, she glanced over her shoulder in confusion. Luca's house backed onto a forested area. Was that where Kye was taking her?

She opened her mouth to ask, but then snapped it shut again. She didn't actually care where the guy took her. She trusted him. And if she was honest with herself, she really liked the feel of his hand around hers.

So, yeah, he could lead her to the state border and she'd probably follow.

"You're not going to ask where I'm taking you?" Kye asked, finally breaking the silence.

"I figure if you're taking me out here to kill me, you wouldn't tell me, so what's the point in asking?"

She expected a laugh at her joke. At minimum, a small

chuckle. Instead, his fingers tightened around her hand. "You're safe with me."

She warmed at his words. Yeah, she knew that.

They walked for another couple minutes, food in one hand, fingers still entangled, until finally, something came into view.

A small double-seat swing, surrounded by green, freshly cut grass. The manicured lawn was a stark contrast to the wild nature growing all around it.

"How…how is this here? In the middle of the woods?" It was completely out of place. But also romantic. Not to mention beautiful.

Kye took a seat on the swing first, and Samantha sat beside him. "Luca built it for Evie. She was attacked in these woods by her ex. He wanted to make new, happy memories here."

Oh, well, that was sweet. "Is the ex—"

"He's gone."

Gone. That meant dead, didn't it?

"That's good." Old Samantha probably wouldn't have said that. New Samantha felt safer with her enemies gone, and she was sure Evie felt the same. "You know what's funny, Tori has a swing just like this at the house her mother left her. Well, not exactly the same. It's not hidden by a million tall trees. But the swing itself is almost identical. We used to sit on it for hours, talking about any and everything."

Kye nodded as he lifted his burger to his lips. "I saw it when I went with her, Ax, and Jobs to search the house."

Her fork stilled midway to her mouth. "When…I mean, was that the day they were taken?"

She noticed the muscles tense in his arms. "Yeah. The day Jobs and I couldn't protect our own."

Did he blame himself?

She touched his arm. "Hey. It's not your fault. From what I've heard, you were outnumbered. The odds were stacked against you." There had been two of Carter's men for every one of Kye's. It was a fight he was never going to win.

Kye nodded, not looking all that convinced.

"If anyone should feel guilty, it's me." Samantha looked down, pushing her food around her plate. "There are so many things I should have done differently. Like not involving Tori. Investigating the truth earlier. And once I did learn the truth, I should have suspected that her home would be bugged rather than running over there and letting them hear exactly what I said to her."

Kye reached for her hand and gave a little squeeze. "Everything you did, you did with the best intentions."

True. Didn't ease the guilt, though.

"Do you think one day I'll be the woman I used to be?"

The words were in the air before she could stop them, and she immediately wanted to pull them back.

Where the hell had that come from?

She stared at the rocks on the ground like they were the most interesting things she'd seen all day, until Kye's fingers went to her chin, lifting her head.

"I don't think you'll ever be the woman you used to be." Her heart dropped. Until he spoke his next words. "I think you'll be stronger. Tougher. You already are. The difference is that, one day, the strength won't be weighted down with pain."

The heaviness on her chest lightened at his words. God, she hoped he was right. She wanted to believe him so badly.

"The pain will ease," he whispered. "Give it time."

Almost involuntarily, her gaze dropped to his lips. When it raised again, it was to see his eyes had darkened. He was looking at her with a new intensity.

She wanted to kiss him. His lips called to her on such a rudimentary level.

Do it.

Before she had a chance to act on the whispered words, Kye

let out a soft growl, his lips landing on hers. His hand went to the back of her neck, his mouth pressing firmly on her own.

Samantha's blood heated. Her chest hummed in awareness.

Then his tongue invaded her mouth, massaging hers.

Samantha lost herself. Lost herself to the beautiful man who eased her pain. Replaced it with goodness and light and peace.

She leaned into him, pressing her body against his. Her hand smoothed over his chest, feeling every hard ridge through his shirt.

She was seconds from brushing her plate from her lap and climbing on top of the man when he swiftly pulled away.

A soft protest escaped from her lips as her eyes snapped open. She was about to ask why he'd stopped when she saw him studying the forest around them. His gaze was still intense, but this time out of anger.

Suddenly, he was on his feet.

She sucked in a quick breath as his plate dropped to the grass. "Kye—"

His finger went to his lips.

He was listening.

Wait...was there someone out there? Her head shot around to scan the trees.

"Stay here." Kye whispered the words so quietly she almost didn't catch them. Then he disappeared into the forest.

He was only gone for a minute before he returned, holding a guy by the collar.

Kye shoved him against a tree. That's when Samantha recognized who he was. Phillip Barret, the reporter.

Samantha jumped to her feet.

"Calm down, man!" Phillip held his hands in the air in a gesture of surrender.

The move didn't seem to calm Kye one bit. "What the fuck are you doing here?"

His gaze shot to Samantha, then back to Kye. Some of the fear left his expression, replaced with a confident, almost arrogant smile. "Listening. Watching. Seeing if I could pick up anything for the story. I'd be interested to know how you knew I was there, by the way. I certainly didn't make any noise."

The guy had balls of steel.

Kye moved his face closer to Phillip's. "Here's what's going to happen. We're going to walk you to your car, and you're going to get in and drive away. If I ever see you again, either on one of our properties or harassing one of our women, you'll regret it."

"Is that a threat?"

When Kye lowered his head another fraction, their faces almost touching. "Yes."

CHAPTER 13

*S*amantha wasn't sure how long she'd been standing in the bathroom, staring up at the shower like it was a bomb about to explode, but it was a long time.

Her feet itched to walk away. To throw some clothes on and start the day. But she didn't. *Couldn't.* Something inside Samantha stopped her.

Part of it was that her therapist, Grace, had encouraged her to give it a try. The woman was young but good at her job. The sessions were healing. So far, two weeks' worth of appointments every three days were helping Samantha put her fragmented parts back together again.

Every so often, she swore she saw strain lines around her therapist's eyes. Like she had some of her own pain or trauma to deal with. Maybe that's why Samantha felt comfortable talking about things she never thought she'd want to say out loud. Because Grace's empathy felt real.

So, yeah, Grace was a big part of the reason why she wanted to try this.

But it was also an internal need to prove to herself that she was okay. That her past didn't control her future. That dead men didn't still have a say over her actions.

"If you feel up to it, give it a try."

Grace's words replayed in her head. *If she felt up to it.* She should feel up to it, shouldn't she? Her mind had always been faster than most, it made sense that it would heal faster, didn't it?

Sucking in a deep breath, Samantha reached into the enclosure and turned the shower on. The light pitter-patter of water hitting tiles echoed through the small bathroom.

There. Step one done. That hadn't freaked her out.

Grace had suggested focusing on small details. The smell of the water as it fell around her. The temperature of the drops. Even the coolness of the tiles beneath her feet.

She could do that.

Closing her eyes, she gave herself a silent pep talk before stripping off her sleep top and shorts. She wriggled her toes on the cold tiles. Touched the glass enclosing the shower, reminding herself that she was here, in Marble Falls, in Oliver's home.

Safe.

She repeated the word in her head as she lifted a leg inside the cubicle.

When the water hit her foot, she quickly pulled it back. Dread of what was to come making her hesitate.

"It's also okay to stop. Walk away. Try again another day."

Grace had given her permission to stop. But, dammit, she didn't want to! She wanted the past to leave her alone. She wanted to recapture the confident woman she used to be.

One step. Then another. That's all she needed to do.

Clenching her jaw, Samantha lifted her leg again, this time stepping under the water. She was careful to keep her head out of the spray as she shifted her body to stand in the enclosure.

The warm droplets hit her chest hard and fast. She lifted her trembling hands, watched as the water ran through her fingers. She gave herself a second. Waited to see if panic would set in.

It didn't.

Good. This was good.

She remained as she was for a couple of minutes, appreciating how far she'd come. A quiet voice in her head whispered that this was good enough for today. This was progress, and she could take the next step tomorrow.

But again, her own stubborn pride stopped her from listening. She wanted to be okay. And okay people were capable of putting their faces under a spray of water and *not* having panic attacks.

Swallowing, she closed her eyes. Slowly, Samantha stepped forward.

Immediately, her breath shortened. Her heart began to gallop.

She quickly pulled her head back. Took a moment to concentrate on the line of grout beneath her big toe. On the way the water trickled down her shoulders, heating her skin.

She took a few moments to calm herself.

Minutes passed before she felt okay enough to try again. Samantha lifted her head and looked at the water coming out of the showerhead. Who would have thought that this would be one of the greatest challenges of her life?

Breathing out a long, slow breath, Samantha tilted her chin up and stepped under the spray of water.

It hit her head, her face, soaking her hair.

Her heartbeat took off again. But this time faster. Unrelenting.

Her lungs constricted in her chest.

Samantha choked on the water. The damp cloth over her face made it impossible to breathe, to scream, to cry...to do anything.

She was drowning.

Or maybe she wasn't. And that was worse. Feeling like she was drowning, but continuing to live through it. To experience the same horror over and over again.

She attempted to move her head. Her arms. Strong, punishing hands manacled her to the board. The board that was tipped backward, causing water to fall into her nose. Suffocating her.

Like she'd done so many times before, she gagged. As she opened her lips, water filled her mouth. Her chest.

She needed air. There was none. There was only water.

The towel was whipped off her face. The strong, punishing hands on her wrists tugging her up.

"Are you going to agree to make the microchips?"

She sucked in greedy breaths. Cackling noises sounded from her chest. Everything in her hurt.

The hands on her arms tightened. But she was past the point of pain.

Hylar's rough fingers wrapped around her chin, forcing her to face him. "Answer me."

Her throat barely worked. She opened her mouth but couldn't make any noise. It didn't matter. They knew what the answer was. It was the same as it had been all day. All week.

Hylar sighed. "Again."

She wanted to scream. Cry. Beg them to just kill her.

She didn't do any of that. They threw her onto the table and covered her face in the soaking cloth.

All she could do was hope that the pain would stop, even if it meant dying.

KYE KNOCKED on Oliver's door. It had only been a few days since he'd seen Samantha, but hell, it may as well have been a few weeks. He was drawn to the woman, and he was no longer afraid to admit it.

To himself, that was. He hadn't said it to her. Not yet anyway.

Oliver opened the door, a smile on his face. "Cage, buddy, come in. We were just getting the coffee going."

Kye trailed behind Oliver into the kitchen.

Tori straightened from the fridge, milk in hand. "Hey, Kye. Coffee?"

"That would be awesome, thanks."

Taking a seat at the island, he heard the shower upstairs switch on. A smile tugged at his lips at the thought of seeing her again. He'd been visiting often over the last two weeks. It never seemed enough.

Tori crossed to the cupboard, pulling out an extra mug. "So, breakfast...Joan's Diner, Mrs. Potter's Bakehouse, or am I whipping up some eggs and bacon?"

"Tough call." Kye tapped his fingers on the island. "Joan's Diner has bacon but Mrs. Potter's Bakehouse has cake."

She frowned. "Ah, *I* offered you bacon."

"Tori. You know how much bacon Ax and I can eat."

She raised a brow. "You think I can't accommodate your bacon needs?" At his silent grin, her eyes narrowed. "Challenge accepted."

He chuckled as she abandoned the coffee and headed back to the fridge. He hadn't meant it as a challenge, but if the lady wanted to cook him a mountain of bacon, who was he to stop her?

"I'm making waffles too." Her words were muffled from inside the fridge, but they still made Kye laugh.

Oliver shook his head.

Kye opened his mouth to suggest adding some hash browns to the mix when a noise sounded from upstairs. A whimper, maybe?

He caught Oliver's gaze. His friend had clearly heard it also.

Tori was just placing the bacon on the counter when she stopped to look between the men. She frowned. "What?"

Another whimper sounded. This time, there was no mistaking it.

Kye was on his feet and up the stairs in seconds. He knocked on her bedroom door, but there was no answer.

From this close, he could hear Samantha's heart pounding

much faster than it should, louder than the stream of water. Kye moved into the bedroom, stopping at the closed bathroom door.

"Samantha?"

He knocked loudly, hoping to be heard over the water and her breaths, which were loud and fast. The next sound she made was a low, guttural cry.

It was heart-wrenching. Soul-destroying.

Screw it!

Opening the door, he pushed inside the small bathroom and opened the glass shower door.

Samantha sat on the floor of the shower, water pounding down on her. Her hands were wrapped around her legs so tightly her knuckles were white. Her head was tucked into her knees, wet hair fanning around her back and shoulder.

Christ...

Kye reached across and turned off the water. Grabbing a towel from behind him, he flung it over her back, covering her. She began to rock. The same terrified sounds escaping her at regular intervals.

"Samantha, honey. It's Kye."

She didn't move a muscle. Kye heard the soft gasp from Tori behind him, followed by words from Oliver and their retreating steps.

Kye tried speaking again, but it was no use, nothing was pulling her out of her panic.

Reaching into the shower, he wrapped one arm under her knees and the other behind her back, then he lifted her, taking her to the bed.

Sitting, he rocked her slowly in his arms. Whispering soft words, promising she was safe.

It took about three minutes for the trembling to lessen. For the pained sounds vibrating from her chest to soften. When she finally looked up at him, her eyes were glazed over with fear and confusion.

"Kye?"

"Yeah, baby. It's me."

She slowly glanced around the room, then back at him. "What —" She looked down at the towel covering her body. "The shower."

Tears misted her eyes, and she tried to blink them away. Lifting a hand, Kye caught one that fell. "What happened?"

He'd felt her hesitation to shower back in Louisiana. Now he wanted to know why.

She swallowed, her gaze lowering to her hands. "One of the methods Carter and Hylar used, to try to make me do what they wanted, was…They waterboarded me."

Rage pumped through his system. He'd feel sorry for any person who'd been subjected to that kind of torture, but Samantha? No. She didn't deserve it.

Samantha curled herself into him, her words muffled against his chest. "They kept dipping me backward on that table. I wanted to give in so badly. I didn't. I couldn't! Instead, I…I got to the point where I didn't care if it killed me anymore."

And just now, the feel of water falling on her had brought it all back.

Kye fought for calm. To not show the absolute fury that was overwhelming his system. Blinding him.

Samantha didn't need anger right now. She needed him to be stronger than that. She needed peace.

Lifting a hand to her wet hair, he stroked her, thankful that her heart rate was evening out. "I'm sorry, Samantha. I wish I could take away your pain." He wished he could go back in time and switch places with her. Save her from all of it.

He felt her cheek press harder against his chest. "I *am* getting better. Grace has been helping. She suggested I give the shower a try if I felt up to it…"

"It's okay not to be ready yet. Healing is a process, and it takes time."

She glanced up, vulnerability bleeding out of her. "That's what she said."

He brushed some hair away from her face. "Smart woman."

Raising her hand, she touched his cheek again. "Thank you."

For a few seconds, they both remained still, their gazes holding. Then she dipped her head again and nuzzled into him. Kye tightened his arms.

Holding her felt so right. He wanted to be the person she always leaned on when she needed comfort. He damn well craved it.

CHAPTER 14

Samantha smiled as she listened to Quinn talk about her mess of a morning.

The woman was standing behind the counter of Mrs. Potter's Bakehouse recounting to Samantha, Tori, and Maya how everything thus far had gone wrong—her cinnamon rolls had burned, she'd dropped a fresh pile of dough onto the floor, closed a cabinet door on her finger, then proceeded to call Wyatt and tell him why it was all his fault.

"I think he'll forgive you," Tori said with a chuckle.

Quinn sighed. "He usually does. The man's a saint. I'm just hoping my run of bad luck has finally come to an end."

"Don't they say bad things come in threes?" Samantha lifted a shoulder. "So I'd say you're done."

Quinn lowered her voice. "Don't say that too loud, the karma gods will disagree and get me again out of spite."

Was that how it worked? Samantha hoped not.

Maya shook her head. "I don't think you've done enough to warrant that. Do you need any help with the coffees?"

"Well, I guess only time will tell." Quinn swung her gaze to the coffee machine, then back. "I'll say no for now, but if you hear a little explosion, come running, because my bad luck has struck again."

Everyone laughed as Quinn turned and headed toward the coffee machine while the rest of them grabbed a table by the window.

Samantha looked across the room to Bodie, who sat by the door. He was working on an open laptop. Anyone walking in would never guess the guy was protecting them. Watching them without watching. "Is he going to join us?"

Maya shook her head. "No. He'll sit over there and give us the illusion that we have private 'girl time'."

Wow. That was dedication. Hopefully, he was also able to get some work done, otherwise, what a waste of time.

"Maybe we should tell him he can…"

Samantha trailed off as both Tori and Maya shook their heads.

"Won't do anything," Tori said.

"She's right. The guys want us to have freedom, while also being safe." A smile stretched across Maya's face as she leaned forward in her seat. "So, different topic, have you girls chosen your outfits yet?"

Uh, outfits?

Tori shook her head, obviously understanding something that Samantha didn't. "No. But there's this dress I've had my eye on. I might order it online and if it doesn't look good, just return it."

"I've been looking at online dresses too. What color is yours?"

Tori opened her mouth to reply, but stopped at Samantha's waving hand.

"Wait, what are these dresses for, and should I be looking for one?"

Tori appeared confused. "I told you the other day that Evie and Luca's wedding is in a month."

Oh, right. She knew that. "They barely know me, I doubt I'll be invited—"

"You are," Quinn interrupted, setting baked goods on the table.

"Are you sure?"

"As sure as I'm standing here." Quinn crossed her arms over her chest. "It's a small backyard wedding. They're inviting the guys and partners, as well as Logan's team, for extra protective detail."

It made sense then. The whole team was going, and Samantha still needed protecting. No one wanted her to be unprotected.

Samantha lifted a shoulder. "Guess I should start looking for an outfit."

Quinn's eyes brightened. "Hey, let's make a day of it! We can shop, grab lunch, maybe even see a chick flick." She looked over to Bodie and waggled her brows a couple times. Everyone laughed *except* him. She leaned over and whispered. "I actually hate chick flicks, but I'm willing to watch one just to see one of the guys in that cinema."

God, the woman was hilarious. Samantha caught Bodie shaking his head, clearly having heard every word Quinn said.

"I'm pretty set on this dress I saw online," Tori said. "But a girls' trip sounds fun."

"Yay! Done. I'll go grab those coffees."

When Quinn walked away, Maya started listing the stores they could visit. There was a heap of them.

"Guess I'll be third-wheeling you and Oliver again." Samantha had been doing that a lot lately.

A slow smile grew on Tori's face, and Samantha knew what her friend was going to say before the words left her mouth. "*Or you could be Kye's date?*"

A warmth spread through Samantha's chest at the mere mention of his name. "We're just friends."

Friends who'd kissed in Luca's backyard. And had sex in the woods.

Gah, she couldn't even think about the guy without getting all hot and sweaty.

Tori knew about the kiss but not the sex. Samantha was still hesitant to share. Still wanting to keep it private between her and Kye.

Tori turned to Maya, looking way too excited. "He's been at our house *a lot* over the last two weeks—"

"He's Oliver's best friend."

Tori shook her head. "The way he looks at her..."

Maya shuffled forward. "How does he look at her?"

"Like she's the sun, the moon, *and* the stars."

Samantha's breath stuttered. She hadn't caught him looking at her like that. But he *had* been over. A lot. For meals, to hang out. Last night, he'd even stayed for a movie after dinner.

And Samantha was loving every minute of it.

Maya's features softened. "That's so wonderful. He's such a great guy. He always said he wouldn't settle down, and now look at him."

Even though Maya had meant it as a positive, her comment had Samantha pausing. He'd been very upfront with her about his history with women. Was it dangerous of her to want more from him than friendship?

If she was honest with herself, she actually had no idea what his intentions were. He might just be wanting to spend time with her to help her recover from what she'd been through.

"Stop it."

Tori's voice pulled Samantha out of her thoughts. "What?"

"You're overthinking it."

"What? No, I was just—"

"You always get that look on your face, then half an hour later, you'll have spun something around the wrong way."

It was true. All of it. Samantha was a classic overthinker.

Before Samantha could deny it, the door to the bakery opened and Jason walked in. Bodie stood, greeting the guy before he headed to their table.

"Hey ladies." He brushed his gaze over each of them before landing on Samantha. "Samantha, how's the hand?"

The hand? Oh, right. The cut that he'd bandaged. Lifting her hand, she showed him the already-healing skin. "Thanks to your skilled bandaging, it's healing nicely."

He laughed, the dimples in his cheeks showing. "I'm not quite at my sister's level of medical skills, but I like to think I can clean and bandage a cut relatively well."

Quinn returned to the table, holding a large takeaway cup. "Jason, just in time. Here's your order."

He took it from her fingers. "Thanks. Ah, I think I ordered a small, but maybe—"

"You did. Easy mistake from a guy who's never ordered a coffee from me before. Trust me, when you try it, you'll be glad I gave you extra. And don't worry about payment. We're grateful your team was able to go to Louisiana. This is my thank you."

Jason ran a hand through his hair. "You really don't need to thank me. This is our problem as much as it is everyone else's."

She lifted her shoulders. "I know. Still want to thank you."

Turning, Quinn headed back to the counter.

"Want to join us?" Samantha was about to stand and grab another chair, but Jason shook his head.

"Thanks, but I'm on my way to Marble Protection. I'm actually running late." He shot a glance at his watch. "I should get going. Next time."

He gave everyone a smile before leaving the bakery.

Maya leaned back in her seat. "He's nice."

"He is." Very nice. And good-looking. He wasn't Kye, though.

"Okay, three cappuccinos." Quinn placed the drinks in front of them. "Hopefully the caffeine hit will keep you going for a good hour."

"Hour?" A coffee in the morning usually kept her going for the day.

Quinn nodded. "You're right, that's too long. Forty-five minutes, maybe?"

Tori chuckled as she pushed away from the table. "I'm going to the bathroom, then I'll return to my blast of caffeine."

Samantha took a sip of her coffee as Tori left. When she looked up, it was to see Quinn hadn't stepped away. In fact, the woman was watching Samantha closely, an almost expectant look on her face.

"Ah...this is great, Quinn." When the woman's brows rose, Samantha hurried to continue. "No, not just great, amazing."

The smile grew wide on Quinn's face. "I'm glad you like it. A lot of blood, sweat, and tears went into perfecting that."

With a wink, she walked away.

Maya lifted her own coffee, speaking under her breath. "Good answer. Quinn's quite impressed with her newly acquired barista skills. I've heard she was pretty terrible at the start."

Samantha had made coffee with machines plenty of times in her life. It wasn't that hard. But then, some skills come to people easier than others.

"It *is* quite good." And just what her sleep-deprived mind needed.

"Wait until you try these baked treats. They're to die for."

Samantha had been eyeing them since Quinn placed them on the table. Especially the custard-filled tart. She was almost salivating just looking at it. She'd just reached for a fork when a message came through on her phone.

When she looked down at the screen, she couldn't help but chuckle before pushing to her feet. Apparently, her friend needed some toilet paper from the cubicle beside hers. A woman's worst nightmare.

"I'll be back in a sec. Tori needs my help."

Walking across the shop, Samantha pushed into the woman's bathroom—and stopped.

There, on the floor of one of the stalls, lay a woman on her stomach, motionless.

Not just any woman. Tori.

Samantha opened her mouth to scream for help when a hand swiftly clamped over her lips, another wrapping around her waist and tugging her away from both Tori and the door.

For a second, she froze. Too shocked to do anything. Then she felt a light breeze. Was the guy dragging her toward an open window?

Her mind immediately snapped into action. She kicked and hit the powerful body behind her with everything she had. The man was strong. So strong, her efforts got her nowhere.

Panic really started to set in when he removed the hand from her waist and reached for the window.

She fought harder. She couldn't let him get her outside. She'd be thrown into a car and taken back to the same sort of hell she'd just escaped!

She had to make noise. Anything to alert Bodie.

Using as much strength as she could muster, Samantha punched him between the legs. The hand on her mouth twitched, shifting enough for her to sink her teeth into his fingers.

The hand flew away from her mouth.

Samantha screamed. As loud and as long as she could.

The guy was gone in seconds, vanishing out the window. Samantha fell to her knees as Bodie burst through the door. He scanned the small space.

"Go after him," Samantha gasped as she crawled over to Tori. Bodie quickly handed her a phone before hoisting himself out the window and disappearing.

Samantha had just reached Tori when Maya and Quinn all but fell into the room, both gasping before dropping to their knees beside Tori.

Maya took the phone from Samantha's shaking fingers and called an ambulance. Samantha focused on Tori. Blood was seeping from her head, pooling on the ground. The asshole had hit her from behind. God, there was so much blood…

"Yes, hurry! There's a lot of blood."

Quinn grabbed as much toilet paper as she could, applying pressure.

Please hurry. I can't lose Tori. She's the only family I have.

CHAPTER 15

*K*ye pushed through the doors of the Marble Falls Hospital, anger pounding inside him like a drumbeat. Their women had been attacked. Injured. Almost taken. *Samantha* had almost been taken.

Turning a corner, he headed to the end of the hall. Bodie and Maya stood outside a room. Bodie gave him a nod before Kye stepped inside.

What he saw shredded his heart. Tori, so still in the hospital bed. Oliver looking pained beside her. And Samantha, tearstained face, standing to the side, arms wrapped around herself in a protective gesture.

He didn't hesitate. He walked straight over and enfolded her in his arms. She sank into him, arms wrapping around his waist, silent tears wetting his shirt.

A full minute ticked by before Kye pulled away, hands going to her face, wiping the tears. "How is she?"

"She needed stitches in her head. But Sage is concerned about her concussion." She took a shaky breath. "Tori's already had a couple in the last few months. Sage is worried that she could have more memory loss. Or worse."

Her voice cracked on the last word, and Kye tugged her close again.

Christ. He wanted to kill the asshole who did this.

He looked over at Tori, her face unbelievably pale. Then his gaze caught on Oliver. The man looked like hell. Kye wished there was some way he could take away his friend's worry.

Taking Samantha's hand in his, he headed toward Oliver, placing a hand on his friend's shoulder.

"You need anything, brother?" Kye wasn't going to ask Oliver if he was okay. He knew he wasn't.

Oliver shook his head, no words leaving his mouth. Angry energy bounced off him. The air was thick with tension.

The door opened and Wyatt popped his head in. He caught Kye's gaze, giving him a small nod before disappearing.

Kye understood what his friend was saying without any words being spoken. They needed to talk to Samantha. Find out what she knew. He turned to her and studied her face. "Are you okay if we step into the hall and talk to the guys?"

Immediately, her back straightened, and her face hardened. "Yes. I don't know if I'll be any help, but I want your team to find this guy."

So damn strong.

Wrapping an arm around her waist, he turned to Oliver before leaving. "We'll be back."

His friend nodded. "I'll listen from here."

Kye never doubted it.

Heading into the hall, he saw that it wasn't just Wyatt who had arrived. Mason, Quinn, Luca, and Evie also stood there with Bodie and Maya.

Kye walked Samantha to a seat, and she immediately lowered into it. Almost like her legs couldn't carry her anymore. Crouching to his haunches, Kye placed his hands on her knees.

There was no one else around. No one who would hear them.

Still, he kept his voice quiet. "Can you tell us what happened, honey?"

Again, that determination washed over her features. "Tori said she needed to use the bathroom. She'd only been in there a few seconds when I received a text from her saying she needed help. When I walked in, she was on the ground." Samantha swiped a hand over her face. "I didn't see him in the room before his hand came over my mouth. He kept my body angled away from the mirror, so I never saw his reflection. But he was strong. And big. As big as you guys."

More anger. More hot fury that he had to push down until later.

He stroked his thumb over the inside of her knee. "How did you get away?"

"When he lifted a hand to the window, I punched him between the legs and bit his hand. Then I screamed. He obviously knew Bodie was there, because he took off after that."

Kye turned his head toward Bodie. "Did you catch a glimpse of the guy?"

Bodie shook his head. "No. He was gone by the time I got out the window. Didn't hear or see him."

Dammit!

Bodie looked miserable. He shouldn't. He'd done a damn good job of keeping Samantha from being taken. But the guilt covered his face like a mask.

Luca stepped closer to Bodie. "What happened isn't your fault. He obviously didn't make a sound when he attacked Tori. Obviously knew about your hearing. You moved at the first sign of trouble. And to get away from you so easily has to mean he's altered too."

Bodie nodded, but he still wore his guilt.

Quinn took a seat beside Samantha, wrapping her arms around her.

Giving her legs a gentle squeeze, Kye stood and turned to his team. "I want to know who the hell did this." They'd paid their dues. Hunted and eliminated their enemies. And now they'd do it again.

Luca nodded. "Me, too."

Mason's jaw clenched. "We'll alert the rest of the team. Keep the women close. And we continue doing what we've been doing...we watch our backs."

He was right. Whatever it took to destroy every last enemy and gain freedom.

Wyatt added, "We'll dust for prints and look through any street surveillance."

Kye nodded. "I'm going to take Samantha home with me."

No one looked surprised by his decision. He'd stop by Oliver's place and grab her stuff. Then he wouldn't take his damn eyes off her. Not for a second.

Samantha stepped inside Kye's front door. She wasn't feeling good. Her stomach was queasy with concern for her friend, and a chill had taken root in her skin at how close she'd come to being taken again.

She glanced around Kye's foyer. He lived just outside central Marble Falls, and his home was beautiful. Even the outside was pretty jaw-dropping, with its perfectly manicured lawn.

And with his security gates and alarm system, not to mention having Kye close by, she couldn't *not* feel safe.

The place was a single-story but seemed huge. There was an open door to the left of the big foyer, with a large bed beyond, presumably the master bedroom. A family room sat across from it, to her right.

Kye's hand went to the center of her back as he led them down a hallway.

At the end of the hall was a large kitchen, living, and dining area. There was another hallway to the left, where Samantha assumed were more bedrooms.

"Your home is beautiful."

Kye smiled as his hand dropped from her back. "Thanks. We got paid some hush money when we got out of Project Arma. As well as investing in Marble Protection, I bought this place."

For a moment, Samantha wasn't sure how to respond to that. *Congratulations? I'm glad you got something good out of such terrible circumstances?*

"It looks big."

"I like space." He tugged the fridge door open. "But I need to confess something. If you're after a home-cooked meal, not only do I have no ingredients, I'm also a terrible cook. If leftover pasta is your jam, then you're in luck." He closed the door. "*Or*—and this is my preference—we can order pizza."

She looked down at her phone, noticing it was almost dinnertime.

Whoa, she'd spent longer than she'd thought at the hospital. But then, she could have stayed all night just to be close to Tori.

"I actually ate something at the hospital, so I'm not very hungry." Nibbling on some crackers from the vending machine counted as eating, didn't it? Plus, her stomach really wasn't feeling great.

Kye moved in front of her, pushing some hair behind her ear. God, she loved it when he did that. When he touched her in *any* way. She was starting to crave it.

"Are you sure?" He looked worried.

Samantha made an effort to smooth her features. "Yes. I might just take a bath, if that's okay?"

He continued to study her face for another beat with his dark eyes. His hand trailed down her neck to her shoulder. An involuntary shiver ran up her spine.

"Of course." His gaze darted from the hallway off the living area, to the hallway they'd just walked through. He almost looked uncomfortable. "The spare bedrooms are on the opposite end of the house from my bedroom. It might be safer if..."

When he didn't finish, Samantha tilted her head to the side. "If we share a room?" *A bed...?*

The thought had her heart giving a little flutter

One side of Kye's mouth lifted. If she didn't feel so sick and tired, she'd probably be able to appreciate how sexy that smile was. "Yeah."

Samantha lifted a shoulder. "We've shared a bed before. It wasn't terrible." No, not terrible at all. Rather, the best night's sleep she'd had for months. Possibly longer.

His mouth curved into a full-blown smile. He indicated back toward the way they'd come with his head. "This way."

Kye gave her a quick bedroom tour. Once he'd brought her bag into the room, she filled the tub and got into the bath. It was ironic that she'd actually always hated baths. Well, not hated; that was a strong word. Disliked. And now was a perfect example of why.

Her mind *did not* stop.

Today's events were on repeat. Questions kept pinging in her head—what she could have done differently? Could she have gone to the bathroom with Tori? Or what if she'd gone first?

She lasted about twenty minutes before she couldn't stand it anymore. Rising from the water, she quickly dried herself, threw on some shorts and a tank top before tucking herself into bed. It was still early, but exhaustion pulled at her.

Checking her phone for what had to be the hundredth time since leaving the hospital, she gave a small sigh. Still no news on Tori.

Closing her eyes, she tried to sleep. Tried and failed. It was impossible. Yet again, her friend was put in danger, *hurt*, because of her. Samantha scrunched her eyes tighter, hating herself for that.

She didn't know how long she lay there. Probably hours.

Eventually, the sound of footsteps penetrated the quiet, causing Samantha to roll to her side, away from the door.

She could hear Kye moving around the room. It was pitch black, but she knew that didn't affect what he could see.

When the bed dipped behind her, Samantha held her breath. Would he touch her? Hold her like he'd done the last time they'd shared a bed?

If he didn't, she was willing to ask. *Beg* for the physical comfort. She needed it tonight almost as much as she needed air to breathe.

When his arm curved around her waist and pulled her against him, Samantha sighed. Some of the storm inside her settled.

"Oliver texted. Tori's awake." Samantha's heart clattered against her ribs at his words. "Fully conscious and no signs of memory loss or any other problems."

The air whooshed out of her chest. The guilt was still there, but her friend was okay for now. Tori had Oliver with her tonight, and tomorrow, Samantha would see her with her own eyes.

"That makes me so happy. The worry was…it was suffocating me." Pressing down on her chest with the weight of a thousand tons.

Samantha didn't close her eyes straightaway. Her mind was still moving at a million miles an hour. The same questions on repeat. Haunting her.

Kye's lips brushed near her ear. "Sleep."

She almost laughed. How? How did she just switch it off?

Kye's thumb started a slow stroke on her hip. Minutes later, the sleepiness began to seep in. Her eyes fluttered shut. His breath brushed against her neck, a welcome reminder that he was still there. That she was safe.

That's when her mind finally let her sleep.

CHAPTER 16

The most wonderful heat surrounded Samantha, wanting to lull her straight back to sleep. She almost did just that. The thing that stopped her was the thrumming heartbeat against her back.

A smile touched Samantha's lips. And not just because Kye was folded around her body like a pretzel, but also because she felt well-rested. God, that hadn't happened in…well, a while.

Rolling onto her back, Samantha wasn't surprised to see Kye completely awake and looking right at her.

She touched a hand to his large chest. "It's you."

A soft chuckle rumbled through his chest, vibrating into her side. "It *is* me."

She shook her head. "No. I mean, *you're* what blocks the nightmares."

The only other times she'd slept terror-free were the two nights following their escape, when she'd been wrapped in Kye's arms.

His features softened, and he shifted some hair off her face, grazing her cheek in the process. "I take it you slept well then?"

"I did." Now she just had to figure out a way to have this man sleep beside her every night, forever. "My subconscious mind must know that I'm safe with you."

It knew that there was nowhere she felt safer.

"Good. Because you *are* safe with me. Always."

His words melted her. Honestly, she wouldn't be surprised if she ended up a puddle right here on the bed.

Studying his face, she looked for a fault. Because the man was almost too good to be true. A part of her, a large part, wanted to ask about his feelings toward her. She knew how *she* felt. It was way beyond friendship. But what about Kye? Was he just protecting her? Or was something more going on?

Samantha opened her mouth to ask just that, but nerves had the words catching in her throat and her mouth snapping shut.

There was too much other stuff going on right now. They both needed to focus on that. On figuring out who had tried to take her. And whether Tori was okay...

Tori!

Samantha tried to sit up, but Kye moved over her, his hands bracketing her on the bed. "Where do you think you're going?"

For a moment, words were lost on her. Heck, making any noise felt like the hardest thing in the world when he was so close, heated skin touching hers...

"We need to visit Tori," she said quietly.

And just like that, the trance was broken. The soft, playful expression disappeared, replaced by hardness.

The protector was back.

Damn. Why couldn't she have spent a few more seconds with the other guy...

But she already knew the answer to that. Because this was Tori. Best friend, sister-by-choice Tori.

"You're right. We should get ready." Kye removed his arms and seemed to be about to stand, when he hesitated. Leaning down, he pressed a kiss to her temple. The kiss wasn't a quick peck. His lips lingered for seconds on end before he lifted them. "I slept well too, sunshine."

Samantha flushed. Lord Almighty, the man was killing her.

When he climbed out of bed, her mouth went dry. He wore nothing but a pair of briefs and his body was a work of art.

Six and a half feet of tanned muscle.

She swallowed her disappointment when he disappeared into his walk-in closet. But he was only gone for a second, quickly reappearing with a pile of clothes in his arms. "I'll use the other bathroom."

He gave her one of his soul-destroying smiles before leaving the room.

You're screwed, Samantha. So, screwed...

Sighing, she climbed out of bed. She stopped abruptly, hand going to her stomach as a wave of nausea washed over her. It only lasted a second, then it was gone, disappearing as quickly as it had come.

Served her right for skipping dinner last night. She still hadn't gained back the weight she'd lost. Not eating couldn't be good for her.

Grabbing some clothes, she quickly dressed, brushed her teeth, and pulled her hair into a ponytail. It took her a couple of minutes to tame her wild gold curls. That's why she rarely wore them down. Too much effort.

Heading to the kitchen, she noticed that Kye wasn't there yet, probably still showering. She walked over to the coffee machine.

Hm. Question was, could she work it? It was big and fancy but didn't look too different from others she'd used.

Going to the fridge, Samantha almost laughed when she opened it. Kye hadn't been lying about the food situation. The fridge was bare. Other than the container of pasta that he'd mentioned, Kye also had milk, beer, and a couple of apples.

"Men," Samantha muttered under her breath as she took out the milk.

Well, not all men. Maybe just bachelors.

At that thought, the smile wiped clean from her face. He *was* a bachelor, and she needed to remember that. After everything that had happened to her, the last thing she needed to add to the list was a broken heart.

Giving herself a little mental shake, Samantha got to work on the coffees. She'd just finished them when Kye stepped into the room.

"Ah, nothing better than the smell of coffee in the morning." He stopped at the island, lifting one of the mugs. "I should have invited you to live here earlier."

"I would have attempted breakfast but…"

He smirked. "Ah, you have a problem with three-day-old pasta in the morning?"

She chuckled. "Yes. Yes, I do."

He shook his head. "Women. So hard to please. Lucky for you, I'm keen for a breakfast bagel. We can grab a few on the way to Oliver's."

She perked up. "Tori's been discharged already?"

"Yep. Normally the hospital would keep her longer, but there's more security at Oliver's place, so Sage will be paying her regular visits instead."

Samantha sagged in relief. That was good. Being allowed to go home was good, right?

"Tori's been asking for you."

Samantha straightened. "Should I grab my stuff and stay with them? Help out? Or would my presence be more of a hindrance?" She wanted to be there for Tori in whatever way her friend needed.

Kye took a moment to respond, seeming to consider his words. "I think Oliver will be able to look after Tori. You being there might make it harder for him…protecting two women instead of one."

Oh, yeah. How could she forget the big red target on her back.

"If you would feel more comfortable being with them, though, we can ask Oliver—"

"No." She cut him off before he could finish. "That's okay. I want Tori to be as safe as possible."

A slow smile curved Kye's lips. That smile was dangerous. "And you want to stay with me, right?"

Some of the heaviness in her chest lifted. "Right."

So much truth to that statement.

He nodded. "Good." Kye lifted his coffee again. "Does Tori like bagels?"

Samantha took a sip of her own coffee. "Does anyone *not* like bagels?"

He laughed. It was exactly what she wanted to hear. "We'll get enough for everyone."

Once they'd finished their drinks, Kye took both the mugs and placed them in the dishwasher. She expected him to lead the way to the car immediately. Instead, he stopped directly in front of her, hands going to the island on each side of her hips.

Samantha's breath stuttered in her chest at his proximity. At the way he confined her to the island.

"Before we leave, I want to tell you something…I like you, Samantha. I've told you I'm not a relationship guy, but you're making me reconsider that particular lifestyle choice."

His head lowered, stopping near her ear. Lord Almighty, but his closeness made her burn up.

"I'm glad you're staying with me."

His lips pressed to the sensitive skin just behind her ear before he pushed off and walked away, leaving Samantha ridiculously hot and bothered.

～

"How are you doing?" Kye asked Oliver, studying his friend closely beside him on the couch. Mason was on the single chair, while Luca stood, leaning against the wall.

Oliver shook his head. He didn't need to speak for Kye to see he was struggling. "I'm never fucking leaving her side again. She's been hurt too damn often. This head injury could have been so much worse. I can't...I don't know what I'd do if I lost her."

Kye touched Oliver's shoulder. "You're not going to lose her. None of us are going to let that happen."

Samantha and Sage were upstairs with Tori. He could just hear the murmurs of their conversation.

"We're not losing any of our own," Mason added.

Oliver leaned back on the couch. He looked exhausted. Had probably been awake at the hospital all night.

"If you need to rest—"

He was straightening before Kye could finish. "No. I'll sleep tonight with Tori in my arms."

Of course he would. It was exactly what any of the rest of them would say.

When the phone in Oliver's pocket rang, he pulled it out, putting it on speaker. "Jobs?"

"I'm sorry to be the bearer of bad news, but there are no identifiable fingerprints, and no street footage of anyone suspicious in the area."

That left them with literally nothing.

"What about Tori's phone? Was it found?" Mason asked.

Good question. The guy had used it to send Samantha a text. If it was, surely there were prints?

"No, we haven't been able to locate it. Can't trace it either, so it must have been destroyed."

There was a collective sigh in the room.

Oliver scrubbed a hand over his face. "Thanks, Jobs."

When they hung up, Kye took a moment to listen in upstairs. Sage was talking about rest.

Mason headed into the kitchen. "I'll plate those bagels."

Food was exactly what Kye needed. He was starving, and he was sure Oliver had barely eaten. They'd brought over a dozen bagels from the diner and Kye had a feeling not one of them would be left uneaten.

Oliver blew out a long breath. "Help get my mind off yesterday. What's going on with Samantha?"

Ah, his favorite topic. "Well, we're not dating, but—"

"Are you sleeping together?"

Kye was momentarily thrown by Oliver's direct question. "Ax—"

"Because the woman is like a sister to Tori, which means she's like a sister to me."

"Good. I like her circle of loved one's widening." It meant more people looking out for her.

He nodded. "It is."

"I don't know where we're headed, so don't ask if marriage and kids are in my plans. But I do know that I like her. A lot." And he may just be willing to break his own "no commitment" rule to see where the attraction led. "We're not dating yet, because we haven't actually been on a date. I'm not opposed to the idea though."

The energy in the room shifted. Oliver even offered up a smile. "The last man has started to crack."

Was he cracking? Who the hell knew.

"All I know is that the woman's affected me. And I can't *not* want her."

CHAPTER 17

When Samantha's eyes opened, her stomach rolled. The room was pitch black, so it was either the middle of the night or very early morning. Kye's arm was heavy around her waist, just like it had been every night for the last week of sleeping together.

Another round of nausea swelled in her stomach.

Oh no. Was the fish she'd had for dinner about to come up?

Closing her eyes, Samantha tried some deep breaths. *In... out...in...out.*

Her eyes snapped back open. Not working. Not even a little bit.

"Are you okay?"

Kye's rumbly voice vibrated from his chest to her back. She was about to answer when suddenly, her mouth filled with that acidic, about-to-throw-up sensation.

Rolling off the bed, she landed on shaky legs, running to the connecting bathroom. She'd only just made it to her knees in front of the toilet when her stomach heaved. Everything she'd eaten the previous night came up.

She was vaguely aware of Kye's warm fingers brushing across

her neck, pulling her hair up. She almost wanted to yell at him to go away. To close the door and block his ears. There was no part of her that wanted the man to see her like this.

Samantha was about to do just that, she even lifted her hand, but suddenly her stomach heaved again, and she quickly put her head back into the toilet bowl.

A slow rub started on her back. His strokes were warm, firm, and soothing. And, suddenly, his touch was too comforting to send away.

They remained like that for a long couple minutes. Until she had nothing left to give. Then Samantha sat back, exhausted.

Kye stepped away for a second. And even though she'd been wishing him away, she now wanted to call him back.

He returned immediately, warm cloth in hand. When he placed it across her forehead, her eyes fluttered shut. His hand began those heavenly strokes on her back again.

What had she done to deserve him?

"How are you feeling?"

Her eyes popped open. He was beside her, worry in his expression. "Now that the fish is all gone, better." She just hoped that was it. That there would be no more surprise nausea spells.

One thing was for sure, she wouldn't be eating the stuff again for a very long time.

"Should I call Sage?"

Samantha shook her head. "No. I don't want to bother her in the middle of the night with food poisoning. I'll just sleep it off."

The intensity in Kye's features didn't lessen. Reaching a hand out, he touched her cheek. "You're not hot."

No. She didn't have a fever. In fact, now that she'd been sick, she felt completely fine. "I'm okay, Kye."

"It was definitely something you ate...?"

His thumb caressed her cheekbone. Oh, how she loved his hands on her. "What else would it be?"

He seemed to take a moment to consider his words. "That

night when we got out, when we made love in the cave...we didn't use anything."

Her eyes widened at his insinuation. He thought she might be *pregnant*?

No. No, no, and no. "I'm not pregnant. I've had a period since that night."

Kye nodded, not looking relieved or disappointed. In fact, his features were surprisingly smooth.

Rising to her feet slowly, she grabbed her toothbrush and scrubbed her teeth and mouth for several long minutes before thoroughly rinsing. When she was done, she looked down at her sweaty tank. "I could use a sh—A bath."

Argh. This phobia of hers was so annoying. Grace had told her that it would take time. That at some point, she would work through the fear of water falling on her.

But right now, in this moment, it was frustrating as hell because the last thing she wanted to do was run a bath. She wanted to get clean as quickly as possible, then crawl straight back into bed with Kye.

His features immediately softened in the mirror, obviously having heard her fear. Kye shot a quick look at the shower before returning his attention to her. Her heartbeat sped up at what she just knew he was going to say.

"Do you trust me?"

To keep her safe physically? Yes. Absolutely yes. But there was another enemy in her life. One that she felt completely alone in battling...her mind.

"Kye, I don't think—"

"Then don't think, sunshine." Both his hands went to her waist. He didn't pull her close, just rested his hands there. "Trust. Trust me to keep you safe."

Goose bumps rose over her skin. Her mouth opened, ready to say yes, but fear rendered her silent.

She wanted to say yes. Oh, God, did she want to. Accepting

help from this beautiful man should be easy. But the last time she'd stepped under a stream of water, she'd relived one of the worst moments of her life. She'd tasted the absolute terror of drowning all over again.

Would her mind pull her back there again? To that moment when she'd almost begged for death?

Kye was patient as he waited. He didn't speak. Didn't apply any pressure. He just watched. She knew with a hundred percent certainty that if she said no, he would support her. He would run her a bath before crawling back into bed.

Her calm protector.

She looked over at the shower. Her heart raced in her chest.

Trust Kye. And trust your strength.

The whispered words in her head had her straightening. She'd survived everything that had been thrown at her in that hell. She'd defeated them. She would defeat this too.

Before she could talk herself out of it, Samantha nodded.

Kye stroked his thumb over her hip. "Say the words sweetheart, so I know for certain."

"Yes. I want to shower with you. I trust you."

Having the words in the air made them real. She really did trust him. He wouldn't be able to rid her of the demons, that would take work on her part, but he could be her pillar of strength, holding her up if her knees caved.

Kye turned her around before taking her hand in his. He didn't let go as he walked to the shower, reached in, and turned it on. The sound of the water hitting tiles made Samantha want to turn and run.

She locked her knees.

Kye's hand tightened around hers. His features tranquil as he turned back to her.

When he let go, his hands went to the bottom of her top. She lifted her arms as he tugged it over her head. His eyes didn't leave hers as he continued to her shorts, pulling them down her legs and allowing her to step out of them.

Kye stripped off his briefs before stepping under the spray of water. She didn't have time to appreciate his body naked of clothing, not when he was pulling her into the shower stall.

Her steps were small. She could feel the glass door along her back as it closed. The water barely touched her.

Kye's hands went to her hips, holding her steady. Stroking her skin with his thumbs. His touch and closeness almost distracted her from the falling water.

"You're so beautiful. A sunrise that most people only get for a couple of minutes every day...I get every second I'm with you."

Water hit his shoulders, running down his large chest.

Samantha touched his warm skin. Watched the water bounce off her arm. "And you remind me of a gladiator. So big and strong. But you fight for freedom. You're a protector."

"Your freedom and mine." His head lowered, his mouth going to her hair. "When we were in those cages, I barely knew you, and it still tore me apart that I couldn't help. That I couldn't stand in front of you every time that asshole put his hands on you."

Her fingers glided up his wet chest, grazing across his skin until they wrapped around his shoulders. "You being there, in the same room, was a lifeline." She wet her lips, debating over whether to tell him the next part. "When Hylar was alive, I'd almost given up. Almost stopped caring whether I lived or died. I think that's why I could withstand what they did to me. You go into your head and wait for death. When Hylar brought Tori in, a part of my soul came back to life...but it wasn't until you were placed in the cage beside mine that I could really breathe again."

She was still damaged. Still tortured by her memories. But her soul no longer wished for death. Her heart beat in her chest with purpose.

Kye lifted his head. His gaze intense. "I'll help you breathe anytime you need me, Samantha." Bending slightly, he pressed his lips to hers.

Samantha rose to her toes, pressing her chest against his.

There was so much emotion in the way he kissed her. So much unspoken passion. Promise.

Her hands glided up his neck, running through his hair. She moaned softly. The heating of her skin having nothing to do with the water.

The hands on her waist tugged her closer. The water now hit her lower half, but she barely noticed. Kye consumed her senses.

At the feel of his tongue pushing through her lips, tasting her, connection like she'd never experienced washed over Samantha. Connection to the man who held her. The vibrations he brought to her life.

Her back bowed, her chest pressing harder to his.

She forgot everything. The time, the day...everything but him and the way his arms felt around her.

When Kye lifted his head, a small groan of protest left her lips. She looked up to see his eyes were just as glazed over with desire as she was certain hers were.

He took her hand in one of his and lifted it into the water. She watched as droplets rolled from her hand, along her arm, down to her chest.

Kye stepped back behind the spray, and she knew what he was waiting for. What he wanted her to do. Fear began to flutter in her stomach.

"Keep your eyes on me, honey."

Eyes on him.

"Feel my hand against yours."

He gave her a gentle tug. It was so soft, she easily could have resisted and remained rooted to the spot. She didn't. She stepped forward, the water hitting her head, dribbling down her face.

Fear sliced at her fragile mind. Darkness tried to edge her

vision. Memories she'd rather forget were right there, threatening to take over. Blur her reality.

She tightened her grip on Kye's hand. Refusing to look away even as water dripped into her eyes, her mouth.

This was it. The moment she took control of her future.

A second passed. Then another. Her heart still beat too fast, and her chest was still rising and falling in quick succession, but she didn't let the terror consume her.

A slow smile spread across Kye's lips. "That's it, sunshine."

He stepped close, lifting her into his arms so that they were both under the spray of water. His head lowered, his mouth stopping just above her ear. "We'll make new memories for your mind to hang on to. Just you and me." Kye's hand went to the back of her neck, his eyes boring into hers.

"Just you and me," she breathed.

"So damn proud of you." He growled the words before his mouth slammed down on hers. Taking. Claiming.

His fingers entwined in her hair, tugging her head back. Her groan was swallowed by his lips, which moved across hers. Gentle but firm.

A deep ache entered her body, making any fear from moments before feel distant. She rubbed her center against him, a desperate need for the man growing inside her.

A long sigh emerged from her throat when his lips finally released hers and trailed down her neck.

One of his hands went to her breast, closing over the soft mound and massaging. Samantha's breath stuttered in her throat. Her head flinging back.

Kye's thumb touched her pebbled nipple, brushing over the peek. Pleasure blasted through her system, a cry tearing from her chest.

Pivoting, he pressed her against the wall, his body surrounding her. Slowly, his hand shifted down the side of her body, moving between them. The moment he touched her core, every limb of her body jolted. Her fingers dug into the skin on his shoulders.

His thumb rubbed her throbbing clit slowly. *Agonizingly* slowly.

Her head rolled against the shower wall. Her body trembled under his touch.

"You are fucking breathtaking."

His words only just penetrated her heat-fogged mind. She was struggling to concentrate on anything other than his touch on her center, torturing her.

When a finger slid inside her while his thumb continued to glide over her clit, a small whimper released from her chest.

"Kye…" Her voice sounded almost pained. The gentle invasion intoxicating her.

He pulled his finger out slowly before sliding back in. Repeating the action over and over again as her hips rose to meet him.

Her breathing grew more labored by the second.

Kye's head lowered to her neck, his mouth latching onto her skin, biting gently. Then he slid a second finger inside her.

Her entire body tensed. Her nails digging into his shoulders so violently, she was sure she was breaking skin.

She was right there on the edge. He sucked her delicate skin harder, continuing his onslaught on her throbbing center. Pushing all the way inside her before pulling out.

"Let go, baby."

Her body trembled. His fingers moved in and out again. Her back arched as a scream erupted from her chest. Samantha shattered.

CHAPTER 18

The sound of Samantha's fiery cry had blood roaring in Kye's ears, deafening him. And the feel of her wrapped around him, trembling in his arms, had every possessive and territorial instinct inside him screaming to keep this woman. To never let her go.

Keeping his arms wrapped firmly around her, he spun, turning the taps off and stepping out of the shower.

Samantha was quiet, tremors still pulsing through her limbs.

Grabbing a towel, he quickly rubbed it over both of them. It in no way dried them completely, but he didn't have the patience for that.

Stepping into the bedroom, Kye lowered her to the bed. He didn't join her straightaway. Instead, he took a moment to take her in. Lose himself in the sight of such beauty.

Her wet curls fanned her head like a halo. Her creamy skin glistening in its dampness.

She wasn't just sunshine. She was every radiant thing of beauty on the damn planet.

Lowering himself atop her, he fused his lips to hers. Tasting her sweetness. Drinking her in. He spent countless minutes devouring her. Drowning himself in all that was Samantha.

Eventually, he trailed his lips down her neck, her chest, never losing contact with her flesh.

When he reached her breasts, he paused. *So fucking perfect.*

Lowering his head, he took a hard nipple between his lips and sucked.

"Kye...!" Her desperate cry was loud. Her fingers scraping over the skin of his back.

He didn't stop. He couldn't. He sucked her sensitive peak, hard, only pausing to switch to the other side.

Her hips thrust up, her fingers now tugging at his hair. Those soft whimpers sounding from her chest...

Damn, they shattered him.

Coming off her nipple, he trailed his lips down until he finally reached the junction between her thighs. He heard the stutter in her breaths. The quickening of her heartbeat.

Placing a thigh over each shoulder, he widened her legs.

"Kye." This time she whispered his name.

"I've got you, sunshine."

Lowering his head, he closed his mouth over her bundle of nerves. Her back immediately arched. A strangled cry piercing the silent room.

He didn't stop. He licked and sucked, dragging every last moan out of her. He alternated between swirling his tongue and sucking her clit. Loving the way her body responded to his touch.

"Kye...please!"

He knew what she wanted. It was exactly what he wanted. What his body was screaming for. Hell, he was so hard it was bordering on painful.

Rising, he quickly grabbed a condom. Before he could cover himself, Samantha sat up, taking it from him and opening the foil wrapper. Instead of putting it straight on him, her fingers wrapped around his length.

His eyes flared. A deep growl vibrated through his chest. "Samantha." He spoke her name like the warning it was.

Her hands began to move slowly. Exploratively.

Kye had to clench his fists to stop himself from grabbing her, throwing her down, and taking the woman there and then. He closed his eyes. Her touch was both heaven and hell.

The second he felt her lips around his tip, his eyes snapped open.

She was on her back and he was sheathed in seconds. Samantha gasped.

He took her mouth with his before whispering, "I need to be inside you *now*." He'd never needed anything more in his life. "You annihilate me."

Lifting her arm, he pressed a kiss to the inside of her wrist, feeling her pulse exploding against his lips. He positioned himself at her entrance.

A slow smile curved her lips. "Then get inside me, handsome."

Fuck. He didn't need to be told twice.

Pressing her hand to the mattress beside her head, he pushed inside her heat. Every muscle in his body tensed in an effort not to come apart right there and then. He had to physically restrain himself from driving into her hard and fast.

He wanted this to last. He wanted to spend endless minutes inside the woman. All damn night wouldn't be long enough.

Samantha's eyes fluttered shut. Her head tipping back, exposing her creamy neck.

Kye started to move his hips, easing out and pushing back in at an excruciatingly slow pace.

"Faster." Samantha's whispered word was accompanied by a leg curving around his hip, tightening, urging quicker movements.

His muscles strained as he forced himself to calm. Then Samantha leaned up from the bed and nibbled on a spot below his ear. "I need more of you, Kye."

The last thread of his control snapped. He drove into her hard and fast, almost completely pulling out of her warm, soft body before pounding back in.

Samantha scrunched the sheets with her fist. Her ragged breaths and moans filled the room. Every time his body returned to her, it was like coming home. Returning to the only place he wanted to be.

Reaching his hand between their bodies, he pressed his thumb to her clit. Another cry pierced the room. He started to move his thumb rhythmically, his brutal thrusts never pausing, until finally, her walls clenched around him

Samantha screamed his name.

Fuck, he loved hearing that on her lips in the throes of passion. It's what tipped him over the edge.

A sound that was almost animalistic, even to his own ears, released from his chest. Then he was tensing. His heart soaring, his body pulsing inside hers.

He stilled above her. Her chest rose and fell in quick succession, every breath pressing her against him.

A whole minute passed, maybe more, before either of them could speak. Then she smiled. Lit up his damn world. "Thank you."

He couldn't stop the chuckle. "You're thanking me for sex?" He felt like he should be thanking *her*. Dropping to his knees and worshiping the woman.

Her voice softened. "I'm thanking you for everything. Supporting me. Being here for me. Making me feel alive and cared for." Reaching up, she touched the side of his face. "You make me happy."

Good. Because she made him fucking ecstatic. Lowering his head, Kye paused just above her lips. "I'm glad, baby. And I feel the same."

Then he was kissing her again. And he couldn't see himself stopping for a long while.

KYE FELT like he'd only just closed his eyes when noises from outside his room woke him. First, the front doorknob jiggling. Then the soft creak of it being pushed open and footsteps as people walked inside. Two people.

Adrenaline flooded his system.

Who the hell had managed to breach his security system and enter his home?

Crawling out of bed, he noted the soft rays of sunlight penetrating the room, telling him it was early morning. He shot a quick glance across the bed to Samantha. She remained under the covers, her chest rising and falling with quiet breaths.

Throwing on a pair of briefs, Kye opened the bottom drawer beside his bed. Reaching under his socks, he pulled out a gun, immediately taking the safety off.

Silently, Kye moved to the closed bedroom door.

If the intruder had altered DNA, they'd hear him coming. There was no way around that. Maybe they weren't altered, though, because the two intruders had walked straight past his bedroom and down the hall.

He still wouldn't be lowering his guard. Not with Samantha here.

Opening the door quietly, Kye moved down the hall. He was seconds from stepping into the kitchen and pointing the gun when familiar voices sounded.

"What are you doing? We had a coffee at my place less than an hour ago," Mason muttered.

"Why are you always up in my grill about coffee? I love it, I'm reliant on it to fuel my day, deal with it."

Sighing, Kye walked out of the hall, lowering the gun to his side in time to see Quinn taking a mug from the cupboard.

"So, knocking and waiting by the door isn't a thing anymore?"

Quinn shrieked, slamming the cupboard door shut and spinning around. Her hand went to her chest as she shot a look over her shoulder to her brother. "You didn't care to warn me that Kye was up?"

Mason lifted a shoulder. "It was more fun this way."

Kye switched the safety back on the gun, only looking up when a soft gasp sounded from Quinn.

"A gun?"

He lifted a shoulder. "If you guys had waited by the door, there would *be* no gun." Well, not in his hand, anyway.

"What's the point in having a key if you can't use it?" Mason asked, looking about as far from remorseful as one gets.

"A key for emergencies. Is this an emergency?" Kye was guessing not.

Quinn frowned. "You're asking if today's shopping trip is an emergency? Yes. Yes, it is."

Kye looked at the time on the wall. "Do all shopping trips start at seven a.m.?"

"Only when breakfast is required first, and one of the shoppers needs to get back to the bakery for a midday start."

Mason shook his head. "Don't try to understand her. I've known the woman her entire life and most of mine, and I still don't get her."

Quinn nodded. "And you never will."

Jeez, they were quite a pair. They reminded Kye of his relationship with his own sisters.

Quinn got a twinkle in her eyes as she took a step closer to Kye. "So, while Samantha's asleep, tell us how it's going with her. Sparks flying? Promises of forever floating around?"

Yes. Plenty of sparks. The sparks lit a damn fire. But he wasn't about to say any of that to Quinn or Mason. Not when he'd barely said it to Samantha.

Soft footsteps sounded from the front of the house, followed by a door opening. He almost smiled when Samantha didn't immediately step out of the bedroom.

You listening, sunshine?

Maybe he'd share just a fraction of how he felt, then...

"The woman's amazing. She makes me feel and want things I've never felt or wanted before. There's a future there."

He almost smiled at the slight elevation in heart rate from the bedroom. Quinn sighed happily, while Mason lifted a brow, obviously having heard Samantha down the hall.

"That is so dang beautiful. See, all that 'I'm gonna be a bachelor forever' crap was just you waiting." She looked at her brother. "Didn't I tell you he'd come around when he found the right person?"

Mason nodded. "You did. But then, you think every person on the planet is destined to be coupled up."

Quinn lifted a shoulder. "Of course. Is it too optimistic of me to think that everyone should find their soul mate? The other half of themselves? Someone to complete them?"

Is that what Kye had found? Strangely, the idea didn't scare him. It felt too early to be confessing undying love, but it didn't feel out of the realm of possibility that he might be doing just that in the future.

Mason coughed. "So, breakfast before stalking the women around the shops?"

Samantha chose that moment to walk down the hall. She stopped beside Kye. She'd thrown on one of his shirts and a pair of sleep shorts that were only just visible.

Seeing her in his shirt made him want to do things that he *could not* do with company present. Almost involuntarily, he tugged her against his side and pressed a kiss to her temple. "Morning, sunshine."

Her smile grew slowly. "Morning."

Quinn's next sigh caused Samantha to look her way. "So. Cute."

Samantha's cheeks tinged pink. "I didn't realize you guys were getting here so early."

"Blame her," Mason muttered.

Quinn rolled her eyes. "Wyatt started work early, and Sage is doing some house visits for Fletcher and Tori. So here we are. Breakfast?"

He felt the slight tensing from Samantha. "I feel bad going without Tori."

The humor dropped from Quinn's features. "She gave us her blessing and has already ordered her dress. She's resting, and she's demanded we visit her afterward to show her what we bought."

Samantha nodded. "And she threatened that if we didn't go, she'd unleash Oliver on us."

Kye scoffed. "That pretzel doesn't scare me." His arm went around her shoulders. "Don't worry, baby. You're safe."

They all chuckled.

CHAPTER 19

Samantha stepped into the pale pink dress, fully prepared to step right on out when it turned out to be too small.

Despite the tiny waist on the thing, Quinn had insisted she try it on. And Samantha was quickly learning that there was rarely, if ever, a time a person could say no to Quinn.

Wriggling her hips, it took her a good couple tugs to get the material over her waist and chest.

Snug. Very snug. But surprisingly, it didn't cut into her. In fact, it almost felt like she was wearing nothing.

Glancing up, Samantha took in her reflection. She almost gasped. Holy crap on a cracker. The dress looked…amazing. Like, better-than-she'd-ever-looked amazing.

Turning to the side, she glided her hand up the soft material. It gave her an hourglass appearance that she'd never had before. The deep vee at the chest made her breasts look bigger than they were, while at the same time, not looking too "on display". And the pale pink was just the right shade to make her feel beautiful and feminine.

"Come on, woman. We don't have all day. Let us see."

Quinn's loud voice pulled her out of her awe. She and Maya were waiting outside the dressing room while Mason, Kye, and Bodie were in the main part of the shop.

They'd been shopping for a couple of hours while the men had followed them around, keeping their distance. It was almost laughable seeing the huge guys crowd into so many women's clothing stores.

Both Quinn and Maya already had dresses, while Samantha had begun to wonder if she'd ever find one for herself. Until now...

Pushing the curtain aside, Samantha stepped out. Maya's mouth dropped open while a smile a mile long stretched across Quinn's face.

Quinn shook her head. "Man, I should be a personal shopper. You look *a-mazing*!"

Maya nodded. "You really do."

"You don't think it's too much?" The hem stopped above her knees, so it wasn't overly formal. And even though she didn't think her chest looked too exposed, the dress was in no way modest.

"Nope. Not too much at all." Quinn folded her arms. "Woman, you need to get it. It will drive Kye nuts."

Hm. That didn't sound terrible.

"I agree. It would be a crime not to," Maya said.

A small smile curved her lips. "I'm going to get it."

Maya clapped her hands. "Yay! We've all got our outfits just in time for you to get to work, Quinn."

"Perfect. This has been fun. We'll have to do this again before the next wedding." When Quinn lifted her brows suggestively toward Maya, Samantha grinned.

"Yeah, I think there are a few women in line to be married before me. *You* being one of them." She lifted her hand and started counting. "And Shylah and Lexie and Sage..."

Samantha lifted her shoulders. "Could always do some joint

weddings." She didn't know exactly how that would work, but she was sure it had been done before.

"Or we could just skip the wedding and go straight to babies, like Lexie," Maya suggested.

Quinn scoffed. "Yeah, right. The guys would have a fit if any of us got pregnant right now. Can you picture their anxiety skyrocketing at the level of security that woman would need?"

It would definitely add another layer of stress. "Don't worry. I don't plan to get pregnant anytime soon," Samantha assured her. She had to spend some time working on herself first. Figuring out who this new Samantha was.

"Me either," Quinn sighed. "One day, though, Wyatt will make me some beautiful, nerdy, super-fit babies."

Everyone laughed at that. Wyatt may be smart, but he was not your typical nerd.

When the women headed back into the shopping area, Samantha tugged the curtain over the entrance to the changing room. She didn't take the dress off straightaway. It was too pretty. She needed to look at it, admire it, for just another moment.

Gah, she couldn't wait to do her hair and wear this in front of Kye. She knew he wasn't superficial. How could he be? He'd spent over a week with her looking dirty as hell and still seemed to like her. But she wanted to look pretty for him.

Smiling to herself, she peeled the dress off her body—yes, literally peeled, that's how tight it was. Putting her own clothes back on took a quarter of the time.

She was still smiling when she put the dress back on the hanger.

Turning, Samantha was about to walk out when a hand pushed the curtain back and a man stepped inside. Surprised, she immediately backed into the corner.

When her brain caught up with what was happening,

Samantha opened her mouth to scream, but a hand covered her lips, silencing her.

Phillip Barret. The damn reporter.

Instantly, her fear was replaced with anger. Was the jerk really stooping so low as to harass her in a woman's changing room? How the hell had he gotten around the guys?

She brought her knee up in an attempt to nail him between the legs, but he saw it coming, quickly stepping closer, eliminating any small space between them and halting her ability to move.

Her fingers went to the wrist of the hand covering her mouth, but it did nothing. The man was stronger than he looked.

He smiled. An arrogant "I've won" kind of smile. When he lifted his free hand, she saw he was holding something. A folded piece of paper.

He waved it in front of her before pushing it into her pocket. There was nothing sexual about the way he did it, but still, the touch felt like a violation and had her skin crawling.

He continued to stand there for another moment before winking and moving away, disappearing out of the changing room as quickly and quietly as he'd entered.

For a moment, Samantha just stood there, dumbfounded. Wondering what the hell had just happened. Shaking her head, she forced herself to snap out of it. "Kye."

Her call for him wasn't loud, but it wasn't soft. She knew he was listening, knew he would hear her voice.

Phillip also knew about the hearing thing. Kye had given himself away in the woods at Luca's. Why else would he have been so careful about not making a sound?

Suddenly, the curtain was pushed aside and Kye was there, looking tall and fierce, scanning her from head to toe. "Are you okay?"

"I'm okay." She nibbled her bottom lip as Mason and Bodie showed up beside him. "Phillip was here."

"*What?*" The word was spoken quietly, with underlying fury.

Mason and Bodie scanned the changing area before moving away. She heard the sound of other curtains being pulled back.

Kye stepped closer, hands going to her shoulders. "Did he touch you?"

"Yes." The muscles in Kye's arms bunched, and Samantha hurried to continue. "He just put his hand over my mouth to stop me from calling for you. He didn't make any noise while he was here. He stood too close for me to attack him."

That seemed to enrage Kye further.

"You're safe. That's what's important." He rubbed her arms with his hands. She could tell he was making an effort to tame his emotions. But the anger was just visible below the calm. "What did he want?"

Oh—the paper!

Reaching into her pocket, Samantha yanked it out, quickly opening and reading it. Her heart stuttered.

Quinn and Maya approached, Maya stepping beside Samantha. "Are you okay?"

She looked up, unsure what to make of the words in front of her.

Kye frowned as he gently slid the piece of paper out of her hands.

Quinn looked confused for a moment before reading the note over Kye's shoulder. "*I saw who attacked you at Mrs. Potter's Bakehouse. Give me the information I want and I'll tell you who it was. P.S. Watch your back, it's someone you trust.*" She looked up, scowling. "What the hell?"

His number was also below the message.

The last bit had to be a lie, if not the entire thing. The only people she trusted were here in Marble Falls—Tori, Kye, and the team. None of them would have hurt Tori the way they had, or try to kidnap Samantha. She knew that better than she knew anything.

Kye lowered the note, his jaw visibly tense. The guy looked like he was ready to punch something. That or just combust.

Bodie was the first to return. "There's a back storage room off the changing area, with access to an outdoor delivery area. The locks on both doors have been tampered with. Mason's still searching."

Even though Kye looked ready to kill, when he took her hand, his touch was gentle. "Let's get out of here. Then we're going to find that reporter and bury him."

~

"I WANT BARRET FOUND. I want him found and threatened so badly that he doesn't even *think* about showing his face in Marble Falls again, let alone cornering my woman in a damn changing room!"

Kye raged to Wyatt on the phone, his frustration clear. And yes, he was referring to Samantha as *his woman*. He didn't give a rat's ass who heard him. He was already kicking himself for not staying closer to her in the shop.

Imagine if it hadn't been Phillip? Imagine if it had been someone else? Someone like *him*?

No. He couldn't think about that right now. It would tip him over the boiling point.

"I'm working on it, Cage. He shouldn't be too hard to find." Wyatt sounded just as angry. It wasn't a surprise. Quinn had been there. It could have easily been her in that changing room.

Kye ran a hand through his hair. He needed to calm the hell down. "I know. I appreciate it."

"Is Samantha okay?"

"Surprisingly, yes. I think she was more angry than anything else. She's pretty strong."

Stronger than him, that was for sure. He was here in his study, ready to blow up, while she was in the living room, on the couch, looking completely fine.

"So his note didn't scare her? Make her question any of us?"

Kye frowned. Did it? He'd been so focused on Barret getting her alone, *again*, that he hadn't considered that. Now that he thought about it, of course, it might freak her out.

To him, the concept was beyond ridiculous. A pathetic attempt by the asshole to get information from her. To Samantha, though…who knew? She hadn't been around his team as long as he had.

"I'll ask her."

"Good idea." Wyatt sighed. "When we get him, we need to find out exactly who his sources are. How did he even know to come looking for us? That there was a story at all?"

"We'll find out everything he knows." Kye would put enough pressure on the guy that he would spill his guts. It wouldn't take him long. Not with the methods he planned to use…

"You know, an easy way to gain access to him—"

"No." Kye didn't give Wyatt a chance to finish. He knew what his friend was about to suggest, and the answer was no. "We're not sending her to him."

"Obviously we'd have her covered."

Still no. "We can't be certain that he's not a threat. We also don't know what his true motives are. Yes, he's a reporter, but he could be working for this mystery woman. And if we set up a meeting, it could be an easy way for them to capture her."

No way in hell was he letting that happen.

"I understand." And Kye knew that his friend did; he'd react the same if they were talking about Quinn. "We'll get him another way."

"Thanks, Jobs. Thanks for everything."

"Of course."

Hanging up, Kye headed out of the study and into the hall.

When he reached the living room, rather than going straight to Samantha, he stopped, taking a moment to study her.

She lay on her side on the couch, pillow beneath her head, looking all kinds of adorable…peaceful, even. And so damn beautiful.

This woman, who had been thrown into a nightmare with him, was now in his life to stay.

Walking over, he gently lifted her head, replacing the cushion with his lap. His hand went to her hip.

"No luck?" She looked up at him.

"Not yet."

Nodding, she looked back to the TV.

"I need to ask you something." He paused for a second, nerves at what she might say suddenly eating at him. "You're not concerned about what Barret wrote, are you?"

She rolled onto her back, a frown pulling at her brows as she looked up at him. "Concerned?"

"About me or my team?" God, even saying that out loud sounded absurd to him. "Because you can absolutely trust me and every one of my brothers to keep you safe."

She slowly sat up and straddled his lap, a leg going to each side. "Kye, I know I can trust you. I trust all of you."

His hand went to her cheek. It was like he was addicted to touching this woman. "Good. Because I would never hurt you." Conversely, he was utterly consumed with keeping her safe and protected.

"I know."

She leaned forward and pressed her lips to his. The kiss was soft but so damn powerful. It made his heart beat faster than it should. It touched his soul.

She pulled back. "I trust you with my life, Kye."

He touched his temple to hers. "Good. Because I'll take care of your life like it was my own. Like it's *more* than my own."

He would sacrifice himself for this woman, any day of the week. The thought should scare the crap out of him. It didn't. Not in the slightest.

CHAPTER 20

*S*amantha quickly trailed behind Kye, struggling to keep up as he entered the Marble Protection office. "Let me call him."

"No."

It was an effort not to grind her teeth at Kye's instant and unyielding refusal. It was the same each and every time she'd asked over the last few days.

But she wasn't about to stop. She couldn't. Not when the reporter might have answers that could help everyone, dammit.

"Have *you* called him?"

Kye pulled his shirt over his head before rifling through the closet for a fresh one. "You know we have. A few times. As soon as he hears our voices, he hangs up because he knows we're not telling him shit except to stay away from our women."

Argh. And they still hadn't allowed her or any of the other ladies to make the call.

She stood behind him as he tugged the white shirt over his head. When he turned and attempted to step around her, she mirrored his movement, blocking his way. "Then let me call. A call won't put me in danger."

Kye's eyes narrowed. Most would probably back off at the look he gave her. He'd perfected the intimidating I-could-squash-you glare.

She wasn't scared. And she wasn't backing down.

"I don't want you in contact with him."

He took a step to the side, attempting to step around her.

She shadowed him again, blocking his exit. Nope. He wasn't getting away that easily. "I'm not a delicate flower, and I would appreciate it if you didn't treat me as such." She smoothed her hands up his chest. "Please. Let me help."

He lowered his head, lips hovering just above her ear. At the feel of his hot breath against her skin, a small shiver coursed down her spine.

"No."

Dammit! Why was the man so goddamn stubborn?

He pressed a kiss beneath her ear before his hands went to her hips, holding her in place as he stepped around her and headed toward the door.

Did he think this conversation was over? Hell no, it wasn't.

Racing in front of him, Samantha pushed the door closed before barricading it with her body.

Kye lifted a brow. "Really? You're blocking me from exiting with your body. Do you think that's a smart idea?"

No. It was stupid. But she'd tried doing the smart thing, asking; it had gotten her nowhere. "I think *you* need to be smarter about this whole Barret situation and let me help."

"Do you?" He stepped closer, a hand going to either side of her head, his chest almost touching hers.

Her breath caught in her throat. The man smelled too good. Looked too good.

No! She had to be firm. Stick to her guns and help them end this. Otherwise, they could spend years looking over their shoulders. Kye would spend years protecting her.

"Yes. Let me call him. You can be right there beside me,

protecting me from his dangerous voice." One of his brows quirked up at her sarcasm. "Face it, you have no other options."

It had been days, and Wyatt and Evie still had no idea where the guy was. They'd even called *The Hidden Outpost* to report him, but the magazine didn't give two hoots about his actions. In fact, they seemed pleased with his tenacity.

Kye dipped his head again, this time his lips going to her neck. She almost whimpered when he pressed a fluttery kiss against her skin. "And what happens when he refuses to tell you anything on the phone? When he demands to see you. In person. Alone."

She swallowed when she felt his tongue swipe her skin. Thinking was almost impossible. The guy was turning her brain to mush. "I don't agree to meet him alone."

One of Kye's hands lifted off the door and trailed over her shoulder, down her body, grazing the side of her breast.

Okay. It was official. The man was trying to kill her.

"Like I said, I don't want you anywhere near him, and that's what he'll demand." His hand lowered farther, curving behind her, clutching her ass. Then he jerked her closer. Allowing her to feel his hardness pressed against her belly.

Holy crap.

"Please, Kye."

He paused. Hope began to rise in her chest. Then…

"I'm not risking you. The answer is no."

His teeth nipped her neck, causing a small yelp to release from her throat and goose bumps to rise over her skin. Then he straightened, removing all contact.

A knowing smile curved across his lips.

Oh…that no-good asshat.

Shoving his chest, she wasn't surprised when he didn't move an inch. Squeezing around him, she headed to the desk.

"Lucky for me, I don't actually need your permission. I was just being polite."

"You need his number, honey."

Lifting the company phone, she put it to her ear, tapping her head with her free hand. "I have a near photographic memory. No paper needed."

She started dialing. She'd gotten halfway when the phone was yanked from her fingers. Christ, the man was fast. He'd made it across the room in under a second.

"Samantha—"

"Don't 'Samantha' me." She poked his big chest. Fully aware it was infantile but not caring in the slightest. "This guy might know who attacked Tori. Who tried to take me. I will *not* go back to being a prisoner and I do not want the people I love put at risk! I've given you guys time to find him. You haven't. Now I'm going to call."

"I won't allow them to take you."

Samantha tilted her head to the side. "You can't guarantee that. Not while the threat is still out there. I'm sorry, Kye, but I'm making the call whether you like it or not. You can either be present, or I'll do it at the first opportunity I get alone. And sooner or later, there *will* be an opportunity."

Seconds of tense silence ticked by. Kye's jaw clenched.

This time, she almost *did* want to step away. Almost took back what she said, hating that he was unhappy because of her.

No. Hold firm, Samantha. Remind the man that you're strong and capable.

She straightened her spine.

"Fine." The word was low and deadly. It actually had the fine hairs on her arms standing on end. "But, if I tell you to hang up, you hang up. And under no circumstances do you agree to meet up with the man without my say so. Got it?"

"Got it."

His pause was heavy. "I don't like it."

She wished they had a plan everyone liked. But they didn't. And she couldn't back down. Someone she loved had been hurt. Could be hurt again. Not to mention the danger Kye and his team were in if she was taken and forced to make more chips to control them.

Lifting a hand, she pressed it against his cheek. "I know. I'm sorry."

She almost sighed in relief when he took her hand in his, turned it, and kissed the inside of her wrist.

KYE, Wyatt, Luca, and Asher stood around Samantha while she sat behind the desk in the Marble Protection office.

Kye's hand twitched with the need to reach over, yank the phone away and hang up. He didn't. But only because Samantha hadn't left him much choice. It was this, or she called him on her own.

Yeah, not an option.

He didn't want Samantha to be involved in finding Barret and taking him down. She'd suffered enough. She needed time to recover. And he'd do everything in his power to protect her.

The phone rang three times before it was answered. "Barret speaking."

"Phillip. It's Samantha Jacobs."

"Ah, Samantha. I was wondering when I would finally hear from you. I would ask you to take me off speaker, but the guys would hear me either way."

Frustration pinched Samantha's face. "Tell me what you know, and I'll tell you what I know."

His chuckle made Kye's temper flare. "This isn't my first rodeo. We either meet in person, and I make sure we both get what the other person wants, or we both get nothing."

Not gonna happen.

Samantha sighed. "You know that I can't meet with you."

"Come on, Samantha. Don't you want to know who I saw

climbing out of that bathroom window? I promise, it will shock the pants off you."

Samantha looked up at Kye. He shook his head.

"We all know you need me more than I need you," Phillip continued. "I mean, my story is all but written. I've done my research. I know those guys were part of a government project that was suddenly shut down. I have eyewitness accounts of super-human strength and speed—Oliver outside AJ's Bar; Eden over a year ago, racing through town at record speed. Hell, I even have a report from a guy in Keystone, Colorado, claiming bones were broken in his arm from Bodie exerting very little pressure."

When Samantha didn't respond, Phillip continued.

"It's not difficult to put two and two together. All of which will be laid out in the article I've almost completed."

Kye had to breathe deeply to stop from blowing up.

There was another beat of silence. Kye could practically hear Samantha thinking. And he was almost sure he wouldn't like anything she was considering.

Placing his hand on her shoulder, he gave it a gentle squeeze. A reminder of what they'd agreed on.

"If you legitimately saw someone climbing out of the bakery window, then you already know why I can't meet you alone."

Exactly.

"Fine. Tell me what you know over the phone, then I'll tell you what I know. I've got to warn you, though, I'm recording."

"No."

"Then no deal, buttercup. We done here?"

Kye heard the slight increase in her heartbeat.

"Samantha—"

"If we meet, Kye will be with me."

No. No, no and *no*.

He reached out to hang up but Samantha stood, putting her body between him and the phone. He easily could have shifted her to the side, but the expression on her face stopped him.

Desperation.

She needed this to be over. Maybe even more than he did.

Phillip sighed. "I'll tell you what...there's an office on the outskirts of Marble Falls that's been unoccupied for a good year. I'll wait there for you. I'll allow Kye to be with you—but that's it. None of the others. I'll know if any of the other guys are close. I have eyes everywhere. And I won't hesitate to leave, which means you won't find out who the attacker was."

Kye didn't believe for a second the guy had "eyes everywhere," but he was still furious, not wanting to agree to a single part of this. Samantha reached up, placed her hand on the back of his head, and pulled him close. She muffled the receiver before whispering, "I trust you to keep me safe. Please. This is all we have."

Goddammit.

He looked up at his team. Like he suspected, they weren't agreeing or disagreeing with the plan. They were leaving it up to him, because it was his woman.

"Fine."

A small smile touched Samantha's lips. "I'll be there," she said into the phone.

Even though he'd just agreed, Kye's stomach still dropped at her words. God, he hated this. It was only Samantha's lingering touch that calmed him.

"Good. I'll be there in an hour. Don't be late. Oh...and just so you know, a trusted friend has a copy of my story. So if something were to happen to me, it still goes out to the masses. Got it?"

This guy just became more and more of a scumbag.

Samantha nodded. "Got it."

CHAPTER 21

Samantha snuck a peek at Kye. He sat behind the wheel, looking just as mad as when they'd left Marble Protection.

She hated that he was angry because of something she'd asked him to do. And it would be a hundred percent her fault if something went wrong. But really, what other choice did they have? Sit and wait for someone to attack again?

She was desperate. Desperate to put everything behind her and really focus on living her life.

Slowly, Samantha slid her hand over the middle console and placed it on his thigh. His hand immediately covered hers. At least he wasn't shutting her out. Treating her like the bad guy.

"Thank you."

He took his eyes off the road for a second to look at her before flicking them back. "For what?"

"For doing this with me."

She hadn't exactly given him a choice, not with how she'd threatened to call Barret when Kye wasn't around. Samantha cringed at the memory.

But the truth was, Kye could have hung up the phone before she'd agreed to meet him. Or just not driven her here.

Deep down, he knew this was the best way forward right now.

He squeezed her hand. "We're only doing this because my team is going to listen to what's happening, wait close by, and come at any sign of danger." She knew all that. They were going to listen from a device in Kye's pocket. "You remember what I said?"

How could she forget? He'd told her half a dozen times in under an hour. "Stay behind you at all times. If you say go, we go."

He nodded. "Even if we don't have the information we need."

Of course. She wasn't stupid. She knew their immediate safety came first. "Even if we don't have the information we need," she confirmed. Turning her head, she watched the blurry trees through the window.

A few minutes of silence passed.

"You know, my mom and I used to go for drives when I was younger. We'd search out new cafes and try all their desserts. I went from ordering babycinos to hot chocolates to coffees."

Kye frowned. "What's a babycino?"

"You never had babycinos when you were a kid?" At the shake of his head, her mouth dropped open. She'd thought they were a rite of passage. Customary in every childhood. "It's a small cup of frothed milk with some chocolate powder sprinkled on top. Some places add little treats on the side, like marshmallows or cookies or chocolates. Toddler Samantha thought they were the bee's knees."

"Hm, toddler Kye never had the privilege. Although there was dessert in my childhood. It was usually a race between me and my sisters to see who ate it first."

Samantha chuckled. "Who usually won?"

He smiled for the first time that afternoon. "Who do you think?"

"You?" The man ate *a lot*. It wouldn't surprise her if he was able to down three-quarters of something before either sister got a bite in.

"Yep. They hated it."

She always loved when he spoke about his family. The stress lines around his eyes faded, and a calmness settled over him.

"When this is all over," Kye continued, "I'd love for you to meet them."

Her head snapped around, her chest constricting. "Really?"

He chuckled. "Yeah. Does that surprise you?"

Surprise? More like settle some of the ragged nerves inside her. If he wanted her to meet his family, that meant he saw a future with her, didn't it? "A little."

"When the danger is gone…what are your plans?" There was a hint of strain in his voice. Because he hated that she wasn't safe? Or because he was scared about her answer?

"I'm not sure. I'll need to look for a new job. But wherever Tori is, that's where I want to be. She's the only family I have. So even if the job was out of town, it wouldn't be far."

She could have said that she didn't want to be too far from Kye either. It would definitely be true. But fear stopped her. Stole the words right out of her mouth. They'd made no long-term commitments to each other.

He squeezed her hand. "I like the idea of you being close."

Her heart sped up a notch.

Kye lifted his hand to the wheel and turned the car left. He only drove another half mile or so before they stopped in front of an old building. Graffiti covered the exterior bricks. Even if Barret hadn't told her the place was empty, she would have been able to tell just by looking at it.

"I don't like this," Kye muttered, leaning back in his seat.

She didn't either. But if there was even a slim chance that she'd find out who was after her, then it was worth it.

Samantha unclipped her seat belt. "I know. But if he really does know who attacked Tori and me at Mrs. Potter's Bakehouse, then we're one step closer to eliminating all enemies."

To safety.

Kye nodded. It was a completely noncommittal nod. And she knew why. He didn't think Barret had any answers. But then, how did he know Tori had been attacked? Sure, it could have been word of mouth, someone in town seeing Tori get taken to the hospital, but the guy had specifically mentioned the attacker climbing out the window...

Kye took the listening device out of his pocket, switched it on, and clipped it to the inside of his shirt. It was small and completely undetectable unless he was searched.

He climbed out first, coming around to Samantha's side. There was one other car in front of the building. A blue jeep. The reporter's, no doubt.

You better have some information for us, Barret.

Kye opened her door and helped her out. He led them to the entrance of the building slowly. There was no one else on the street. It felt like a dead part of town. She didn't even know such a deserted section of Marble Falls existed.

Kye stopped at the door and paused. She watched as he listened to everything on the other side. A small frown crossed his face. He looked down at her and shook his head. "I can't hear anyone."

Her heart sank. What did that mean? That Phillip wasn't there? He'd stood them up? Why would he do that?

"Maybe he's running late?"

Kye frowned, casting a quick glance above Samantha's head at the jeep. "Maybe."

He pushed the door open. Samantha didn't miss the fact that it wasn't locked.

The space was dark. So dark, she could barely see a thing. There were two small windows at the front of the room, both with coverings.

She heard Kye try a light switch, but it didn't work.

"You guys can come, there's no one here," he spoke to his team. They'd be about five minutes away.

"This doesn't make sense." Barret had been trying to get her to talk to him for weeks. They'd followed all his instructions today, he wouldn't have just *not* shown up...

Kye touched her arm. "Let's wait outside for the guys."

She frowned. "Wait...can you smell that?"

It was kind of like a metallic, rusty sort of odor. Barely noticeable.

Grabbing her phone from her pocket, she turned the flashlight on. Scanning the room, she saw that random desks and boxes filled the cavernous space. Paper and stationery scattered across every surface and the floor.

Jeez, whoever had been working here had left the place a mess.

Kye moved a few steps in front of her. Pausing beside a desk, he bent down to look beneath it, swearing under his breath.

"What is it?" She stepped closer when suddenly her foot slipped. She was halfway to the floor when Kye's strong arms caught her, pulling her back to her feet.

"What the heck?" Was there liquid on the floor? She pointed the light toward their feet.

Her lungs seized. Was that *blood* seeping from beneath the desk?

Oh, God...

Like they had a mind of their own, Samantha's legs propelled her forward. She knew she shouldn't look, but she did anyway.

The second the light lit the area under the desk, her stomach dipped, the urge to throw up almost overwhelming her.

Barret. He'd been stuffed under the desk, a bullet wound right between his eyes.

Samantha gagged, Kye's arm immediately going around her waist.

"Barret's dead. Gunshot wound to the head," Kye said into the device before urging Samantha back toward the door.

They were almost out of the office when he pulled her to a stop. Oh, jeez. There wasn't another dead body, was there? Her stomach couldn't handle that.

Kye had just shoved her behind him and was mid-turn when his body went flying, thrown through the air.

A scream caught in her throat. She heard the shatter of glass as a figure appeared right in front of her. The phone dropped from her trembling fingers, plunging her into darkness. She couldn't see a face, only the outline of a body. He was tall, and she was almost certain a hood covered his head.

She opened her mouth to cry out, but no sound emerged.

Pulled off her feet, Samantha was flung over a hard shoulder. Before he could straighten, he was thrown to the side.

Samantha flew with him, unable to extract herself.

She hit the wall right beside the body they'd just uncovered. A brutal thud sounded before she fell to the floor. Stars dotted her vision, a light buzz sounding in her ears. Blinking a few times, she heard the sound of fists colliding with flesh.

Samantha tried to push to her feet, but her knees wobbled, sending her back to the ground. Scrunching her eyes closed for a second, she decided staying low was best when the sound of fighting continued. Almost in a daze, she started to crawl toward the door.

When she passed the desk, her hands landed on wet, sticky liquid. Immediately, she jerked away, only to have her hands slip from under her. Then her entire body was coated in the stuff.

No, not stuff—blood. Barret's blood.

Her stomach began to heave, an anguished sob leaving her chest.

Loud car engines sounded from outside.

There was the shuffle of movement. A curse—from Kye—followed by heavy steps racing toward the back of the building.

Then Kye was at her side, hand on her back. "Are you okay?"

She began to hyperventilate. Dread rising. "It's…it's everywhere. Barret's…his blood!"

"Shh, it's okay, baby. I'm going to get us out of here."

Samantha felt herself being lifted into Kye's arms and carried out of the room, toward the light. She almost didn't want light. Didn't want to see the crimson liquid covering her hands and chest.

He stepped outside at the same time a team rushed forward.

"He took off toward the door at the back." Samantha didn't need to be looking at Kye to know he spoke between gritted teeth.

"Barret?"

"Under a desk inside."

Most of the team moved forward, while Luca remained. He nodded his head toward Kye's car. "I'll drive you two home."

Home. It felt too far. Too much time for her to be sitting in this blood.

As if sensing her unease, Kye dipped his head to her ear. "It won't take long. And I won't let you go."

Samantha held him tighter, some of her panic lowering.

CHAPTER 22

*K*ye stepped out of the bedroom. He could hear his team in the backyard. They'd texted to let him know they were coming over and bringing food. It was easier than calling a team meeting at Marble Protection, especially with it being evening.

He and Samantha had stood under the hot water in his shower for a long time. He'd scrubbed her body until every drop of blood was gone. There'd been a hell of a lot of it. On her chest, her hands, her arms…even her face.

Christ, he hated how much it had shaken her.

He wanted to kick his own ass for not shielding her from Barret's body. Where Kye and his team had been around death enough to be immune to its effects, Samantha hadn't.

Stepping outside, he saw most of his team and their partners already present. Pizza and salad sat on the back deck table. Mason and Sage were the only people yet to arrive.

It felt good to have his brothers around after the day he'd had. Dinner already being organized didn't hurt either.

Kye stopped beside Oliver. "Thanks for coming over."

Oliver nodded. "Of course. How is she?"

"Better. Not great. But the blood's off her skin."

Thankfully, her fear of showering was all but gone. He'd showered with her every day since that first time. And every day, she got better. He couldn't imagine trying to wash all the blood off in the bath. It would have been a nightmare.

Today was already bad. But it could have been worse. A lot worse. Kye ran a hand through his hair. "Thank God he didn't get his hands on her."

Oliver pressed a comforting hand to his shoulder. "I'm glad she's safe, brother."

One by one, the rest of the guys came to stand with Kye and Oliver.

"Did you get a look at him?" Asher asked.

A muscle ticked in Kye's jaw. He'd known this question was coming. Had been anticipating it, knowing no one would like the answer.

"No. The guy had the hood from his sweatshirt over his head when I threw him across the room. As he jumped up, I tackled him and he landed on his stomach. I got some punches in, then he flipped me off and I was on my back...then we heard you guys coming. He ran."

Kye couldn't even tell them the color of his fucking hair. It was beyond frustrating.

"I called it in to our CIA contact," Wyatt said, eyes on Kye. "They're handling the body. Asked if there was anything they could do for us."

Yeah, they could figure out who the hell this new unknown threat was.

"I told them I'd get back to them," Wyatt continued, not waiting for a response, likely thinking the same thing.

"I didn't feel a gun on him," Kye said quietly, brushing a hand over his face. "After a few punches, I tried to check him for weapons, thinking I could grab the gun and shoot him. There wasn't one."

Wyatt looked surprised. "You're sure?"

"Very sure."

Eden frowned. "It wouldn't make sense for him to get rid of the gun before you arrived..."

"Unless he never *had* a gun," Bodie finished. "And Barret was shot by someone else."

It was possible. Hell, anything was possible. A moment of silence passed between them.

"We'll get to the bottom of it," Wyatt said.

"I just...I need her to be safe. Not because of the microchips..." Which was important, but not at all what he was focused on. "Because I can't lose her."

He'd never felt this way before, and he wasn't going to hide it. He was falling for Samantha. Hell, he was pretty sure he'd already fallen. If someone had told him he'd feel this way about a woman a year ago, he would have laughed in their face. What was the saying? Make plans and God laughs?

At the sound of footsteps on the deck, Kye swung his head around to see Samantha stepping outside. No one just looking at her would guess what she'd been through today. The woman was unbelievable.

He took a step, intending to go to her, when Tori jogged across the lawn toward her friend, propelling herself into Samantha's arms.

Kye turned back to Oliver, wanting the women to have a moment together. "How's Tori doing?"

Oliver's gaze went to her. "She's getting there. Headaches are lessening. Today's only our second trip out since the attack. She keeps telling me she's fine, but I want her to get as much rest as possible. To be honest, if it was completely up to me, I'd keep her inside the house for months."

Kye didn't blame the guy.

"When we find the man who did it..." Oliver trailed off, never finishing that sentence. He didn't need to.

The attacker was a dead man.

He'd hurt one of their own, almost caused long-term harm to Tori. That wasn't a person they could afford to keep around.

"I don't know if Barret really knew who attacked the women at Mrs. Potter's Bakehouse," Kye said. "But someone clearly went through the effort of murdering the guy before he could say anything to Samantha."

Asher nodded. "I'm betting the CIA finds a bug on Barret's phone. Either that, or someone was trailing him and listening to everything he said."

Luca frowned. "What about the stuff Barret wrote in the note? About the attacker being someone Samantha trusted?"

Oliver was already shaking his head. "That part can't be true. The only people she has in this town are us."

Kye's thoughts exactly.

At the sound of people arriving, Kye turned to see Mason and Sage walking across the lawn. They weren't alone. Jason and Logan trailed behind them.

Sage headed toward the women while the men continued their way. Except for Jason, that was. He beelined for Samantha at the food table.

Instant annoyance filled Kye. It shouldn't. He knew it was a ridiculous reaction. But the memory of them together on the couch all those weeks ago, Jason touching her, and now the way he headed straight for her...Yeah. It made him mad.

Mason began chatting with the guys. Kye tried to ignore Samantha and Jason, but the more seconds that passed, the harder it became.

A couple of minutes later, Logan nudged his shoulder with his own. "You okay?"

"I don't trust your friend." He wasn't going to lie or sugarcoat the truth; there was no point.

Logan frowned. "He's a good guy. One of the best."

Kye wanted to trust that. But when he saw Jason put his hand on Samantha's knee—*again*—he lost it.

SAMANTHA TUGGED a shirt over her head. She still didn't feel clean. She had a feeling it would be a while before she did.

Blowing out a long breath, she headed out of the bedroom. Kye had mentioned everyone was coming over. He'd asked her if it was okay, and she said yes, genuinely grateful they were here. She needed people around to take her mind off the day. And she'd never turn down an opportunity to catch up with Tori.

Samantha stepped outside. The second Tori spotted her, her friend ran forward, throwing her arms around her.

"I'm so glad you're okay," Tori whispered, seconds before she pulled back. "We aren't having a good run, are we?"

Samantha couldn't help but chuckle, even though there was nothing remotely funny about it. "That's putting it lightly. But we're still alive and kicking. We're kind of indestructible."

Tori laughed in return. "Don't say that too loud, they'll hear you." She shook her head. "I've decided next time you want to play detective with Kye, I'm vetoing it. In fact, I'm locking you in the house and not letting you come out. Oliver's already agreed to have my back on this."

Samantha wouldn't put it past her. She was badass when she wanted to be. "I think that's probably a good idea."

After today, she'd decided chasing down leads wasn't for her. She would leave that to the guys who had trained for it.

Tori studied Samantha's face. "Are you okay?"

She'd been through worse. But her therapy session scheduled for Tuesday couldn't come quick enough. "I'm okay. Are you?"

Tori lifted a shoulder. "If you mean is my head okay, then yeah, it is. I'm kind of going crazy, though. Oliver's had me on bedrest for forever. But I know I'm lucky to have him looking out for me."

Yeah, Samantha was just as lucky to have Kye as her protective detail.

Tori threaded her fingers through Samantha's and began to tug her toward the women. When they passed the food table, the smell of pizza had her stomach growling, reminding her that it had been a long time since she'd eaten. She'd been feeling sick since the attack, so she'd declined any offer of food from Kye.

"I'm just going to grab something to eat, then I'll come over," Samantha said, coming to a stop.

"Okay." Tori squeezed her hand before returning to the women.

Samantha studied the pizzas. Usually pepperoni was her favorite, but right now it didn't look appealing at all. In fact, just the sight of it almost made her stomach rebel.

God, what was wrong with her? Had the attack put her off one of her favorite foods? It was just a bit of blood. It was gone, it should not be affecting her like it was.

Grabbing a plate, Samantha popped two slices of margarita on it. She was about to head toward the women when Mason, Sage, Logan, and Jason walked down the steps of the deck. Jason's gaze immediately clashed with hers, a smile lifting the corners of his lips.

She smiled back. She liked Jason. He'd stopped and chatted with her a couple of times when they'd both been at Marble Protection. The guy always made an effort to check in on how she was doing, which was nice.

He walked over to her. "Hey!"

"Hey, yourself. You're still in town." She'd thought his team had left.

Jason nodded. "Yep. The rest of the team has returned to be with Blake and his family in case there's any trouble there. Logan and I will stay until after the wedding. Gives me a bit more time with my sister."

"We can never have enough big bad protectors in Marble Falls."

Jason took a small step closer. "Are you okay? I heard it was a bit of an ordeal today?"

She lifted a shoulder. "Yeah. I'm not used to seeing…dead people." Or falling into a pool of their blood while the assumed killer fought Kye. "Kye's been amazing. Although, I think he's frustrated the guy got away and he didn't see his face."

"Yeah. I'd be frustrated, too. But we'll catch him. I have faith."

Good. They could definitely use of bit more of that.

He seemed to consider his next words before asking, "How's it going with the therapist?"

She'd almost forgotten that she'd told him about her sessions. There was just something about Jason that made him easy to open up to. Maybe it was because that first time they'd met, he'd caught her in a moment of vulnerability.

"She's great. I've come such a long way with her help. Her, Kye, and Tori have kept me sane."

"Good. A strong support network is important. If I hadn't had the guys…" He shook his head. "Let's just say I wouldn't be the jovial man I am."

Samantha laughed. "Jovial?"

"Yeah." He pulled back, frowning. "You don't think I'm jovial?"

Before she could answer, her stomach growled.

Her cheeks immediately flushed. *Classy, Samantha.*

She'd heard that, so there was no way Jason with his above-average hearing hadn't.

He chuckled, putting a hand on the small of her back and leading her to a chair. "Eat."

She took a seat but kept her eyes on Jason. "You don't have to sit with me."

"I don't mind. The guys are talking shop. Logan will catch me up later."

Samantha took a bite of her pizza, her eyes sliding over to the women. "How's Sage doing with everything?"

"She's incredible. The woman is so focused on helping everyone that she doesn't seem to let any of the other stuff faze her."

The doctor *didn't* look fazed by any of the danger in Marble Falls. But then, Samantha hadn't known her for long.

"Do you have any sisters?"

She looked back to Jason at his question. "Tori. Not a blood relation, but it feels like she is."

Jason nodded, his gaze landing on Logan. "I know what that feels like. What about parents? You keep in touch with them?"

"My mom passed away from cancer a couple years ago."

Jason frowned, his hand going to her knee. "God, I'm sorry, Samantha."

"Thank you." She gave him a small smile.

She felt his hand tense seconds before he stood.

Samantha's head shot up to see Kye walking toward them.

No. Not walking. *Storming*. And looking ready to kill. Placing her food on the grass, Samantha rose to her feet.

Kye stopped a foot away from Jason.

Jason didn't back away. "Everything okay, Kye?"

His eyes narrowed. "No. Someone attacked us today. Tried to take her from me."

"I can understand how that would make you angry."

Kye stepped even closer. "Get. Away. From her."

Oh, for heaven's sake! Samantha stepped to the side of the men, placing a hand on Kye's chest. "Kye—"

He tugged her back gently, away from Jason, not taking his eyes from the other man. "I think you should leave."

The crowd had quieted. She could see the guys close by, seconds from intervening.

Jason didn't appear intimidated in the least. "I'm not a threat to you *or* Samantha."

Kye smiled, but there was no humor behind it. "Really? Because the reporter insinuated Samantha's attacker was someone she trusted." Samantha opened her mouth to speak, but Kye continued. "And today, she was almost kidnapped by a man about your height and build, wearing a sweatshirt with a hood."

Samantha gasped. "Kye!"

"Look around you," Jason said quietly. "*Everyone* here is my height and build."

Kye's eyes narrowed. "Difference is, I trust the others."

Samantha saw Sage step forward, only to have Mason pull her back. He stepped up to Kye and placed a hand on his chest. "Kye, he's not the guy who attacked you today. He was with me and Sage."

He turned to look at his friend. "And you had your eyes on him every second of the day, did you?"

At Mason's silence, Kye nodded. "That's what I thought."

CHAPTER 23

Samantha watched the muscles in Kye's back strain the fabric of his shirt as he deflected a blow. He was running the last class of the day at Marble Protection, and the teenagers were in awe. *Had* been in awe since he and Bodie started the session. Not that it surprised her. She was a full-grown adult, and *she* was in awe.

She hadn't missed the fact that Bodie had done most of the talking, though. Kye had been quiet all day. Ever since his confrontation with Jason last night.

She hated that. She'd hoped that coming to work would turn his mood around.

It hadn't.

Was he angry at her? Angry that she'd been speaking to Jason? That she didn't believe he was the bad guy? Or was he just angry and frustrated in general?

"Any chance you could help me pack these chairs up?"

Her head shot up at Logan's request before she scanned the scattered chairs from the previous class on the other side of the large room. "Sure." She pushed to her feet. "How did you get roped into helping out around here?"

Logan lifted his large shoulders. "I'm the one who asked. We're setting up a business of our own, so the guys have been talking us through a lot of stuff."

Ah, that explained it. Lifting a chair, she started walking it to the side. "In Lockhart?"

"Not quite." Logan held a chair in each hand as he headed in the same direction. "Heard of Cradle Mountain?"

"No. Is that in Texas?"

"Idaho. It's a small town near Ketchum. Flynn's mother lives there. She's not doing so great so he wants to be there for her."

"Didn't you move to Lockhart because one of the guys has a daughter?"

He nodded, stacking his chairs before taking hers to pile on top. "We did. Fortunately, the mother has agreed to move as well."

Being close to a parent was a very good reason to relocate. Samantha had been by her mother's side every day during her illness. "That's great. Will your business be similar to this one?"

"We'll be focusing more on security but will offer whatever our clients need. Personal protection, security advice, self-defense lessons. We'll even perform search and rescues if required."

Logan grabbed more chairs, and Samantha did the same. His biceps rippled, highlighting his immense strength.

Well, that job would be right up their alley. "The business sounds perfect for your team." They stacked the chairs before going back for more. "Will Sage be sad that her brother's farther away?"

Logan lifted a shoulder. "From what I've heard, she'll be flying up to see him regularly."

Didn't surprise Samantha.

She continued to chat with Logan about his team until all the chairs were stacked. Once the last one was on the pile, she was about to walk away when Logan touched her arm. He paused, seeming to debate over his next words.

"I hope I'm not overstepping here, but I just wanted to say something. And I've said similar to Kye." He shot a look over her head, presumably at Kye, before looking back at her. "Jason would never hurt an innocent. Especially a woman…not with having a sister and mother who mean so much to him. He's a good guy. I trust him with everything I have."

She shook her head. Logan didn't need to tell her that. She knew. "Before last night, the thought had never even crossed my mind that Jason might be the person who attacked Tori or attempted to take me. And even after Kye insinuated it," she couldn't help but cringe at that, "I didn't believe it. Not for a second."

She barely knew the guy, but there was a gentleness about him. A kindness that couldn't be faked.

"Yesterday was just…a hard day." She felt like she needed to explain Kye's behavior. "I think it all got to Kye."

Logan nodded. "He cares about you."

She smiled. Good, because she cared about him too.

"Anyway, I just wanted to say that. Try and provide you with some reassurance." He nodded toward the class. "I think they're done. I'm gonna get going now."

She shot a look over her shoulder to see Kye packing up. He didn't look any happier than the last time she'd looked his way.

She turned back to Logan. "Thank you. And good luck with your business."

He chuckled. "Thanks. I think it will be a big learning curve, but worth it."

Logan headed out. Everyone from the class began filtering out the door, leaving just Bodie and Kye.

Samantha walked toward them. "Good class?"

Bodie straightened. "Yeah, they're good kids. Very receptive."

Kye didn't look her way.

"Are all students not like that?"

Bodie laughed. "Ah, no. There have been a few fights. A few kids who couldn't care less." He lifted his shoulder. "You get that. I'm gonna get going. Maya's probably dying to see me."

They both laughed as he waved goodbye. Once the door closed behind him, there was silence.

Samantha went to stand beside Kye. "Are you angry at me?" The man still wasn't looking at her, and it was frustrating as heck.

"No."

"Really? Because you *seem* angry."

He headed to the office, Samantha trailing him. He lowered himself behind the desk and began shutting down the laptop. "Samantha, I'm not really in the mood right now."

"Because you're angry." She knew she was pushing him, but she wanted him to admit how he was feeling so they could deal with it.

When he didn't answer, she pressed the screen of the laptop down. He only just moved his fingers before the top closed on them.

"Kye...can you please talk to me?"

He finally looked up. "I wasn't angry before, but you're starting to make me angry now."

Good. Angry people were more honest. She rounded the desk. "Tell me what you're feeling."

He stood, towering over her. "I'm feeling frustrated, Sam. And confused."

Sam? Since when did he call her Sam? "Why?"

"Because I almost lost you yesterday! And it was my fault for agreeing to go to that office. Then a guy I barely know touches you. A guy who, as far as I'm concerned, could easily be the man who attacked us."

Her features softened. "Kye. You didn't lose me. You fought

the guy off and we're both alive and safe. And you heard Mason. Jason was with them yesterday. It wasn't him."

His jaw visibly clenched. "I'm not used to feeling like this."

Was it her, or was there some anguish in his voice? "Like what?"

"Like if I lose you, I lose myself." He ran a hand through his hair. "I'm not this guy."

She almost didn't want to ask...but she did. "What guy are you?"

"The one who only dates casually. Who doesn't get caught up in relationships." He scrubbed a hand over his face. "This is uncharted territory for me. This jealousy. This gut-wrenching fear of losing you."

She touched his chest. "You won't lose me, Kye."

His eyes darkened, his hand going to her cheek in a gentle caress. "Good. Because I love you. And it's driving me insane. I never expected to fall in love like this, but I have. And I refuse to let you go now."

KYE HADN'T PLANNED to say those words, and by the expression on Samantha's face, she hadn't expected to hear them. But now that they were out, he sure as hell didn't regret them. It was how he felt, and the woman needed to know.

"Love?" Her voice was quiet.

A smile stretched his lips. The first all day. "Yeah, sunshine. I love you."

Her eyes misted. "I love you, too."

He closed his eyes. Hearing her say those words...damn, did it felt good.

Wrapping his arms around Samantha, he lifted her up against his chest, resting his forehead to hers. "Glad to hear it. Because I wasn't going to let you go either way."

Well, he probably would have if she really wanted, but it would have broken him. Torn his heart right out of his chest.

Her arms tightened around his neck. She didn't so much as crack a smile. "I told you. I'm not going anywhere."

Kye pressed his lips to hers. The kiss was sweet. It felt different to any other they'd shared, because this one had no uncertainty. They knew exactly where they stood with each other.

He swiped his lips across hers, loving the small shiver that raced up her spine. Then he deepened the kiss. Tasted the intoxicating woman in his arms. Feasting on her.

Sliding a hand up her body, he stopped when he reached her breast. A soft purr released from her throat, causing the blood to rush in his veins.

"We should stop." It killed him to say those words, but if they didn't now, he didn't know if he'd be able to later.

Her lips tore from his but didn't leave his body, instead moving over his cheek, his neck. "Why?"

Why? Because the woman was destroying the small tendrils of self-restraint that he possessed.

Her lips shifted to his ear before she whispered the words that set his body ablaze. "Make love to me, Kye. Here and now."

For a second, he stilled. He wanted to give her more than a quickie in the office. She deserved more than that. But then she nipped the skin below his ear. Wriggled her hot little body against his.

And right or wrong switched off. Want became need.

Swinging around, he sat her on the edge of the desk. In seconds, he moved the laptop and every other item on the desk to the floor.

Samantha giggled. Shit, even that made him harden.

His hands went to the hem of her top, tugging it off in one fell swoop before removing his own. Samantha reached her hands behind her and unclipped her bra. Her perfect breasts bounced as they broke free. His heart sped up in his chest.

"Where have you been all my life?" he whispered.

She bit her bottom lip. "Waiting for you. The world made us wait, didn't it?"

It did. But never again would they be without each other.

She kicked her shoes off. He did the same. Then he was with her again. Arms wrapping around her waist. Mouth going to hers.

He felt her hand ease down his chest, stopping at the top of his shorts before shoving down his last items of clothing. Then her fingers were wrapping around his hardness, making his heart jackhammer in his chest.

Kye groaned deep in his throat. Jesus Christ, the woman was killing him.

When her hand started to move over him in gentle exploration, every muscle in his body tensed. Her touch firmed. Her movements becoming more rhythmic.

His breaths whooshed in and out of his chest. It was the perfect combination of bliss and torture.

Tearing his lips from hers, he grabbed her wrist. "Honey, I can't let you keep doing that."

"I want to touch you."

"You have no idea how much I *like* you touching me. But right now, I want all of you." He used his other hand to graze her cheek.

Her eyes heated. He took her mouth again, using his body to press her flat against the desk. He didn't separate his lips from hers as he removed the last of her clothes.

He wanted to stop and look at her. Admire his beautiful woman. But he couldn't. Even the smallest bit of separation seemed too much.

Moving his lips down her neck and chest, he took one stiff

nipple into his mouth. Her fingers grabbed at his hair, her soft cries filling the room.

He spent endless minutes sucking and tasting, enjoying every little sound and reaction from his woman. He moved across to the other nipple and did the same.

Her body writhed beneath him.

Slowly, he trailed his mouth down her stomach, reaching the V between her legs. When he swiped her clit with his tongue, she immediately whimpered. He did it again. Same reaction.

So damn sensitive.

Kye sucked until her groans became louder and heavier. Then he lowered his mouth, penetrating her with his tongue.

A primal cry released from her lips, urging him on. He continued to slide his tongue in and out, wanting to push her to the very edge.

Samantha tried to buck her hips, but he held her firmly, devouring her softness.

"Kye...!" Her cry was breathy and desperate.

Slowly, he made his way up her body, lips caressing her skin, wanting to taste every inch of her.

He quickly moved across the room, grabbing a condom from his gym bag before returning to her. She was still on her back. Looking at him with desire-filled eyes. Desire and trust.

Kye leaned over her and she immediately wrapped her legs around his waist. Pausing at her entrance, he took in her face. The woman he loved. The woman who loved *him*.

"You're mine, Samantha."

Her hand went to the back of his head, her eyes never leaving his. "Yours."

Slowly, he slid into her, feeling her walls stretch around him. Neither of them made a sound, but words weren't needed. They both felt it. The intensity of their connection.

Kye began to move his hips. Easy, rhythmic thrusts. He

watched her eyes shutter. Her head tip back against the desk, exposing her long neck. Kye latched on, sucking the creamy skin.

He would never tire of this woman. Not if he lived a hundred more years with her. She made him feel alive. And he wasn't giving her up. Not for a second.

Each deep thrust brought them back together. Brought Kye back to his love.

Her breasts brushed against his chest, her hands clutching his neck and shoulder.

Lifting a hand to her breast, Kye rubbed his thumb over the peak. She cried out. Arched her back. He did it again, then pinched the hard nipple, and Samantha fell over the edge.

He kept driving into her, but the feel of her walls throbbing around him was too much. With one final thrust, his entire body tensed and then shuddered. He growled deep in his throat before lowering his body to her chest, just keeping his weight off with his elbows.

They both breathed heavily, Samantha's arms wrapped around him, holding him close.

Kye wasn't going anywhere. Not now. Not ever.

CHAPTER 24

"*C*all me in if you need anything."

Samantha smiled at Kye. They stood at Oliver's front door but had yet to knock. "Thank you, but I don't think I'll need anything. We'll be celebrating Evie inside, while you guys are just out back."

It was two nights before the wedding, and this was their own versions of bachelorette and buck's parties for the couple. They were all at Oliver's house.

Everything in Marble Falls had been quiet the last couple weeks. It was the only reason they'd decided to go ahead with the wedding. Logan's team would still be present as added security.

Kye smiled. "Okay, what about if *I* need something?"

She almost laughed. "What might you need?" She had a feeling she knew but wanted to hear the guy say it.

Kye bent his head, his lips so close to hers she could almost feel them. "You. Always you."

Her cheeks heated at his words. He'd been saying sweet things like that ever since they'd declared their love for each other. And she would never tire of it.

"You can survive without me for a couple of hours." Whether she could survive without him was an entirely different matter.

Kye growled before kissing her. She heard the door open behind her and almost wanted to tell whoever it was to get lost.

"My God, you guys are too cute." Tori. Of course. "But..." Fingers wrapped around Samantha's upper arm, tugging her toward the house. When Kye let her go, she almost wanted to groan in disappointment. "This is a girls' night. Boys are out back."

Tori swung an arm around Samantha's shoulders, throwing a sweet smile Kye's way.

He shook his head, but still smiled. "Call if you need me."

Tori rolled her eyes. "She won't. But thanks."

Samantha just caught the wink Kye sent her way before the door all but slammed in his face.

"Would it have been so terrible to let the guy kiss me for a bit longer?"

Like a minute. Or ten.

Tori scoffed as she pulled Samantha into the living room. "You two have been all over each other for weeks. A couple hours' break will be good for you."

Hm. She wasn't sure "good" was the right word. Hard maybe?

She was glad to be spending the night with Tori and the rest of the women, though. She'd really grown to like everyone in Marble Falls. It felt like a real community.

When she stepped into the room, she saw she was the last to arrive. The six other women were scattered around the living area, all smiling and laughing.

Samantha crossed over to Evie, sitting on the couch, and gave the woman a hug. "Happy bachelorette party, Evie."

When they separated, Evie had a huge smile on her face. "Thanks for coming, Samantha. It's so nice to have all the girls together before the big day."

Lexie sighed. "Unfortunately, the boys vetoed the stripper idea. Party poopers."

Samantha took a seat beside Evie.

Tori shook her head. "Unbelievable."

"Actually, the guys offered to come and give us a show," Maya said with a smile. "Bodie was pretty keen. He probably still is."

Laughter filtered across the room. That didn't surprise Samantha.

"I don't know how Eden would feel about me looking at other men naked, friends or not," Shylah added from across the room.

Samantha didn't know how *she* felt about ogling other naked men. The guys were all gorgeous, but the only man she cared to look at was Kye.

Evie shook her head. "No naked men. I just want to spend the night with my girls."

"Then a girls' night you will have." Quinn jumped to her feet. "Okay, first thing on the night's itinerary is crazy cocktail creations!"

Samantha followed the women into the large kitchen. She hoped this wasn't a competition because she'd never made a cocktail in her life. Not that she intended to drink much. She hadn't been feeling her best for weeks now. There had been so many times she'd been about to mention it to Kye. But too often, she caught the worry in his eyes. The strain on his face.

The guy tried to hide it, but he was stressed.

So, she'd made the decision to check in with Sage before worrying him. She shot a look across the kitchen island to Mason's girlfriend. Would it be terrible for her to ask about it tonight? Only if there was a quiet moment, of course.

She felt bad, because tonight was Evie's celebration, but maybe if she caught the other woman alone...That way, no one would be bothered, and Samantha wouldn't have to stress Kye further if it was nothing.

When the room fell quiet and seven sets of eyes landed on

Samantha, she suddenly realized that they expected some sort of answer from her...to a question she hadn't been paying attention to. Crap.

Tori nudged her shoulder. "Well? What kind of alcohol do you want to use for the base of your cocktail?"

Quinn leaned over the island. "And remember, make the wrong choice, and you could lose."

So it *was* a competition. Dang it. She had no hope. "Brandy," she blurted.

Quinn lifted her brows. "Same as me. No copying my secret recipe."

Hm, copying wasn't the worst idea.

As if reading her mind, Quinn shifted her body, attempting to cover the ingredients she'd already grabbed.

"Evie's the taste tester, right?"

Evie's brows shot up at Sage's question. "Wait, what?"

Lexie nodded. "Sure is. No one can get too drunk tonight, but a bit tipsy won't hurt."

Samantha laughed as she got to work, mixing anything and everything that looked like it may taste good. She was going for sweet flavors. They went with brandy, right?

The women started talking around her. About the men. About the wedding. About the way Luca agreed to anything and everything for the big day.

Over the next couple hours, Samantha laughed more than she had in years. They played half a dozen bachelorette games, one involving a life-size cardboard cutout of Luca. Everyone put on lipstick and a blindfold and had to attempt to kiss his lips.

Everyone was way off—very intentionally—so that was an easy win for Evie.

As the end of the night neared, most women seemed to be at least a little drunk, Evie included. Luckily, everyone had a day to recover.

She was pretty sure that her and Sage were the only sober

ones. Lexie might have been sober, too, but it was harder to tell because the woman was already so extroverted.

Tori just about fell onto Samantha's lap. "God, I love you."

Samantha chuckled. "I love you, too."

"I'm so happy you and Kye love each other. Think of all the extra time we can spend together. The breakfast dates. Gym dates."

"Tori, there will be no 'gym dates'. And even if we weren't dating, I plan to see you all the time anyway."

Her friend smiled. A very glassy smile, but a smile all the same. "Can we still marry our men?"

Samantha chuckled again. "Yeah, we can."

"Good." Tori lay her head on Samantha's shoulder for a moment before quickly straightening. "Hey! You're not drunk."

The accusation in her voice had Samantha biting back another laugh. "That is correct."

Tori reached for something on the coffee table, almost falling to the floor in the process. Samantha just saved her with a hand to her waist.

She grabbed a random glass and pushed it toward Samantha's lips. "Drink."

The moment she got a whiff of whatever was in the cup, her stomach rolled. "Uh, no thank you."

The smell of alcohol didn't usually make her nauseous. In fact, she normally loved celebrating with a few drinks. What the heck was wrong with her?

Tori giggled drunkenly, keeping the glass close.

Suddenly, nausea began to crawl up her throat.

Moving quickly, Samantha shifted Tori away, stood and speed-walked to the hall bathroom. She'd just dropped to her knees when her entire dinner came up.

She didn't know how long she remained there, maybe seconds, maybe minutes, but at some point, she felt a hand on her back, rubbing in circular strokes.

When she looked up, she saw Sage kneeling behind her, as well as Lexie, by the door. Embarrassment tinged her cheeks pink.

"Are you okay?" Sage asked calmly.

Samantha nodded, pushing to her feet and moving straight to the sink. "Sorry, I haven't been feeling well." She caught Lexie's frown in the mirror before dipping her head, rinsing her mouth.

"You hardly drank anything," Lexie said. "I'm pretty sure I saw Tori sculling your cocktails."

Sage moved to stand beside her. "You look pale. Any other symptoms?"

Samantha wet her lips. Now was probably as good a time as any to bring up how she'd been feeling. "I was actually wanting to talk to you, if that's okay, but tonight probably isn't the right time."

"Don't be silly," Sage said softly. "You can talk to me anytime."

"I should probably..." Lexie started heading out, but Samantha quickly shook her head.

"It's okay, it's probably nothing." She didn't want to make it into a bigger deal than it likely was. "I've been feeling nauseous on and off for a few weeks, and a bit lightheaded. Tired...really tired."

And she shouldn't be tired, because since she'd been sharing a bed with Kye, she'd been sleeping better than ever.

Sage seemed to consider her words. Samantha caught Lexie's brow hike up seconds before she disappeared out of the room. When she returned, she closed the door and handed Samantha a small box. "I carry this in my bag since Fletcher. You never know when you'll need one."

Lexie's words confused her...until she looked down. A gasp escaped. "Um, I'm not."

Again, Lexie raised a brow. "Really? Because I had those same symptoms. And they continued to get worse until I started seeing Sage."

No. No, no and no. She was not pregnant and did *not* need to take a test. "We did it without protection one time, but I've had a period since then."

Sage nodded, looking far too calm under the circumstances. "Some women can experience a small amount of bleeding, particularly in the early weeks."

What? Samantha had never heard of that before. But then, she'd never properly researched pregnancy.

Sage placed a hand on her arm. "You don't need to take it now."

Oh, yes, she did. She needed to debunk this idea right the heck now. "I want to."

The women nodded before stepping out of the room.

Samantha quickly peed on the stick, trying to calm her racing heart by assuring herself it wasn't possible. She *was not* pregnant.

A couple of minutes passed before Sage knocked, entering the room alone and closing the door after her.

"Lexie rejoined the group. She won't say anything about this." Sage stood close. "Do you want me to call Kye?"

Call Kye? To tell him she was taking a pregnancy test at Evie's bachelorette party? "That's okay. I'm pretty sure it will be negative, so there's no point in—"

Samantha stopped mid-sentence when the single word appeared on the stick.

Pregnant.

Holy crap on a cracker. Her breath cut off in her throat. For a moment, she felt lightheaded.

Sage must have noticed because she took Samantha's elbows and directed her to sit on the lid of the toilet, crouching in front of her. "Are you okay?"

Honestly? She wasn't sure. "We love each other...but we're still so new."

Sage nodded. "This must be a bit of a shock."

A shock? It felt like someone had pulled a rug out from under her feet and now she was flailing on the floor.

"I can't...I mean, this must be wrong."

Another calm smile from Sage. "We can do a blood test tomorrow. But those tests are rarely wrong."

Rarely wrong. So Sage was saying Samantha was more than likely pregnant.

She ran a hand over her face. "The wedding is in two days. We're spending the entire day tomorrow helping with everything. Kye has so much going on right now. I can't imagine dropping this on him, not to mention taking the attention away from Evie and Luca."

And truth be told, Samantha was a bit scared about Kye's reaction. She knew he loved her, but were either of them ready for a baby?

God, just thinking about his reaction made her feel shaky with nerves.

As if sensing her fears, Sage moved closer. "How about we organize a blood test for three days' time? That way, you can tell him after the wedding, and he can come with you to the appointment. In the meantime, I'll get some supplements to you tomorrow."

Some of the tightness in her chest eased. "You think that's okay? To wait a few days?"

She sure could use the time to rack her brain on the best way to tell Kye. And to work up some courage.

"If you feel better waiting, then we wait. You're not waiting long. I'll give you the supplements tomorrow while we're setting up for the wedding," Sage continued, hand going to Samantha's leg. "Lexie had some higher nutritional requirements, and I suspect you will too."

Samantha nodded. Blood tests. Supplements. Because she was pregnant. With Kye's baby.

She needed time for it to sink in. At least a day. Or maybe a century.

CHAPTER 25

*H*eat radiated off the fire. The flames were bright in the night. Kye lifted a beer to his lips as his team spoke around him. Tonight was about Luca. His wedding the day after tomorrow.

Kye couldn't be happier for the guy.

Logan's team also sat around the fire, beers in hand. The extra layer of security was definitely needed. Luca wouldn't have gone ahead with the wedding without them.

With sixteen DNA-altered men, in addition to the recently installed security fence around Luca's property, it was highly unlikely anyone would get through.

Luca threw his head back and laughed at something Asher said. Kye smiled. His friend was happy. Good. They'd all been through a lot over the years. Too much.

And the reality was, they didn't know when this would end. When one threat died, another seemed to pop up. It was like they were playing Whac-A-Mole. And the game could go on for years.

They couldn't put their lives on hold forever. The wedding had to take place.

Kye took another sip of his beer, darting his gaze to the house.

The sound of female voices drifted through the night air, penetrating his ears. Voices and laugher.

He almost smiled himself.

He didn't listen to what was being said, he only needed to know they were safe. They deserved their privacy for the night. Christ knew they barely got it any other time.

Shooting his gaze back to the guys, he saw Jason standing. Before the man had taken a single step, Kye knew he was heading his way. He'd been expecting this. Probably should have been the one to initiate it after how he'd acted during their last confrontation.

Jason took a seat beside him on the log. "Hey, Kye."

He gave the man a nod. "Jason. Look, I'm sorry—"

Kye stopped as Jason shook his head. "Don't. It's not necessary. You don't know me, it's understandable that trust doesn't come easy. Particularly after the day you'd had." Jason looked to the fire, the gold flames reflecting in his eyes. "I wouldn't hurt her. I saw Samantha in the kitchen that day at Luca's. She looked tortured. Like she was in her own head, battling demons, and couldn't get out." He swallowed. "It's something I'm familiar with."

God, now he felt like even more of an asshole. "I'm sorry to hear that."

Jason lifted a shoulder. "Hylar could have made our time in captivity worse, but it was still hell." He scanned the guys around the fire. "The only good thing that came out of that place was my team. They became my family. Even then, while we all experienced the same thing, we're all handling it differently."

"I can't imagine what it would have been like."

"The worst was worrying about my sister." He shook his head. "Some days, the worry would consume me. These guys kept me sane. Assured me that she was okay because we were following orders. Hylar had no reason to harm her."

"If I was in that position, my worry would have been with my family too."

Jason swung his attention back to Kye. "When I saw Samantha, it was almost like I was seeing myself. In those moments where I lose my mind to the memories. She was held for less time than me, but she had it a lot worse."

Kye tried not to tense at the reminder.

Jason's sincerity made him feel like even more of an asshole for how he'd overreacted. "I shouldn't have gotten so defensive that day. And I shouldn't have come at you at my place, either."

"I'm glad you did." That surprised Kye. "The few times I've run into her since we've met, I've noticed that she's been different. Less guarded. More at ease. I'm sure that the pain of what she went through is still there. It'll probably never go away completely. But she's getting there. I'm sure you have a big part to play in that."

"Her therapist has been amazing for her, too." He ran a hand through his hair. "If I have it my way, no harm will ever come to her again. Emotional or physical."

Jason nodded. "Good. I've been raised to believe it's a man's job to protect women and treat them with respect."

Damn straight. "You sound like my kind of guy."

Jason cracked his first smile. "Glad we're finally on the same page. Took enough time."

"Better late than never."

KYE GLANCED beside him at Samantha. It was nearing midnight as they drove home, and the moonlight cast a glow over her skin from the passenger seat.

Was she sitting unusually straight? Not only that…but her shoulders also looked tense, her features pinched.

Reaching out a hand, he touched her knee. "You're quiet."

He'd expected to be driving home with a giggly, glassy-eyed woman who'd consumed one too many cocktails. Most of the women had looked exactly like that when he'd gone inside to get her, but Samantha wasn't one of them.

She glanced at him and smiled. The smile was tight. "I didn't feel like drinking. I've had a bit of a headache all day."

His grip on her knee tightened. She'd felt unwell a couple of times in the last month. "Everything okay?"

"Of course." She placed her hand over his. "How was the guys' night? Luca have fun?"

Was she deflecting?

He wanted to push, but he didn't. Not when she looked so tired. And maybe a bit anxious. Her nervous energy just about bounced around the car.

Perhaps it was just that tonight had been a big one. After all, it was a large group of women, and some of them—in particular, Quinn and Lexie—had big personalities.

"I think he had a great time. There were no games for us, just beers around a fire."

She chucked softly. "So no kiss the fiancé or cocktail competitions."

He laughed. "Not really our style."

She quietened for a moment, and he could almost hear her thinking. "Were you listening to us?"

"We listened in to make sure you were all safe but didn't listen to any conversations. I basically heard a lot of chatter and laugher."

He was almost certain he felt some of the tension ease from her body.

She stroked her thumb over his hand. "Do you feel better about Jason?"

"Yes. He came over and spoke to me, and I acknowledged that I jumped the gun. Judged the guy before I knew him. I'm grateful to him and his team for helping out with security at the wedding."

He caught Samantha's smile. It was radiant, especially after how somber she'd seemed just seconds ago. "Does this mean you regret what happened at your house?"

"It wasn't a stretch to assume it was him after the note Barret left you."

"Well, yeah, but you could have approached the situation differently."

"You're right. I could have."

"He was just checking in on me," Samantha said quietly.

And Kye should be grateful for that, shouldn't he? "I'm glad you feel comfortable talking to him."

"Have you looked into Barret?"

"Jobs hacked into his email and social media accounts. He was looking for anything the guy had written about us or the project. Came up empty."

A part of him had been hoping Barret had emailed a colleague or friend, detailing what he'd seen at the bakery. He hadn't. Wyatt had hacked everything and found nothing.

Samantha stroked the back of his hand. "I'm sorry you haven't been able to find any information."

He tried to hide his stress from Samantha, but he was almost certain he was doing a shit job of it. She watched him too closely. Saw the emotions he tried to mask.

"We will. It took us a long time to take down Project Arma. To kill Hylar, Carter, and the other men on his team who posed a threat. But we did it. Whoever this new enemy is will be no different."

One way or another, they would take them down.

"I know you will." A couple minutes of silence passed, with just the dull vibration of the car as background noise. "Could I ask you something?"

Kye laughed. "Of course, sunshine. Ask me anything."

"Do you see kids in your future?"

Okay, whatever he'd been thinking she was going to ask, it sure wasn't *that*. Kids? Like living, breathing small humans who were a hundred percent reliant on him to be kept alive?

"Truth?" He shot a look across to her, seeing her small nod. "I can't imagine being a father anytime soon. Protecting you is new to me, and it's all consuming. Hell, it keeps me awake at night. The idea of losing you kills me. So, protecting an infant..."

Christ, the very thought had spikes of panic shooting up his spine.

Samantha's energy seemed to shift. Almost like she was retreating from him emotionally.

That wasn't the answer she'd been looking for.

He wanted to take it back, but he couldn't. He couldn't lie to her because that wouldn't be fair to anyone.

"In saying that, a couple of months ago, I couldn't imagine being in a relationship. And now that I am, I'd never go back." If he'd learned anything in his life, it was that you had no idea what the future held. "Maybe after everything calms down, I'll feel differently."

Who knew, maybe in as short as a year's time, he'd want four kids, a puppy, and a yellow family van.

"I'm sorry if that wasn't the answer you were looking for." He really was. He wanted to give the woman the world.

"You don't need to apologize for telling me how you feel. I want your honesty. Always."

But she sounded sad. And her hurt made Kye hurt. "How many kids do you want? And remember, I can tell if you're not being honest."

A small smile returned to her lips. He wanted more of those.

"I always wanted two. I imagined having them close so they could play together. Be best friends. Even twins don't sound terrible."

Kye had to really school his features to hide his reaction. He couldn't imagine having *one*. Having two at the same time…it filled him with very tangible terror. Give him a couple of terrorists over two babies any day.

He kept his voice level. "I always loved having sisters growing up. It's like being born with friends you can never get rid of."

She chuckled. "Yeah. That's the idea."

He squeezed her thigh. "Maybe one day."

"Hm."

CHAPTER 26

Samantha wriggled her hips into the pink dress. Holy heck, it was tight.

It was the dress she'd loved from the shopping trip with the girls. She hadn't purchased it after the drama with the reporter, but unbeknownst to her, Quinn had gone back to the store and grabbed it for her. Something Samantha had learned a few days later.

It was definitely tighter now, and she'd had to struggle her way into it *then*.

Was that because she was pregnant, or had she consumed a few too many slices of pizza over the last few weeks?

It took at least half a dozen tugs before she was able to get it where it was meant to be. Turning sideways, Samantha immediately inspected her reflection in the bedroom mirror, noticing there was the tiniest hint of a bump. Barely visible. So small, it was unlikely anyone would know it was the beginnings of a baby.

Baby...holy crap, that sounded strange, even in her head. She was having a *baby*...with Kye. Wow.

She'd spent the last two nights tossing and turning. And yesterday, even though she'd been busy all day helping with wedding setup and prep, thoughts of the future and Kye's reaction plagued her mind.

The third time Kye asked if she was okay, she'd almost told him. The words had been right there on the tip of her tongue. She'd only just stopped herself.

Today was the wedding of one of his best friends. If she told him, he would tell his team, and it would be something else for everyone to worry about.

No. She could wait. She planned to tell him tonight, after the wedding. Either that or tomorrow morning. It depended on whether she chickened out when they got home.

A whistle from the door snagged her attention.

Kye leaned against the bedroom entrance, arms crossed and a heated look on his face.

Her mouth went dry. She should be the one whistling. His perfectly fitted black suit and tie with a white shirt had him looking like the sexiest James Bond she'd ever seen.

"That dress is dangerous, sunshine."

The dress? Nope. He was the dangerous one, and she wasn't talking about his above average speed or strength.

He moved toward her slowly. His steps almost predatory.

She smoothed her hands over the material of the dress, palms suddenly feeling clammy. "It's a bit tight."

He stopped in front of her, hands going to her hips, tugging her close so that her body collided with his. "I like it. Not sure I'm gonna like other people seeing you in it."

Yeah, it was kind of like a second skin with how it fit right now. "No one will be looking at me. All the attention will be on Evie and Luca."

He lowered his head, lips hovering over hers. "Good. Because I don't want to be causing any scenes today."

She giggled before he kissed her heatedly.

When he pulled away, he studied her face. "You doing okay

after such a busy day yesterday? You didn't seem to sleep very well again."

Her gaze immediately lowered to his chest. "I'm okay. I just…" She sighed. "Tonight, I have—"

The sound of the doorbell ringing cut off her words. Immediately, she started to pull away, but his hold on her waist tightened.

"What were you going to say?"

She smiled up at him. "After the wedding."

When he remained where he was, continuing to hold her tightly, she almost squirmed. It took the doorbell ringing a second time for him to finally loosen his hold. For his intense stare to look somewhere other than at her.

His hands didn't drop though. "Come in."

The jiggle of a key in the doorknob sounded, followed by footsteps leading right into the bedroom.

"Oh my gosh, you two look amazing!" Tori approached with Oliver by her side. "And although you look unbelievably adorable in that couple's embrace, there's no time for smooches." She clapped her hands. "We've got a wedding to go to, people."

Finally, he stepped back.

Samantha just held back the relieved sigh that threatened to release from her lips. When she looked at her friend, she smiled. "Tori, you look absolutely gorgeous."

Her navy-blue dress had off-the-shoulder straps and was tight down to her knees. It suited her to a T.

"Why thank you, my friend. Don't even get me started on your dress." Tori took Samantha's hand, tugging her toward the door. She grabbed the small handbag from the bed on the way. "Now, we ready to go and celebrate love?"

The guys cheered while Samantha chuckled, everyone following Tori out to the car.

The drive to Eden's place was filled with excited chatter. When they arrived, Oliver keyed in the code at the gate before driving in. By the look of all the cars in front of the house, they were one of the last, if not *the* last, to arrive.

The second Samantha stepped into the backyard, her breath caught. The lawn was separated into two sections. The section closest to her was set up for the ceremony.

Rows of chairs were divided by thousands of deep red rose petals scattered along the grass. At the end of the makeshift aisle sat a timber arbor decorated with the most beautiful arrangement of flowers.

The other section of lawn held an array of tables—some cocktail tables, some lower round tables. There was also a long food and drinks table.

The space was beautiful. Gentle orchestra music played from speakers, adding to the romantic aura.

Kye slipped an arm around her waist.

"It's beautiful," Samantha whispered.

"Not as beautiful as you," he breathed softly, pressing a kiss to her cheek.

She smiled as Kye tugged her toward Eden and Shylah.

She noticed who she assumed to be a celebrant standing near the arbor, Luca and Asher standing beside him, Fletcher wriggling in Asher's arms, clearly trying to break free. There was also a photographer, and caterers were scattered around the other section of lawn.

"Great day for a wedding," Kye said, coming to a stop at the group.

"Oh my God, it's perfect, isn't it?" Shylah gushed.

Samantha cast a look around. "Is Lexie inside with Evie?"

Shylah nodded. "Yep. I only just left them."

Eden smirked. "I've barely seen Lexie all day. It's been oddly quiet."

Samantha grinned as Tori came to stand beside her. Samantha eyed the food on a passing caterer's tray as he headed toward the long table. "Mm, food smells good."

Eden nodded. "Tastes good too. And Mrs. Potter is doing cake and dessert later."

Tori's eyes lit up. "Well, I won't be needing much savory then."

As the group chatted around her, Samantha took in what others were wearing. Everyone was dressed immaculately, men in black suits and women in beautiful dresses, some long, some short. She noticed Jason standing by the chairs, and one of his teammates guarding the house, both looking incredibly serious.

Kye inched closer to Eden. He spoke in a hushed tone, but Samantha still heard. "Security all set up?"

"Guys are all stationed."

And just like that, Samantha was sucked back into reality. Everything may look picture-perfect and carefree, but it didn't mean that was their reality.

Almost instinctively, her hand went to her stomach. She could only hope the danger was gone before their baby was born.

"Is your stomach okay?" Kye's question pulled her attention. "Are you feeling sick again?"

Her hand dropped. "I'm okay. I can't wait to try the cake." Samantha was careful not to lie, knowing Kye would see right through it.

Just like he had that morning, he studied her face so closely that she wanted to squirm. "You sure?"

"Could all the guests please take a seat?"

The celebrant's voice over the microphone saved her from answering. People moved around her. She went to take a step, but Kye's hand on her wrist stopped her.

"Samantha—"

"Everything's okay, Kye. Come on. It's time to watch Luca and Evie get married."

Sighing, he led her toward the seating area. Samantha swallowed, wetting her dry throat.

It didn't take long for everyone to be seated, even Lexie. Samantha only half listened as the celebrant began to talk. The other half of her attention remained on the pregnancy. That was, until Kye's fingers begun to run gentle circles against her hip.

When everyone stood, Samantha forced herself to concentrate, not wanting to miss a moment of what was coming next. The second Evie walked out, Samantha's mouth dropped open.

Beautiful. No, not beautiful—that didn't do her justice. The woman was stunning. She wore a strapless ivory gown that pulled snuggly against her chest, hanging loosely from her hips.

Yeah. Evie looked breathtaking.

Samantha swung her attention across to Luca, and suddenly emotions welled up in her chest. The man actually had tears in his eyes. It made tears form in Samantha's.

So dang beautiful.

Kye's arm around her waist tightened. She looked up, noticing he was watching her. She held his gaze for a few seconds. Calmness, which had been missing for days, settled in her heart.

It may have been the music, or the way he had his arm around her. But it was most likely the fierce emotion she saw staring back at her.

She'd been trying to ignore the bubbling panic and fear since the stick read "pregnant." She'd been telling herself she was waiting to tell Kye because she wanted to protect him.

But suddenly, she knew that wasn't true.

Her biggest fear was his reaction. No, not fear—terror. She'd been terrified that the man would look at her differently. Like she was a problem rather than a partner.

But at that one shared look, the fear eased.

Samantha leaned into him, feeling safe in the knowledge that this was Kye. And she could trust him.

~

THE MID-AFTERNOON SUN beat down on Kye as he sat at a table, arm strung over Samantha's shoulders.

Perfect. All of it. The ceremony, the photos...not to mention having Samantha by his side the entire time. The entire day conspired to make him want things he'd never wanted before. Marriage. Kids. A family.

Who the hell was he?

Not the guy he used to be, that was for damn sure.

He looked around at his friends. Everyone sat at scattered tables, eating and laughing. Like they didn't have a worry in the world. Exactly how it should be.

Quinn leaned back in her seat across the table, hand going to her stomach. "I think I ate my weight in food. Or Wyatt's weight. How on earth am I going to fit dessert in?"

Kye shook his head. "I swear I've told you about the two stomachs, Quinn. The savory and the sweet. If you haven't eaten any sweet yet, then it's empty and ready to go."

She rolled her eyes. "I am ninety-nine percent sure that's a made-up thing."

"Nope." Wyatt shook his head from the seat beside her. "Cage is right. And I would know."

She scoffed. "How would you know?"

Kye already knew what his friend was going to say before he said it.

"Because I'm the brainy one."

She tilted her head to the side. "Last weekend you put a nonstick fry pan in the dishwasher."

Wyatt lifted his shoulders. "And?"

Samantha giggled while Kye hid a smile. He knew his friend well enough to know he was just trying to get a rise out of Quinn, and by the look on her face, it was working.

She leaned forward. "That destroys the pan, Wyatt."

"Really?" He scratched his head like this was news to him.

They all laughed.

Well, all except Quinn. She shook her head before her eyes landed on something behind Kye. Turning, he saw Mrs. Potter standing by the dessert table. She was directing Logan and Jason on where to put the cakes.

Quinn pushed to her feet. "The woman's already putting our security to work. I'm going to give Mrs. Potter a hand. Maybe while I'm gone, you ladies can give the guys a lesson on kitchenware and cleaning."

Samantha glanced over her shoulder. "So that's the famous Mrs. Potter?"

"The one and only. The absolute queen of cakes." Kye frowned. "You haven't met her?"

She shook her head. "No, Quinn's always been at the front of the shop when I've gone to the bakehouse."

"She must have been in the back whenever you popped by." Where the magic happened.

"Or maybe she wasn't there," Maya said. "Quinn mentioned she's barely been there the last couple months. She was also out of town when you first got to Marble Falls, Samantha. Family stuff, I think."

That was news to Kye. "I didn't know."

Wyatt lifted his shoulder. "Visiting a son or something. Wasn't really important. Not with everything else."

True. Him and Samantha had just been freed.

Mrs. Potter had a son and daughter, both of whom were living in a different state. Connecticut, maybe? "Hope her family's okay," Kye said, lifting a beer to his lips.

Quinn returned to her seat, frowning. "She doesn't need my help."

Wyatt slung an arm over her shoulders. "Good. I get you back."

She nodded absently, attention seemingly with Mrs. Potter.

Kye returned his beer to the table. "What is it, Quinn?"

It took a moment for her to turn her gaze to Kye. "I don't know, she was just...distant? I'm not sure. Actually, she's been a bit distant since she got back to town."

Kye shot another look over his shoulder at the older woman. He saw her whispering something to Logan.

Suddenly, Logan straightened, his eyes going almost blank, looking forward.

A sliver of unease slid up Kye's spine. *What the hell?*

Straightening in his seat, he turned his attention to Jason, noting the other man was standing in exactly the same way on Mrs. Potter's other side.

Oddly rigid, the same vacant look on his face.

Mrs. Potter scanned the crowd. Then she spoke.

"Good evening, everyone."

Samantha's body went rigid beside him. There was a sharp intake of breath. When he looked her way, her face was pale.

Everyone went quiet. Even the person controlling the music turned it off, clearly expecting a speech of some kind. It made the sound of Samantha's heart pounding against her ribs that much louder.

"That's the voice." Samantha whispered the words so quietly, Kye almost didn't catch them.

He touched a hand to her knee. "What voice?"

When she looked at him, there was cold, stark terror in her eyes. "The voice from the facility. She was the one talking to Carter."

No. That wasn't possible. This was *Mrs. Potter.* The sweet old lady who ran the bakery down the street from Marble Protection.

"It's so nice to have everyone together like this." Mrs. Potter scanned the crowd again.

Was it just him...or did her voice sound different? More formal. An underlying anger to the words.

The usual smile that sat on her face was missing. "It's like you knew I wanted everyone in the same place at the same time."

Luca stood slowly. "What have you done to Logan and Jason?"

Suddenly, the other five members of Logan's team emerged from their stations around the house, surrounding them.

The smile on Mrs. Potter's face returned, but it wasn't a smile he recognized. He may as well be looking at a stranger. "They're following my instructions. Just like Jason did when I told him to take Samantha at the bakery. Of course, I told him to protect his identity first and foremost, which is why he took off. Oh, and also when I asked Logan to wait for Samantha at the office. After I'd killed the journalist, that is."

She paused, her gaze going to Samantha.

"Your design is flawless. Instant obedience—followed by no recollection whatsoever of what they were made to do."

Kye shook his head. No. It couldn't be true. "How are you controlling them?" A sick feeling had begun to churn in his gut.

"Isn't that obvious? These men are the originals. At a routine medical appointment while in James's care, the microchips were inserted. At the time, the chip only responded to a female voice. Which works well for me right now."

"James?" Kye asked through gritted teeth, moments away from jumping to his feet and attacking the woman.

The phony smile slipped from her lips. The next expression was full of anger. *Rage*. It was spine-chilling. "My name isn't Potter, darling. It's Maeve Hylar. I'm James Hylar's mother. Tanya's mother. My children were *both* killed at the hands of you murderers."

That wasn't true. Hylar had ordered the kill on Tanya, and Carter had pulled the trigger.

She took a step forward. "And let me tell you, there is nothing —*absolutely nothing*—more dangerous than a mother who has had to bury not one, but *two* of her babies."

CHAPTER 27

a chill swept over Samantha's skin. She couldn't move. Couldn't speak.

Jason and his entire team were under this woman's control because of the original microchips she'd completed. Chips she'd assumed had been destroyed when they didn't work the way Hylar wanted them to.

"You took the remote."

Mrs. Potter didn't answer. Instead, her gaze shot across to Kye. "Stand."

What happened next shook Samantha to her core.

Kye stood.

His body rigid, his eyes blank—just like the members of Logan's team.

No. How was that…

A gasp slipped from her lips as suddenly, she realized. The chip she'd created in Killeen. The one she'd assumed had been lost in the chaos. Carter must have taken it. Had a surgeon implant it in Kye before throwing him into the cell.

Her lungs seized. Gasps sounded from around the lawn. The sound of chairs falling and people standing.

Samantha couldn't move. She felt paralyzed. Her mind struggling to comprehend what was going on.

"Cage," Bodie said from the other side of the table.

"The only person he'll listen to is me. He's waiting for further instructions. Isn't he, Samantha?"

The woman's eyes fell on her. Samantha couldn't see a scrap of humanity in her. She was all rage.

"Carter was supposed to lead this army. Once everyone from Kye's team was microchipped, we were going to replace the older chips in Logan's men." She shook her head. "That boy really wanted it all. The power. The control. And you had to kill *him*, too."

Samantha finally found her voice. "Don't do this. Let them go."

If Kye hurt her or his friends, if Jason hurt his sister, it would destroy them all.

Maeve took a small step forward. "You think I'll let the deaths of my children go unavenged? *I* will finish Hylar's work. *I'll* ensure his death wasn't for nothing."

Samantha shot a quick look up at Kye. His eyes were so empty. She wanted to cry. No, she wanted to grab his shoulders and scream at him to snap out of it. But that wasn't going to happen. She knew the power of what she'd created.

She looked around the yard, saw the men on their feet, moving in front of their women, ready to protect them with their lives.

Maeve's gaze returned to Kye. "Kye, take Samantha. We'll need her to make more microchips. The rest of you, knock out the men, tie them up and throw them in the van parked out front."

When Kye turned his gaze to her, it was like looking into the deadly eyes of a stranger. A killer.

His hand shot out and strong fingers wrapped around her arm, digging painfully into her skin, dragging her to her feet.

Kye had taken a single step when a large body collided with his. Samantha was thrown to the grass as his menacing grip released her.

He and Oliver began to grapple on the lawn. It was loud and violent.

"Run!"

It took her a second to process Oliver's command. When it finally penetrated her cloudy mind, Samantha pushed to her feet and took off. She stumbled multiple times before Tori was there, grabbing her arm and tugging her forward.

Tori all but dragged Samantha through the yard. At one point, Samantha turned her head, took in the chaos. Where seconds ago there had been laughter and love, now a war raged. Men who were allies, *brothers*, fought like they were prepared to kill.

The women were running toward the house. The few outsiders who had worked at the wedding were screaming, fear thick in the air.

Samantha swallowed a sob as Tori tugged them around the house and toward the front. Her hand was steady as she opened the passenger door to Oliver's car, shoving Samantha inside. A second later, her friend was in the driver's seat.

Reaching into the middle console, Tori yanked out a key before attempting to start the car.

The engine didn't make a sound.

Panic crawled up Samantha's throat. They'd done something to the car. And she was betting if they'd done it to one, they'd done it to all of them.

Samantha looked up to see Maeve in front of them, gun in hand, pointed directly at the windshield. She screeched when Tori's hand went to her head, shoving them both down.

The bullet pierced the glass, hitting the driver's seat, right where Tori's head had been.

Tori opened the middle console again, grabbing everything and throwing it out. Then she tried the glove box, clearly not finding what she was looking for. When she reached under the driver's seat, her hand retreated, clutching something silver.

A gun.

She reached under the other seat. "Bingo."

Tori pulled out a second gun, pressing it into Samantha's hand.

A small gasp released from her lips. "Tori—"

"Logan's coming." Samantha looked up, and sure enough, she saw Logan walking straight toward the driver's side. "I'll go for him and shoot to incapacitate, not kill. You go for Mrs. Potter—I mean Maeve. Then *run.*"

Samantha nodded, tears in her eyes. Oh, God! She didn't want to leave her friend with Logan, but Tori was trained in combat. Samantha wasn't.

Samantha was also the one Maeve wanted.

Tori's hand went to the door. The second it opened, bullets hit the metal. Tori shot a quick look outside before aiming her gun and shooting.

Samantha inched her own door open. She'd only shot a gun once in her life, and that was over five years ago. But she had the fact that Mrs. Potter needed her alive working in her favor.

The woman wouldn't shoot to kill.

She took a quick, calming breath before glancing over the door and shooting.

Miss. Big miss.

She was about to aim again when suddenly Quinn rounded the building at a sprint, throwing herself at the older woman. The two fell to the ground.

Samantha heard Tori grappling with Logan. Glancing across the car, she saw Logan throw her friend to the ground. She was about to move toward her, help in any way she could, when Tori kicked a leg out, catching Logan at the knee.

"Run, Samantha!"

She shot a look back to Maeve and Quinn grappling in the

driveway, then glimpsed Sage coming their way.

It wasn't until she saw Kye rounding the corner that she took off, running toward the forest behind her.

Shadows fell over her as she ran through the trees. Her breaths began to whoosh in and out of her chest quickly, from adrenaline and fear.

She didn't focus on any of that. She fixed her mind on putting one foot in front of the other. Pounding her feet against the uneven ground.

Every step she took surprised the hell out of her. Why hadn't Kye caught her yet? He must not be running. Was he walking? So confident she'd run out of steam that he didn't need to rush?

Sobs released from her chest as branches flicked against her face. At one point, her foot caught on a tree trunk, sending her flying. The gun fell from her fingers, losing her precious minutes as she had to rummage through the dirt to find it.

Her chest struggled for air and her knees ached as she pushed back to her feet and kept moving.

It wasn't until she reached a river that she stopped, pain zipping through her chest.

The Colorado River. It had to be. It ran through most of Marble Falls.

Samantha bent over, unable to suck in enough breaths, her lungs screaming for air.

She was about to keep moving when rustling sounded behind her. Branches snapping...

Spinning around, she caught sight of Kye's large frame stepping out of the trees. Her heart soared wildly in her chest.

He stopped, vacant eyes boring into hers.

She took a small step back. She was close to the riverbank. She couldn't afford to get much closer. "Kye. Please don't do this."

Not even a hint of recognition or compassion looked back at her.

When he began moving forward, Samantha lifted the gun.

He stopped, studying the weapon in her hand.

"I don't want to shoot you, Kye, but I will." Her voice trembled. Every part of her rebelled against the words that left her mouth.

"You're lying."

Crap...

He began walking again, and out of instinct, Samantha stepped backward, all but forgetting about the river.

The gun slipped from her fingers, her arms flailed. She hit the water hard, immediately sinking beneath the surface.

Ignoring the immediate cold and shock, Samantha lifted her feet and pushed off the bottom, propelling her body away from Kye while remaining under the water. She kicked her legs, swimming as fast as she could. The current pulled her down the river, threatening to drown her, lungs screaming for air.

She didn't make it far before a strong arm wrapped around her middle, a hard body pressed against her back. It was a body that normally signified safety.

Now it meant danger.

He lugged them both back to the bank, his strength impossible to fight against as water whooshed over her face, causing her to swallow more of it than she should have.

Kye climbed out of the river, lifting her into his arms. Instead of throwing her over his shoulder like she'd expected, he cradled her to his chest.

Good. This was good. She could see his face, and he could see hers.

Was there a chance she could get through to him? Could his heart suppress the microchip's control over his mind? Chances were slim. But she had to try. She couldn't just accept her fate.

"Kye, please listen to me! You don't want to take me back there."

He continued to march through the trees, not acknowledging her words.

Lifting a hand, Samantha touched his face, cradling his cheek with her palm. "I love you."

Was it her...or did a flicker of humanity cross his face?

She wet her lips, forcing calm into her voice as she said the next part. "If you take me to Maeve, she'll kill me."

He swallowed. Another flicker of emotion. Another crease between his brows.

"But before she kills me, she'll make you hurt me. Force Logan's team to hurt me, until I agree to make more microchips to control your brothers." She didn't miss the way his steps slowed. "You can't let that happen, Kye. I'm pregnant."

His feet stopped. His breathing deepening.

She needed to keep appealing to his emotions. She had to believe that they could give him the strength to fight this. "We're having a baby. You and me. And I'm asking you to protect me. To protect our child."

The frown between his brows deepened. His arms tensed seconds before they dropped, causing Samantha to fall to the dirt.

She shuffled back, never taking her eyes off Kye. Should she run? Would he *let* her run?

"Kye—"

"Go back. Get the gun. Shoot me." Every word was a growl torn from his chest.

"Kye, I can't—"

He clutched his hair, pain marring his features. "She's in my head." He shook his head now, seeming more frustrated by the second. "I'm going...to come for you again. I need you...to be protected!"

When she continued to remain still, Kye suddenly looked up. Pure rage in his eyes. "*Now!*"

She pushed herself up. She was running on empty, barely able to feel her feet beneath her. But she didn't let that stop her. She'd move until she couldn't move any more. To save her baby.

Would she be able to find the gun? She had no idea where it

had fallen. Was it on the riverbank? In the water? And if she did find it, would she be able to shoot him?

Samantha's chest constricted.

Minutes passed before she reached the river again, then more before she found the place where she fell in. When she spotted the gun lying in the dirt, she dove on it, lifting the weapon and turning.

Just like he had moments ago, Kye walked out of the trees. The vacant expression returned to his face.

This was it. This was when she had to decide. Shoot or be taken. She wasn't sure she could talk him around again. And even if she did, how long would it last?

He walked toward her purposefully—and suddenly an idea came to her.

A stupid idea. One that could have deadly consequences. But she was all out of good ones.

Samantha pointed the gun at Kye's shoulder…at the spot where she'd designed the chip to be inserted.

She hesitated, fear paralyzing her.

What if she missed? What if Kye bled out?

Kye lifted a hand toward her, and Samantha pulled the trigger.

His hand dropped as his body jerked. Pain distorting his face as he looked down at the wound.

She'd missed. The bullet grazed the top of his shoulder.

When he glanced back at her, instead of a vacant expression, there was anger. So much anger that when she lifted the gun again, his hand went to her throat, lifting her and shoving her against the nearest tree.

"Kye!" she choked out.

His fingers tightened. "Conscious or unconscious, I must get you back to Maeve."

As his fingers squeezed, Samantha lifted the gun, swiftly pressing it exactly where she knew the chip to be.

She pulled the trigger.

Kye and her both tumbled to the ground. She coughed and choked, sucking in the air that had been stolen from her.

When she looked up, it was to see Kye twitching on the ground. His eyes shut.

Oh, God! What had she done?

Crawling forward, she touched his shoulder, only to have his entire body convulse. His hand flew out, colliding with her face.

Samantha's head flew backward, a cry echoing through the woods. Lifting a hand to her throbbing cheek, she breathed through the pain.

For a second, there was silence. Kye's body as still as her own. Climbing to her knees, she began to creep forward.

Leaves rustled as he pushed into a sitting position. She paused. Studied him.

An odd mix of confusion and anger sat on his face.

Reaching out, she grabbed for the gun that had flown from her fingers. She needed to protect herself and the baby if she was still dealing with a stranger. If the man was still being controlled, she'd shoot again. She'd have to.

Kye's brows pulled together. "Samantha?"

There was warmth in his voice. Worry, even.

The tremble in her hands increased. "Is it really you?" She was scared to believe it. Not daring to have hope, if that hope would only be washed away.

"Sunshine, are you okay?"

Sunshine...

A sob broke from her chest, the gun falling to the dirt. Then she was flinging herself at Kye's big, protective body.

At his slight grunt, Samantha was reminded of his bullet wounds. Immediately she attempted to pull back, but Kye's arms tightened, remaining strong around her.

When he did finally pull back, he grazed her cheek with his finger, looking as deadly as he had seconds ago. But now he was on her side. "What happened?"

CHAPTER 28

$\mathcal{F}$ ire burned from Kye's shoulder. But it was nothing compared to the fire that burned in his chest at what Samantha told him. At the danger she was in. The danger *he* had posed to her.

He swallowed his fury, watching as Samantha finished tying his shirt around his shoulder before taking her hand and standing. "We need to get away from the house."

He stepped forward, but Samantha dug her heals in. "No! I need to go back there."

No way in hell. "Not happening. We don't know what's going on back there right now. It's too dangerous."

He tugged again. When she continued to remain where she was, Kye picked her up, cradling her against his chest, ignoring her struggles. Every second they remained where they were, his anxiety went up a notch. Anxiety that someone from Logan's team would step through the trees. Attempt to take her from him.

"Kye, you need to listen to me! I can stop this! I am the *only* one who can stop this."

He increased his pace to a jog.

"Maeve has the remote!" she continued. "It's the only way she could have activated the microchips with her voice. It'll be on her. We need to get it so that I can enter the code that will cease all commands!"

Kye leapt over a fallen tree trunk, attempting to block her pleas.

"The only other way to stop this is to destroy the microchips. But even then, I'm the only person who knows the exact position of the chip. And the incision point needs to be exact." Her hand went to his chest. "I know that going back is dangerous, but it's a risk we need to take. To save your brothers. Their women. God, even Fletcher is there! That woman that I saw wouldn't hesitate to hurt or kill anyone who's not an asset to her mission."

Kye stopped. Dammit, she was right. His brothers were fighting for their lives right now. For the lives of their women. Women who were basically family. And Fletcher...

"We just need to get to Mrs. Potter," Samantha said quietly. "I *can* and *will* stop this."

Everything in him rebelled against going to the house. He didn't want her anywhere near the fighting. But if they didn't...

"You stay with me at all times." Even as the words left his mouth, they made him feel sick with dread. "If I get there, and I deem it too dangerous, we run."

He would outrun any asshole who came near Samantha.

She nodded.

Blowing out a frustrated breath, he began to move.

His shoulder ached, but the pain was a good distraction from what was going on in his head—red-hot fury. Fury over what had been put into his body. Over what the chip had almost caused him to do. Over the fact that he had to take his woman back to a war zone to try to save his brothers and their loved ones.

And fury at the bakery owner's deceit.

Christ, he felt like a damn fool. So many things suddenly made sense. Hylar knowing about Lexie's pregnancy, about Tori's survival and where she was. Hell, they'd even mentioned to Mrs.

Potter that Bodie was in Keystone, Colorado. Kye had no doubt that was how Sinclair found Maya.

Trust would never come easily to him again.

When he neared the front lawn, his arms tightened around Samantha. He clearly heard the sound of fighting in the backyard, violent and fierce. But at least it was still going. Silence would have been worse.

Silence may have meant it was all over. He was too late.

Kye welcomed the noise.

Stepping out of the forest, he took in the front of the house. The doors of Oliver's car were open. Blood pooled on the ground. But there was no one around.

He didn't move forward, instead taking a moment to listen to everything happening around him. There were people in the house. He could hear heartbeats. Breaths.

Ten, maybe eleven. He was guessing the women were in there. Someone had likely rounded them up. Captured them.

If someone from Logan's team was in there, that meant, without Kye, the fight was seven against seven.

His muscles tensed.

He took a step toward the house.

That was all he got before he heard the footsteps, loud and fast, coming toward them.

He only just had time to put Samantha down and push her behind him when Jason sprinted toward them, his big body colliding with Kye's, sending them both to the ground.

Kye grunted when Jason's body impacted his bullet wound. Jason recovered faster. Jumping to his feet and lunging at Samantha.

Kye reached him just before he touched her, grabbing the man from behind and throwing him to the side.

Landing on Jason's back, Kye threw a punch to his head.

He only managed the single blow before Jason flipped around, throwing Kye aside. The guy didn't even spare him a glance, immediately crawling toward Samantha.

She shuffled back. Jason reached out, grabbing her ankle.

Not a chance.

Kye was on him again, grabbing the wrist of the hand that held Samantha with enough force that Jason growled, fingers releasing her.

Kye went for the gun in his belt, drawing it out. Jason rolled over, his elbow catching Kye in the face. He lost his grip on the weapon, which went tumbling toward the forest.

When Kye caught a glimpse of the man's eyes, he almost paused.

Nothing familiar stared back at him. No signs of recognition at all.

When Jason grabbed something from his waist, Kye saw silver reflect the sunlight before a knife slashed at him. He hit Jason's wrist hard and fast, sending the weapon flying.

As Kye and Jason continued to grapple, he vaguely heard Samantha rushing around them.

What the hell was she doing? She needed to get the hell away from the man.

Jason's head shot up. He jumped to his feet, but Kye was faster, grabbing him by the shoulders and flinging him into a tree.

Jason's body rebounded off the wood and he hit the ground. Kye was on him in a second. He didn't lift his head as he yelled at Samantha.

"Get...away from us, Samantha! He wants *you*."

The woman actually moved closer. "Hold him still and I'll stab the chip!"

Jason threw an elbow, catching Kye in the chin, whipping his head backward. Then he lunged for Samantha, causing her to stumble and fall, knife slipping from her fingers.

Kye dove on top of Jason again, only just able to contain him. "Can you do it from behind?"

"Yes."

With Jason pressed face first to the ground, Kye ripped his shirt from his body. Jason attempted to buck him off. It took three tries to grab his wrists. When he finally got them, he held them out to the sides, resting his entire weight on top of the guy.

"Now, Samantha!"

He heard her heart pounding as she moved in, dropping to her knees beside them. Kye hated her being so close to a threat. Jason was bucking like a madman. Everything in Kye wanted to shove her back.

Samantha's fingers were visibly trembling as she touched his back, feeling his muscles and bones. She positioned the knife right below his shoulder blade.

Jason bucked again and the knife shifted from its position.

Kye tightened his hold. When Samantha positioned the knife a second time, her trembling was worse. Violent, even.

Quickly, so Jason didn't have a chance to react, Kye released one of Jason's hands, placed it over hers and pushed the knife into the man's shoulder.

Jason howled in pain. Then he went still.

Kye tugged the knife out, hand going back to his wrist. He didn't move from his position, not even when Jason began to twitch.

"Move back, Samantha!"

She did as he asked, shuffling back in a crab crawl.

Jason stilled again.

Kye frowned when several long seconds ticked by. "Jason?"

Another moment of silence passed. Then he spoke. "What the hell is going on?" He attempted to buck Kye off. His head lifted. "Samantha? Fuck, are you okay?"

Kye looked over at Samantha to see relief flood her eyes. She swallowed. "It's...it's him."

He turned the man onto his back. That's when he saw what she did.

The old Jason.

Standing, Kye pulled him to his feet with his good arm.

"What's going on?" he asked again, eyes shooting to the house, then beyond it to the yard. Just like Kye, he could hear it all.

"Long story short, your team and I were microchipped." Kye scanned the house as he spoke. "Mrs. Potter has a wireless remote that acts as a connector between the chips and her. It gives her control. We need to find her, get the remote, so that Samantha can deactivate all commands."

Anger—the same anger that was rushing through Kye—flashed over Jason's face. He studied the house again, more than likely thinking about his team's safety, his sister's safety.

"Stay with Samantha. I'm going to check the yard and the house."

Kye crept around the house to the backyard. What he saw had his blood running cold.

It was a damn war zone.

Eden and Aidan were exchanging blows so powerful, a normal man would be left dead.

Luca threw Tyler, the other man plowing into a table and chairs. Tyler remained down for only a second. Coming straight back at him, rage contorting his features.

Mason had Callum in a headlock, which was broken within seconds.

Bodie and Wyatt were fighting Flynn and Liam, frequently swapping their attacks, working as a team.

Each fight was as deadly as the last. Each man fighting for their life.

Asher and Oliver were missing. Where were they? In the house?

Turning back, he carefully scanned a window. Logan and Mrs. Potter were inside. Both had their backs to him. Mrs. Potter holding a gun, while Logan was on his knees tying up what looked to be the last of the women.

No, not last. One was missing.

Lexie.

If Lexie, Asher, and Fletcher were all missing, that likely meant Asher was hiding his family.

Good.

When he noticed Oliver's still form on the floor, Kye's chest tightened. He could only hope his friend was okay.

He returned to Jason and Samantha, noticing how pale she was. But there was also a determined look on her face. Like her body wanted to collapse, but her mind wasn't letting her.

Not much longer, honey.

Kye quickly relayed everything he'd just seen.

"I can go through the glass," Jason said once Kye was done. "Take Logan by surprise, while you guys go for Mrs. Potter."

It was as good a plan as they were going to get.

Kye nodded. "Let's do it."

CHAPTER 29

Samantha remained behind Kye at the front door. She couldn't see Jason but knew that he was by the side window, readying himself to jump through the glass and attack Logan.

Samantha felt sick with nerves as she waited. Waited to hear the smashing of glass. The violence of the attack.

The second it sounded, Kye tightened his hold on her hand as he threw open the door, tugging Samantha behind him, shielding her body with his own.

"Stay the hell back!"

Maeve's voice only just carried above the sound of Jason and Logan struggling on the floor.

Peeking around Kye, she saw the other woman holding a gun pointed in their direction, right at Kye's chest. She was close to the stairs, inching closer.

"You won't shoot me," he said quietly, taking a step forward. "I'm what you want. What you need to finish your son's work."

Maeve's fingers visibly tensed around the gun. "You're so certain?"

From her peripheral vision, Samantha could see Tori struggling in her binds.

"Put the gun down, Maeve." Kye almost sneered her name.

"No." Her hand didn't tremble. Neither did her voice. Both hints that she was either trained, or this wasn't her first brush with danger. "You think after so many years of watching you boys that I'm just going to give up now?"

"So it was all a lie?" Quinn asked, sounding both hurt and enraged from across the room.

"All of it." She didn't take her eyes off Kye as she answered, taking another step closer to the stairs. The other exits cut off by Logan and Jason. "When James returned from the Middle East, he wasn't the boy I raised. They destroyed him. I wanted revenge just as much as he did. He kept me informed of his progress as I watched each of you closely. You boys were an important piece of the puzzle. But you ruined everything!"

Kye scoffed. "You didn't morally object to DNA-altering drugs being injected into the bodies of innocent men? You didn't object to the idea of a microchip that takes away free will?"

The woman snorted. "Dear, there is sacrifice in every war."

And the sacrifice was good men. The thought sickened Samantha.

Kye took another step. When Mrs. Potter took her next step, her heel hit the base of the stairs. "And you're wrong." She said the words quietly.

A small sliver of ice ran up Samantha's spine.

"About what?" Kye asked.

"I don't want *or* need you. I saw you kill him!" Anger twisted the older woman's features. "There were cameras on top of that building. Even through the storm, I saw you pull the trigger. I watched you shoot my son in the head, murdering him. You sealed your fate that day. You're the *only* soldier I'm willing to lose."

In the next second, Kye dove on top of Samantha, sending them both to the ground even as the gun went off.

A loud thud sounded in the living room, like a body hitting the floor hard. Was that Jason or Logan?

Gasps echoed from the women—a second before Samantha looked up to see Logan standing.

"Kill him!" Mrs. Potter cried.

That was all the warning they got before Logan lunged at Kye.

He shoved Samantha to the side quickly. She was only down for a second before pushing to her feet and racing toward Mrs. Potter. Eyes widening, the woman raised the gun.

Before she could pull the trigger, Samantha hit it out of her hand. She reached for the fallen weapon as pounding footsteps sounded on the stairs. When she turned, Mrs. Potter was gone.

Samantha followed the other women, one goal in mind—find the remote.

At the top of the stairs, she spotted Maeve entering the master bedroom. She sprinted inside as the woman ran toward the bathroom.

Samantha lifted the gun. "Stop or I'll shoot!"

Maeve went still.

"Give me the remote." When Maeve didn't make a move, Samantha's grip on the gun tightened. "I don't want to shoot you, but I will." To save Kye—to save everyone—she would a hundred percent kill the woman in front of her.

Maeve turned slowly. Then she reached into her pocket. Samantha felt a prickle of unease at the possibility of the woman pulling some sort of weapon.

When her hand reappeared, fingers wrapped around the small remote, Samantha almost sagged.

"Put it on the ground and kick it this way."

One second passed. Then another. Just when Samantha thought Maeve was going to ignore her, she started bending down. She shoved it across the carpet, but it only made it halfway.

Samantha took two steps toward, then Maeve leapt at her.

She pulled the trigger.

The bullet hit Maeve right in the midsection. The older woman dropped to her knees, hands clutching her stomach.

Closing the distance, Samantha lifted the remote then stepped back. She moved her fingers quickly, keying in the code to deactivate the chips. The code she knew like the back of her hand.

"You've destroyed…everything." Mrs. Potter's voice was weak.

"No. I *almost* destroyed everything by designing this technology for your son." She said, almost to herself, not taking her eyes off what she was doing. "It ends now."

She was almost done. Her heart rate picked up at the thought of this nightmare being over, sweat beading her brow.

"Just like those boys," Maeve said quietly, her voice trembling, "you could have had more. Could have *been* more."

She *was* more. After everything she'd been through over the last year, she had a much better understanding of the world. Of the evil that could live within it. And for that, she was wiser. Stronger.

She keyed in the final digits, and immediately, the noise from downstairs quieted.

Samantha breathed her first easy breath.

It was over.

Samantha's eyes lifted to Maeve. Blood was seeping through her fingers. Her skin so pale it was almost white…

"My son is dead because you sent Kye his location!"

Samantha was just lowering the remote, when, with energy and speed Samantha couldn't believe the woman possessed, Maeve lunged at her, causing the gun to fall to the floor.

The echo of footsteps in the hallway sounded as Maeve snatched the gun and aimed it at Samantha's stomach.

She'd barely managed to grab the woman's wrist before the weapon went off.

Tori's ragged scream was loud from across the room. Her footsteps quick as she neared them.

As if their moves were choreographed, Samantha and Maeve both crumpled to the ground. She vaguely noted Tori securing the gun from the floor. Of another bullet echoing through the room and Maeve's body going still.

More footsteps sounded on the stairs. But they were distant now. Almost like a muffled background noise as Samantha's ears rang.

Her hand went to her side where Maeve's shot had landed. Blood soaked through her fingers, pouring from the wound.

Oh, God, the baby!

Tori dropped beside her, then Kye. His hand moved over hers, stemming the blood. "Get Sage!"

There was movement around her. Tori rose and left.

"The baby…" Samantha barely managed to whisper the panic-filled words. Her gaze bore into Kye's, not wanting to look down and see the blood.

His eyes bulged. "Baby?"

He didn't remember. She'd told him when he'd been under Maeve's control.

Sage knelt beside her. The woman began to speak, but Samantha could barely hear her through the haze of pain and fear.

She looked worried. Kye's face went from worried, to shocked, to even more worried as Sage spoke to him.

Did that mean she wasn't going to be okay? Or the baby wasn't?

Something was placed against her wound seconds before she was lifted into Kye's arms. He pressed a kiss to her temple. Whispered words into her ear.

Closing her eyes, she nuzzled her face into his chest as he moved quickly.

Her and Kye were alive. The danger was over.

Now, she just needed to have faith. Faith that the baby would be okay.

CHAPTER 30

wo months later

EVEN THOUGH KYE'S brothers talked around him, most of his focus remained across his yard, on Samantha. Her bright hair fanned around her shoulders. The rays of sun were hitting her in just the right way to make her look angelic.

What he loved most, though, was the peace on her face. He wanted to see that look for the rest of their days. The woman had seen enough bad in her life.

No more. That was a promise Kye would guarantee.

"I almost don't know what to do with myself," Wyatt said quietly, lounging back in his chair.

Oliver chuckled. "You can rest that big brain of your, Jobs. You've worked hard enough to last you a lifetime."

"We all have."

Kye nodded. Very true. "After years of chasing Hylar and his men, constantly looking over our shoulders and waiting for an attack, it's going to be strange to just live...normally."

Eden scoffed. "We'll never live normally."

"That's okay. Normal is overrated," Bodie added.

As long as abnormal involved safety, it was fine with Kye

"The women will keep us grounded," Luca said.

"And the kids," Asher added, gaze across the yard on Fletcher.

Kids. Because there would be more than one.

For one, Kye and Samantha's kid.

Not a day had passed in the last couple months when Kye hadn't thanked whoever had been watching out for her that day. He hadn't been sure if he'd ever wanted kids before. But now, knowing she was pregnant, it breathed new life into him. He had no idea he'd feel that way, but he did.

"The women are already picking out bassinets and baby clothes together," Luca laughed.

Of course they were—because Evie was pregnant too. Due a month and a half after Samantha. The women were loving it.

His gaze sought her out again. She was talking to Tori, glass of water in hand, beautiful round stomach pregnant for the world to see.

Fletcher ran past Samantha and Tori, closely followed by Lexie. The woman was struggling to catch him.

The day of the wedding, she'd run into the forest to save her son. And the second Jason had become distracted by the return of Samantha and Kye, Asher had gone after them.

Kye couldn't help but grin at seeing the little man so happy today. So loved. It was a look into his own future, no doubt.

It didn't surprise Kye that when Fletcher finally stopped running, it was at the food table.

Asher shook his head. "The kid never stops eating."

Mason raised a brow. "Like father, like son?"

God, if that was the case, Samantha and Kye would have quite the food bill. He'd go so far as to suggest Marble Falls would need to up their food supply, especially if any more kids were in the plans.

"Quinn's all settled with the running of the shop?" Kye asked, turning to Wyatt.

Wyatt nodded. "The refurbishment is complete. As of next week, you'll be able to drink your first coffee at The Coffee Addict."

Very fitting.

After Maeve's death, the bakehouse closed. Quinn hadn't wanted to take over the bakery, not with everything that had happened. Instead, she started her own shop from the ground up.

Asher leaned forward. "There'll be cakes, won't there?"

Wyatt nodded. "She's been working on some new recipes." He patted his flat stomach. "They've contributed toward this gut."

Yeah, right. Kye was pretty sure they were all incapable of losing their muscle. But, hell, why not test it out and eat more cake?

Bodie sighed, the smile slipping from his lips. "I know we've said this a hundred times, but God, I still can't believe she was part of it."

They all knew who he was talking about. Mrs. Potter. The woman they'd had nothing but trust and affection for, watching and reporting back to Hylar right under their noses for years.

Mason scoffed. "The woman killed two police officers and a reporter. Not to mention, she knew how to disable police cameras. We never knew her."

Wyatt shook his head. "It was stupid to talk about the location of the remote at the bakery. If I hadn't, she never would have known where it was."

"Her true identity had been wiped." Luca ran a hand through his hair. "According to Evie, her new one was foolproof. There was no finding out who she was until she wanted us to."

"It makes trusting anyone else very hard," Eden muttered, his voice pained.

He wasn't lying. They'd trusted John Hylar, seen the man as a father figure, and he'd been pure evil. Then trusted Mrs. Potter.

"It just proves a person doesn't need to be six and a half feet tall with a military background to be a threat," Oliver muttered.

That was for damn sure.

When Wyatt's phone rang, the group silenced, waiting for him to dig it out.

It was almost like they were waiting for something to go wrong. *Had* been waiting for the last two months. After years of danger looming, peace seemed almost surreal.

"Hey, Logan. You're on speaker. The whole team's here."

"Great. Just wanted to let you know that some of the boys are about to board a flight for Mexico. Jason, Blake, Aidan, and I will be hanging behind in Cradle Mountain if you need to get in contact with us."

Logan's team had been asked by the US military to complete some "off the books" missions. They'd be doing so while running their business. He didn't know what the current mission in Mexico entailed, but if anyone could get the job done, it was their team.

Kye knew that the men had been struggling in the aftermath of the wedding, even after Sage had removed their chips. Struggling with the fact that the chips had been implanted without their knowledge. That they'd attacked Tori and tried to take Samantha.

Even though they had no recollection of anything they'd done, including fighting Kye's team at the wedding, the guilt seemed to be weighing on them. Time and distance seemed to be helping. Hopefully, steady work would do the rest.

"Thanks for letting us know. You need anything from us?" Kye asked.

"Nah, we're good." Voices and movement sounded in the background. "Just wanted to let you know what's going on. Also wanted to tell you that your names are officially on the books for any missions we might need your support with."

Their team had offered to assist Logan's whenever he

required more men. Now that Kye's team wasn't searching for Hylar, they should have more time to dedicate to helping others.

"Thanks. Stay safe," Wyatt said.

"Always."

Wyatt hung up at the same time as Kye stood. "Okay, boys. Time for me to check in with my woman." As he walked away, he heard the men rising, knowing they were going to do the same.

When he reached Samantha, he gently lifted her from her chair before sitting down and placing her on his lap. Her bullet wound was healing well, but she still needed gentleness.

"How you doing, sunshine?"

Her smile was radiant—and it had him feeling a million different things that he didn't even know were possible a year ago.

She lifted her hand, cupping his cheek. "I'm good. Better now that you're here." She pressed her lips to his. His hand immediately went to the back of her head, his fingers threading through her soft locks.

God. The absolute tranquility that flooded his entire system when he touched her was out of this world. And stronger than any drug or chip that could be put into his body.

"I missed you."

She chuckled softly. "I was only a few feet away."

"Yeah. Too far." He pulled her head back to his for another kiss before finally releasing her. She rested her head on his chest, while his hand went to the small bump of her stomach. "How's Wally doing?"

Another laugh. "Wally, as you love to call the baby, is doing well. A little bit of movement, especially while I was eating the baked treats."

"Ah, already has a sweet tooth like his dad."

The surprise of finding out she was pregnant had been over-shadowed by the suffocating panic at the possibility of losing them both that day. He would protect his family with everything he had.

He gently stroked her stomach, loving the way she sighed, sinking deeper into him.

They remained like that for the next hour, eating, drinking, and laughing with loved ones. Kye appreciating the village of people around him. The family that had grown over time.

Damn, he was lucky. They'd fought a war together, and they'd come out victorious and stronger than ever.

As everyone chatted, Kye heard a car, followed by a knock at the front of the house. His brow rose in surprise. They weren't expecting anyone else.

Mason, who was already on his feet, headed toward the house. "I'll get it."

With a nod, Kye watched his friend go inside. He was only gone for a few seconds. When he returned, he was accompanied by a short, nervous brunette woman.

Kye frowned.

Samantha swung her head around, then immediately straightened. "Grace…"

Why was Samantha's therapist here?

Samantha stood and headed toward the woman. Kye followed. "Grace, what are you doing here?"

Grace wrung her hands in front of her, looking agitated and upset. "I'm sorry. I didn't know you were having people over. I'll come back—"

Samantha touched her arm. "Don't be silly. Is everything okay? Did you want to chat?"

Grace cast a glance over her shoulder before looking back to Samantha and nodding. "Could we talk alone for a second?"

"I'm coming," Kye said. He was sure the woman was harmless, but there was something about the way the therapist was fidgeting that made Kye equally nervous just looking at her.

Suddenly, Wyatt cursed from behind him.

Glancing back, Kye saw him looking at his phone, a scowl on his face.

Christ, what now?

"What is it, Jobs?" Eden asked.

Wyatt ran a hand through his hair before glancing up at the group. "An article has been published. About *us*. It's gone viral on most social media platforms."

The hairs stood up on Kye's arms.

An article about Project Arma? God, that would bring reporters from all over the country to Marble Falls. Hell, it could even prove dangerous for their families.

"Is Jason's team mentioned?" Sage asked.

"Yes. It even states that they moved to Cradle Mountain, Idaho, to open a security business."

What the hell?

"The article is detailed and accurate, going into specifics about the beginning of Project Arma, how it started as a government-sanctioned project before Hylar took over. It mentions our altered DNA, what we can do..."

"How?" Evie asked quietly.

Wyatt looked up, his gaze landing on the therapist. "The main source of information was a therapist by the name of Grace Castle."

Order Logan, featuring Logan and Grace's story, today!

ALSO BY NYSSA KATHRYN

PROJECT ARMA SERIES

Uncovering Project Arma

Luca

Eden

Asher

Mason

Wyatt

Bodie

Oliver

Kye

BLUE HALO SERIES

(series ongoing)

Logan

Jason

Blake

JOIN my newsletter and be the first to find out about sales and new releases!

~www.nyssakathryn.com~

ABOUT THE AUTHOR

Nyssa Kathryn is a romantic suspense author. She lives in South Australia with her daughter and hubby and takes every chance she can to be plotting and writing. Always an avid reader of romance novels, she considers alpha males and happily-ever-afters to be her jam.

Don't forget to follow Nyssa and never miss another release.

Facebook | Instagram | Amazon | Goodreads

CPSIA information can be obtained
at www.ICGtesting.com
Printed in the USA
LVHW100615120422
715974LV00003B/107